EDGE OF
DARKNESS

EDGE OF COLLAPSE SERIES BOOK THREE

KYLA STONE

Edge of Darkness

Printed in the United States of America

Cover design by Christian Bentulan

Book formatting by Vellum

First Printed in 2020

ISBN: 978-1-945410-51-2

 Created with Vellum

PREFACE

Much of this story takes place in Southwest Michigan. For the sake of the story, I have altered certain aspects and taken a few liberties with a real town or two. Thank you in advance for understanding an author's creative license.

1

HANNAH
DAY EIGHT

The monster loomed over Hannah Sheridan, red eyes boring into hers as he reached for her with razor-sharp claws. The monster seized her hand and crushed it, grinding her bones into dust, agony radiating from her fractured fingers, her splintering bones . . .

Pain shattered her into pieces, into shards of herself as she disintegrated into nothing, into anguish and fear and darkness that never ended—

"Hannah!"

Hands on her shoulders, shaking her.

Her eyes blinked open. Blind panic spiked through her. She shot up, the knife clenched in her hand slashing toward her assailant, toward the monster.

"No!" she screamed, her voice ragged, fear a frantic thing in her chest.

A hand caught her by the wrist—strong, but not crushing.

Not yet. The pain would come. The pain always came.

She writhed, struggling to break free, the knife flashing harmlessly in her caught fingers. Her one attempt at striking back was

another failure, just like all the others. Just like everything that
had come before.

"Hannah!"

No . . . A voice in the deepest part of her. A refusal to give in,
to give up.

This was not like before. She was not the same Hannah as
before.

Her deformed left hand flailed. She managed to connect with
soft flesh: a solid strike to the monster's nose. A shockwave of pain
shot through her mangled fingers.

The monster cursed but barely flinched. He leaned his head
back out of her reach. She beat at him anyway, punching uselessly
at his arm, his shoulders, her hands weak against hard muscle.

"Hannah! It's me! It's Liam."

She blinked rapidly. The panicky fog in her brain began to
clear slowly. She forced herself to count, to return to herself. *One,
two, three . . .*

The monster took shape in front of her.

Not a monster, a man.

And not *him*. Not Pike.

The memories of the last week rushed in—the power outage,
her unlocked prison door, the frantic escape through the snow and
woods after she'd freed the dog, freed Ghost. Liam Coleman
saving her life. CiCi's cabin, her kindness.

The exhausting, freezing trek to Branch, the town overrun by looters. The library. The battle with Pike. The panicked flight to the barn.

She went limp against the hay. "Liam."

"That's what I just said." He still held her knife hand, his
fingers encircling her tiny wrist. He watched her like she was a
feral kitten with tiny, needle-sharp teeth that might nip at his
fingers. Annoying, but not a real threat. "Can I let you go now?"

She nodded.

He released her hand and rocked back on his heels. He rubbed his nose gingerly. A bit of blood trickled over his lip. "Didn't expect that. Should've. But didn't."

Guilt pricked her. "I'm sorry, I—"

"Never apologize for defending yourself. It was a solid hit." He rose abruptly to his feet. "Time to go."

In the dimness, she could make out Liam's tall stature and broad shoulders, his chiseled features and bristle of several days' worth of chestnut beard shadowing his square jaw. Those arresting gray-blue eyes that seemed to pin her in place whenever his gaze settled on her.

Everything about him radiated strength, competence, power. A soldier, through and through. He was reticent and aloof. Restless and alert. Shadows behind his eyes.

He'd saved her life multiple times already. She didn't know much about him, but she knew he was good. After Pike, she never thought she'd trust a man again—but now she did. She trusted Liam Coleman implicitly.

The gray light of dawn slithered through the cracks in the barn and leaked through the half-opened barn doors. The frigid air stung her cheeks and exposed ears.

The hat with earflaps that CiCi had given her had nearly fallen off in the night. She pulled it back over her ears, pushed aside the saddle blankets Liam had found last night, and picked several pieces of straw from her oversized brown coat.

Her gaze swept the shadowed barn. The empty stalls. The old, warping slats of the walls. The piles of hay. Where was—?

"Ghost!" She turned, instinctively reaching for the dog.

He lay behind her in the straw, in the same position as when they'd arrived last night. A Great Pyrenees, Ghost was a huge dog the size of a small pony, one hundred and forty pounds of solid muscle covered in a coat of brilliant white fur.

She pressed her hand to his fluffy side. The slight rise and fall of his ribs reassured her that he was still alive.

She rubbed the fur over his belly. His large paws twitched. He let out a low sound that was half growl, half distressed whine.

Though Liam had cleaned him up and tended to his wound last night, a streak of fresh blood matted the top of his head and left ear. He tilted his head and looked up at her, pain and bewilderment in his beautiful brown eyes.

"I'm sorry, Ghost. I'm so sorry."

His long plumed tail thumped weakly. He gave another soft whine, sad and almost regretful, like he was apologizing for his inability to leap up and dutifully act as her furry protector.

"I'm going to take care of you this time, okay? Don't you worry. Just rest. It's okay."

Her heart tightened like a fist. She didn't know what she would do without Ghost. It didn't matter that she'd only been with him for a week. It felt like years. Ghost was loyal, brave, fearless. A magnificent animal, regal and noble as a king.

They'd been trapped together, held captive by the same man.

Ghost had saved her. And not just from Pike. He'd given her the strength to go on. Reminded her of who she was, what she could be.

She swallowed the lump in her throat. "We need to find that vet."

"You feel okay enough to travel?"

She felt stiff and bruised all over, but she didn't hesitate. "Yes."

Liam's penetrating gaze assessed her. "You sure?"

She folded the knife and slipped it into her coat pocket. She wobbled unceremoniously to her feet, holding her basketball-sized belly with her bad hand as if it would help. Movement beneath her hand—the sliding arc of a heel or a tiny fist.

Her gut lurched. She jerked her hand away.

She didn't know how much time she had left. In her basement prison, she'd used chalk marks on the wall to chart passing time. Five years' worth.

That didn't help her know how far along she was. The baby was *his*. That was all that mattered. She tried to think of it as little as possible. She just wanted it out. It was a part of *him*, a living tether to her captor that she loathed and resented with every fiber of her being.

"How do you feel?" Liam asked her again, concerned.

She shuffled toward him with a wince, the pain of Pike's attack the night before making itself known. Bruised ribs. Her right temple pulsed with pain. The skin around her left eye socket swollen, puffy, and tender. But she was up and on her feet.

Her scalp itched, her hair a tangled mess. Her skin had that greasy, unwashed feeling she hated. But her most pressing physical concern lay elsewhere. Her bladder pinched.

"I'll be okay. But I need to pee."

Liam stood guard at the door, gripping the wicked AR-15 he'd stolen from the thugs who'd attacked them in Branch. He scanned the snowy fields while she relieved herself outside around the corner, squatting and balancing against the wall. It was cold and miserable.

She did her business as quickly as possible and used the two squares of toilet paper Liam had given her. She didn't want to think about a time when toilet paper was no longer available. What would people use? Magazines? Corn cobs, like in the old days?

They weren't just running from a killer. The United States had been attacked. An electromagnetic pulse from a nuclear weapon—at least one, maybe more—detonated high in the atmosphere had fried almost all electronics.

According to CiCi's contacts on her ham radio, most of the country had gone dark. And not just the power grid but cell phones and most cars, too.

Short and long-haul trucks couldn't deliver critical supplies to grocery stores, pharmacies, or hospitals. Without the snowplows running, snow drifts had piled dangerously high, effectively cutting off the towns.

Everyone was on their own.

When she returned, Liam gave her a squirt of hand sanitizer, then two granola bars and some water for breakfast. She ate quickly, barely tasting the food. She was hungry, but her focus was on getting Ghost help.

Liam moved gingerly. Dark circles shadowed his eyes. He'd spent the last several nights guarding them. She knew he wouldn't admit it, but he was weary and hurting. Because of her. Because he'd saved her. "Are you okay?"

His mouth tightened. "You don't have to worry about me."

She nodded, worried anyway.

Liam pulled his paper map from his pack and studied it for a few minutes. The barn they'd sheltered in was located outside of Newaygo, just south of the border of the Manistee National Forest.

He showed it to her and pointed to a small dot. "I-31, I-196, and I-131 are the interstates that take us south. Highways are a bad idea. Ashland Center and Bridgeton are off the highway but so small they're unlikely to have a vet's office. Same with Grant, though it's right off the highway. Ashland is about ten miles away. It looks like it's a little larger, large enough to have what we need."

"What if it's like Branch?"

"Not every town will be overrun yet. It depends on their

distance to population centers and highways, and how quickly the residents catch on to their new reality and do something about it. This entire area is rural. We may get lucky. Caution creates luck."

"But Ghost needs help."

He nodded, his expression grim. "I know."

At least with the snowmobile, they didn't have to worry about plowed roads or even roads at all. "How much gas do we have left?"

"It's nearly empty. Only fifteen or twenty miles, I'd guess. We need to refuel. And we need to make a plan."

He spent the next several minutes outlining potential threats, their list of needs, direction of travel, and what to do if they were attacked.

"I hate using the snowmobile," he said. "You can hear it from a mile away. It'll be easy for hostiles to hear us coming, set up a hasty ambush, and pick us off. We can't hear anything, visibility is poor. It makes it hard to see anything but the most obvious threats. I don't like it. That being said, speed is our best defense. We're gonna blow past everything. Keep your eyes peeled for obvious ambushes."

She nodded.

"We'll have to skirt Grand Rapids and Kalamazoo and stay on the backroads. From my calculations, we're still a good one hundred and thirty miles from Fall Creek. More with the detours."

Her heart leapt at the mention of home. She hadn't grown up in Fall Creek, but the small town nestled in the corner of Southwest Michigan had been her home since she'd married Noah Sheridan eight years ago and began a new life as a wife and a mother.

Memories of arguing, crying, and slammed doors echoed through her mind. It hadn't gone well. But that didn't mean she didn't still love Noah. She barely remembered the reasons they'd argued.

The state of her marriage did nothing to diminish her all-encompassing love for her son, Milo. She thought of the last time she'd seen him at three years old—his big dark eyes, black hair curling around his ears, those chubby cheeks she loved to pinch, the clean baby powder scent of him.

Her compass always pointed home to them.

Always.

She slipped her good hand into her coat pocket and felt the compact Ruger American .45. The soothing, comforting heft of it. She'd lost her backpack back at the library, but she still had her weapons.

She'd failed the first time. She was determined not to fail again. Liam had agreed to teach her how to shoot. Next time, she wouldn't hesitate.

Pike was still out there. Still hunting them. Stalking them like a deadly predator. Dogged, tenacious, undeterred.

Ghost had injured him. But Pike wasn't a man who gave up easily. He wasn't a man who gave up at all.

Hannah Sheridan didn't, either.

"We save Ghost. And then home. I'm ready to go home."

2

LIAM
DAY EIGHT

W atery gray light bled into the sky over the trees as the sun rose in the east.

Liam Coleman's gloved hands gripped the snowmobile's handles. The engine roared in his ears and rumbled beneath him. The freezing wind blasted him. Though he was grateful for his helmet to block the worst of it, it also reduced his situational awareness.

Hundreds of stalled vehicles littered the two-lane highway. Too many possibilities for trouble. Too many ways to get pinned down.

Liam avoided the road itself but drove parallel to it along the ridge of a low hill clear of trees. If the woods thickened, he'd be forced back onto the road, but for now, it was faster and safer. He kept one eye on his path ahead and the other constantly scanning the road to the left and right, the treetops, and checking their six.

Hannah rode in front of him, his arms on either side of her tiny figure—slight but for her swollen belly. Ghost rode in the attached trailer behind them.

Liam had spread a few saddle blankets he'd found in the barn beneath the dog and weaved more blankets between the bars, wrapping them with duct tape from his go-bag to keep them in place and block the wind.

It was still no good for a dog, especially not an injured one.

His spine twinged uncomfortably. Hoisting and then carrying the heavy animal across his shoulders had jarred something in his lower back. He wasn't the same after his time with Delta, when jumping from too many helicopters and planes had crushed a few discs.

He was still incredibly strong and fit. A step or two slower, but he could still get the job done. It just took more out of him now. Cost him more.

The rickety snowmobile jarred the aches and bruises from the battle the night before. He was tired and weary, but he was no stranger to exhaustion.

He knew how to function on only a few hours of sleep a night. He was no stranger to pain, either. He'd been trained to compartmentalize and dismiss such things.

He worried about what they would find in the next town. More specifically, what they wouldn't find.

They were low on potable water and lower on food. A pregnant woman ate far more than he'd expected. He knew she needed it. They both needed to keep their energy up and maintain their core body temperature above all else.

They could have built a fire outside the barn and melted snow to drink, but that would've taken more time—and might have drawn unwanted attention. They were both anxious to get Ghost to a vet. They needed to find supplies in the next town. Water, food, and gas.

Liam caught sight of something on the road ahead. Something not quite right. His heart rate accelerated.

He'd learned from experience to trust his instincts; he'd paid the cost for ignoring them.

He coasted to a careful stop, keeping two thick pine trees between them and the road, and switched off the engine.

"Why did we stop?" Hannah asked.

He didn't answer right away. He removed his helmet and slung it on the handlebar. He reached back to his go-bag, pulled binoculars from a side pouch, and glassed the area.

The road twisted into a tight curve that hid what lay ahead. A steep ditch ten to fifteen feet deep lined the left side of the road. Past the ditch, the trees were thinner, which was why Liam had picked this side.

On the right side, a forest of thick, dense pine trees bristled right up to the shoulder. Another reason he'd avoided the road. He hated trees close to the road. Too many places for hostiles to hide. Just the thought made him tense.

A hundred yards to the south, just before the curve, two cars partially blocked the road. They were angled at forty-five degrees, leaving just enough space for a single vehicle to pass through, slowly and cautiously.

Unlike the other stranded vehicles mounded with pristine, untouched domes of snow, these cars showed signs of tampering—crumbling snow along the sides, tamped down powder on the ground to hide fresh footprints.

He couldn't see clearly from this angle, but he sensed a few shadows hidden behind the cars, lying in wait for the next unsuspecting passerby.

"What is it?" Hannah asked quietly.

"Ambush."

He passed her the glass and showed her what to look for.

She studied the scene, nodded. "What do we do?"

He pointed to the hill. "I need to take the high ground. Assess the situation, see what we're dealing with. You and Ghost stay quiet and hidden."

She nodded. Liam was about to get moving when the rumble of another engine reached them.

He pressed his finger to his lips. Hannah nodded.

He eased off the red Yamaha, helped Hannah clamber off, and crouched behind it. She grunted as she squatted, leaning against the side of the machine to keep her balance.

Their boots sank into knee-deep snow. Their breaths expelled white crystalized clouds in the cold air. He lifted the binoculars and watched the road to the north.

A few moments later, a beat-to-hell, late 1970's green Chevy Silverado 4x4 outfitted with snow tires appeared. It was driving slowly to navigate the deep snow and stalled cars, maybe ten miles an hour.

Hannah said nothing. She didn't move.

The Chevy slowed further but didn't stop. They didn't turn around and high-tail it in the other direction like they should have. Liam cursed under his breath as the truck attempted to edge between the two angled cars.

Two figures leaped out from behind the far car closest to the woods. Both were rough-looking men in ragged clothes and unkempt beards.

They ran at the Silverado, shouting and brandishing baseball bats. The first thug—a white guy in a khaki canvas coat and a hunter's camouflage winter hat with ear flaps—yanked on the driver's side door. Whoever was inside had locked it. Hunter slammed the baseball bat into the door's window. The glass shattered.

The second thug, a skinny black guy wearing a white baseball cap, reached inside the broken window, unlocked the door, and yanked it open. He pulled out the driver.

The driver, an elderly Caucasian man, stumbled to his hands and knees in the snow. His knit cap fell from his head, revealing a gleaming bald pate and a few wisps of white hair.

A third thug appeared from behind the second ambush car. White guy, big and burly, with a blond goatee. He circled around the rear of the truck and went for the passenger side.

He dragged out an older woman, likely the old man's wife. Goatee grabbed her by her long gray braid and yanked her to her knees.

She cowered in the snow, crying and begging for her life. Liam couldn't make out the exact words at this distance, but he got the gist of it.

On the other side of the truck, Baseball Cap started kicking the old man. He curled up in the snow, arms over his face, trying to protect his head. Hunter clambered into the bed of the truck and began throwing out supplies. Duffel bags. A couple of backpacks. A pile of blankets.

The old woman's scream rent the air.

Anger sprouted in Liam's chest. His hands tightened into fists.

Hannah tugged on his arm. "You have to help them."

"No, I don't," he said gruffly. "We can't help everyone in need."

"I saw the bodies you left behind in Branch. I know what you can do. You can help them."

His instinct was to avoid all people at all times. He was a natural loner. Don't get involved. Stay alive. Get back to his isolated homestead, where he had or could make everything he needed to survive.

After Chicago . . . he'd thought he never wanted to interact with another human being again. But when he'd run into Hannah in the woods—lost, alone, pregnant—his conscience had gotten the better of him.

His conscience was getting the better of him again.

"We don't have the time," he said half-heartedly.

"You can do it quickly. Five minutes."

He glanced at her with raised eyebrows. "Five minutes?"

Her expression was serious, but a hint of humor laced her voice. "I'll time you."

He could do it. He could shoot them in five seconds or less.

His pistol was in his coat pocket, not holstered beneath his coat. He needed quick access when things went pear-shaped. The rifle he wore slung over his shoulder within easy reach.

He needed to conserve his ammo. He had less than two magazines left for his Glock 19. No spare magazines for the AR-15. His Gerber MK II tactical knife was sheathed at his hip.

He was especially lethal with the knife.

Plus, he didn't want to attract unwanted attention. Gunshots had a tendency to do just that.

Liam glassed the area again, checking the trees, behind the cars, searching for anything out of place, anything that jarred his internal alarm bells. He never took anything at plain sight.

Everything was as it appeared to be. None of the three attackers carried guns. No one else hid in the shadows, waiting to ambush Good Samaritans who came to the old couple's aid.

He could do it quickly. Even without bullets.

He would move down from the high ground and attack silently, working his way from the outside in, using his knife.

Give these animals another few minutes, and they'd kill the old couple. They already had their victims' possessions. The beating was just for fun. Just because they could.

A low, burning outrage filled him.

These scumbags were predators. They'd been predators since the day they were born, and they'd be predators until the day they died.

Better to have the dying part happen sooner rather than later.

3

LIAM
DAY EIGHT

"Stay here," Liam instructed. "Stay behind the snowmobile's engine."

Hannah's lips thinned into a firm line. She nodded.

He unhooked the AR-15 from its sling, switched off the safety, and handed it to Hannah. "Shoot anything that moves. When I come back, I'll whistle 'Happy Birthday.' Don't shoot me."

"I'm fine. Don't worry about me."

He turned and quickly and quietly scaled the hill, keeping a line of trees between himself and the road.

He barely felt the cold. He flexed his fists. His leather gloves were soft and supple, easy enough to fight with.

He had the high ground. You can always fight better from higher ground; whether with guns, knives, swords, or your own two hands.

At the top, he went still for a moment, calmed his thudding heart, slowed his breathing. Listened hard.

The screaming of the old woman. Shouts and grunts from the thugs. Dull thuds as kicks and punches landed. Quieter, the rustling of evergreen boughs, the creak of branches all around him. A small creature scurrying beneath the underbrush ten yards behind him.

The crisp scent of pine strong in his nostrils. He was downwind, not that the thugs would smell him. Or hear him.

This was his element. All of his senses were firing. He was in the kill zone.

He moved swiftly and quietly, stepping over fallen logs and low branches, dodging from tree to tree. The snow was soft, and he knew how to step to make as little sound as possible.

He bent his knees and slid down a steep section. His lower spine tweaked. He ignored it. He used the terrain as concealment as he crept down behind them.

The sounds of the attack grew louder. The thugs laughing and hurling insults. Cries for mercy went unanswered.

Liam quickened his pace but remained alert and careful. He judged the likely location of the thugs and his proximity to them, choosing the best spot to emerge from the trees.

He came out of the trees ten yards behind the thugs. They stood to the right of the Silverado parked in the middle of the two-lane highway, both doors hanging open.

All three were engaged with the elderly couple, their backs to Liam. The two victims lay on the snow-covered asphalt, covering their heads with their hands, curling on their sides.

His gaze swept the stalled vehicles and both shoulders of the road, left to right and left again.

No other threats. Just these three.

Adrenaline surged through his veins. He forgot the cold. Forgot his weariness. Forgot everything but the task at hand.

Liam vaulted the guard rail. He moved stealthily, stepping heel to toe. He unsheathed the Gerber and held it low at his side.

The blade was strong and razor sharp. He always kept it sharp.

He maintained a full grip on the knife handle, curling his thumb around the handle instead of leaving it up and exposed to potential injury. It was also more difficult for an attacker to take the knife away. Not that Liam was worried about that with these jokers.

Baseball Cap was the closest thug. He was taking a break from the beating and had stepped back to light a cigarette. His head was bowed, both his hands up and cupped around the cigarette at his mouth. His baseball bat leaned against the opened door of the truck. Out of reach.

Liam took several swift and silent strides. He approached Baseball Cap from behind, grabbed his head, and drove the knife upwards from the top of his spine into his brain.

Baseball Cap dropped like a stone, instantly dead. The cigarette dangled from his dead lips. Liam stepped back and let him fall.

It took a second for the two remaining hostiles to react. Liam didn't waste that second.

The man in the hunting cap whirled, a startled look on his face. He started to raise his baseball bat, but Liam was already on him. He smashed into the man's chest and drove him back into the side of the Chevy. Hunter let out a pained *oomph*.

The third hostile would be reacting now, too, ready to charge Liam at any second. He needed to move fast.

Hunter pummeled at his ribs. Liam took the blows. Hunter tried to push him off, shove him away so he could get some leverage and get a good punch in, use the baseball bat.

Liam didn't let him. Using his left arm to deflect any potential blows, he used his right hand to slash the knife across the side of the hostile's throat, severing his carotid artery.

He stepped back fast but the arterial spray still got him.

Hunter slid down the side of the truck, flailing, gasping. He'd be dead in a few minutes.

"Hey! What the hell!"

Liam spun to face the last thug.

The hostile stood ten feet away, steel baseball bat clenched in both hands. The big burly guy with the goatee. He was a brute of a man. Lots of power behind that swing. One good hit, and he could crack Liam's skull, scramble his brains.

Goatee's gaze flicked from Liam to his dead friends to Liam again. His small beady eyes flashed with fury and hatred. "I'm gonna kill you, you filthy—"

Liam didn't give him the time to finish his insult. Action beat reaction every time. He wasn't going to give Goatee the chance to charge. Liam charged first.

He saw the cut points in his mind, the angles of attack, the arteries he needed to slash: subclavian, carotid, aorta, brachial, radial. The femoral arteries on the inside of each thigh were the most likely to be left unguarded.

That's where he aimed first.

He lunged at the hostile. Liam lowered his shoulders and barreled at Goatee. Instead of head-butting him in the gut, he slashed savagely with the knife and ducked to the left. Two quick, twisting, brutal cuts.

Goatee swung high, aiming for where Liam's head should be. But Liam's head wasn't there anymore, and Goatee didn't have time to adjust the angle. The baseball bat sailed just over Liam's head—so close, the wind rifled his hair.

Liam rolled and came quickly to his feet, his knife up. He circled around to face Goatee.

Goatee collapsed to his knees. Bright red blood spurted from the two gashes, one in each thigh. The blood gushed down his legs and puddled in the snow.

He stared up at Liam, a look of pure dumb shock on his face. "You—you cut me."

He tried to grip the baseball bat, to use it to pull himself to his feet, but his legs were fast going useless on him. He slipped and slid and flopped in the scarlet snow. He tried to shout insults, but they came out like agonized grunts instead.

Liam kicked him hard in the chest. He fell over backwards. Liam kicked the baseball bat away. It rolled and bounced and came to a stop wedged beneath the front passenger wheel of the Chevy.

Goatee's legs kicked uselessly. More blood streamed into the snow. He was covered in it. He opened his mouth, gasping like a dying fish.

It would take a minute or less for him to die.

Liam moved around the side of the truck.

The old woman stood unsteadily and staggered through the snow to her husband's side. She knelt, wrapped her frail arms around him, and helped him sit up.

She turned to look at Liam. Her thin lips were split and bleeding. A bruise was already blooming along her jaw. Fear in her eyes at first, like maybe she thought he'd killed the thugs just so he could turn around and steal their truck.

"I'm not here to hurt you," he said gruffly.

"Thank you," she said in a trembling voice. "You saved my husband's life."

The old man rose shakily to his feet. Blood settled in the cracks and crags of his face and wisps of white hair. A long bloody cut marred his forehead. He cradled his injured arm against his ribs.

Liam knelt in the snow, scooped a handful, and used it to clean the blood from his face and hands, the spatters on his coat. He wiped the blood from his knife and sheathed it. "You should find a doctor. Get someone to look at that arm."

"How can we thank you?" the man said. "We can pay you. We have cash."

Liam stood and spat into the snow. The adrenaline dump hit him, left his legs shaky. "No payment required. Don't tell anyone else you have cash. You'll need it."

He picked up the duffle bags, suitcase, and blankets and slung them into the back of the truck. He repacked everything beneath the tarp.

He offered the old woman his arm. She leaned on him heavily. She was weak, frail, and shivering from the cold. He helped her get situated in the truck.

They continued to thank him profusely, but it only made him more uncomfortable. He didn't like praise. He just wanted to get the job done and move on.

He checked the bodies for anything useful and found nothing but some loose change and a baggie of pot.

He left the bodies where they lay. Let them rot like roadkill. Let them be a warning to the next worthless punks who thought they could prey on the weak without consequences.

He climbed the hill, his boots slipping a little in the snow, breathing hard, and returned to the snowmobile. He whistled "Happy Birthday" to alert Hannah of his approach.

Behind him, the Silverado's engine sputtered and growled to life. He glanced back and watched the truck wind through the roadblock and continue on its way.

He wanted them to make it. That didn't mean they would.

"How long?" he asked Hannah.

She heaved herself to her feet and handed him the AR-15. She pushed up her oversized coat sleeve and pretended to look at an invisible watch on her wrist. "Approximately three minutes for the fight, ten minutes to socialize. If you wanted an exact time, you should have given me your watch."

He reattached the rifle to his two-point sling and shouldered his pack. "I was in a hurry, remember?"

She gave a small shake of her head. "Uh huh."

She still hadn't smiled since he'd met her, but her eyes were brighter. She was transforming from the cowering, timid woman he'd found half-dead in the woods into something else.

He wasn't sure what yet. She probably didn't know herself.

Hannah glanced down at the road, at the bodies sprawled in front of the ambush cars. They were barely visible through the trees. "You killed them."

"You knew I would."

He waited for her judgment, her criticism. Civilians didn't understand what it took. Too many of them got complacent and comfortable in their illusionary bubble of safety and refused to see reality for what it was.

They didn't want to know how good people had to fight and die to give them that illusion.

"They would have hurt someone else as soon as we left." She chewed on her lower lip, considering. "They needed to die."

He blinked, surprised. "Yes."

Most people still didn't understand. As soon as the planes started falling from the sky, he'd known.

The world had changed in a heartbeat. Anyone who didn't get that was already doomed.

Hannah seemed to get it. What she'd been through . . . she understood how everything could be flipped upside down and inside out in an instant. How some people were evil to the core, and the only thing that stopped them was a bullet between the eyes and a grave six feet under.

She watched him for a moment, studying him. "You're going to kill more people."

"Some people need to be killed."

"But not everyone we meet."

"If they deserve it."

"Okay." She nodded to herself. "If they deserve it."

He didn't enjoy killing. He never had. But he didn't shy from the task when it was necessary. He bore the burden because a soldier had to, even if he didn't wear a uniform anymore.

He walked the thin line. Every day, every fight, every kill. As cold and savage as his enemies, move for move. Brutal but not cruel. Walking the lip of a pit without falling in. Without becoming one of them.

Hannah's expression softened. Her green eyes shone bright in the wintry light. The faintest freckles dusted her nose. "I knew you would help."

For some stupid reason, he wanted to look away but wouldn't let himself. "How did you know?"

"Because you're a good person."

He thought of Chicago. All his mistakes. The people he'd failed. "I wouldn't be so sure."

The corners of her lips twitched. "Maybe you just don't know it yet."

Behind them, the dog whimpered.

Hannah stiffened. "Ghost."

Concern lanced through him. Liam grabbed his helmet and handed Hannah hers. He straddled the seat and started the engine. It coughed to life with a throaty growl. "We're still five miles out. We're not stopping for anything or anyone."

Hannah nodded and slipped on her helmet.

4

PIKE

DAY EIGHT

G avin Pike desperately wanted a smoke the entire time the terrified, quaking doctor worked on his injured arm. His lungs craved the sweet scent of cloves, the deeply satisfying inhalation of smoke, the rewarding ritual that settled his ragged nerves.

But he couldn't. Not with his left arm being tended to by the doc and his right hand holding a gun to the doctor's head.

You never knew with these small-town folks. Never knew when they might get dumb thoughts of heroism in their dense skulls. Like killing him would do a thing to bring back their electricity, their cars and phones, and their warm, safe houses.

Their old world was gone, shot to hell.

Safety no longer existed. Not for anyone.

Pike, however, was loving it.

He'd spent his entire life perfecting his masks, crafting his disguises, building his camouflage. He was no one. Bland and unassuming, with his dishwater blond hair, medium height, medium build, and insipid smile. Completely forgettable.

It wasn't just his banal appearance. It was his family, his job, his hobbies—the collection of "normal" characteristics that blinded people to the truth staring them in the face.

His night shift as a correctional officer at the Berrien County Correctional Facility. The volunteer reserve officer hours at fairs and parades. His obligations to his uptight mother, ever the dutiful son. Suffering through tedious council meetings and miserable family dinners. Enduring his insufferable brother, Julian, and his equally detestable best friend, Noah Sheridan.

But all that took time and effort and incredibly draining amounts of energy.

In the blink of an eye, the country had been thrown back a hundred and fifty years. Back to the Wild West. To the dark ages.

Back to the times when a predator could hunt without the worry of computer databases, facial recognition software, DNA samples, or teams of FBI agents hot on your trail.

With the destruction of the grid, all of that was gone. He could travel from town to town, county to county, city to city, state to state.

No digital trail for anyone to follow. No traces of DNA to nail him to the proverbial wall.

He was free. Completely free to do whatever he wanted to whoever he wanted, whenever and however he wanted. Completely untethered from the modern world of laws and rules and police states and tyranny.

The allure was tantalizing. His new future bright with endless possibilities.

He had only this one thing. This one problem that just wouldn't go away, like a thorn in his foot, a papercut that wouldn't heal, an irritant incessantly scratching his eyeball.

The girl. The one who got away.

The only one.

He could walk away. He could leave her to scurry home and

tell whatever tales she wished to whoever she wished. He never had to enter the boundaries of Fall Creek again.

He could stalk the country, plunder the bloody harvest that awaited him, ripe for the picking. A new victim every day if he wanted.

And he would. He would. But no way in hell was he walking away.

Gavin Pike did not lose. Not a game, not a fight, not a victim. Not once. He wasn't starting with her. That timid little sparrow. That cowering mouse.

She belonged to him. She was *his*. What she carried was *his*.

Fresh rage burned through him, boiling his insides, whipping him into a frenzy of fury and hatred and desire. He could not rest until he'd exacted his revenge.

Until he'd crushed every exquisite bone in her body.

"You done yet?" he snapped at the quavering doctor.

The doctor snipped the bandage and finished wrapping his left forearm. "Your layers of insulating clothing and the thick leather coat saved your arm from serious damage. The bite wounds are mostly superficial, with minor muscle tearing and no apparent ligament damage. Still, you need to rest—"

Pike ripped his arm from the doctor's grasp. The doddering old man was seventy if a day. Thin tufts of white hair haloing around his bald head, stooped shoulders, crepe liver-spotted hands.

"I'll rest when I'm dead."

Which would be never, if Pike could help it.

The doctor eyed Pike's Berretta nervously. "You said you'd let me go. I did what you asked."

"You did. I thank you for that." Pike slipped off the examination table. He took two steps backward toward the door. His clothes were folded in a neat pile on a chair. His Winchester 70 rifle leaned against the chair. "However, it still hurts like a mother."

He glanced down at his new pistol, a Beretta F92. He'd always appreciated a good Beretta F-series. The unique slide with the exposed barrel gave the gun that distinct look. He liked the size of it. It felt good in his hands.

He wanted to test it out.

The doctor cleared his throat. "I can give you opioids, but I can't take the pain away completely."

Pike raised the pistol one-handed and aimed it at the doctor's chest. He flicked off the slide-mounted safety. "That's unfortunate."

The doctor's face blanched. His rheumy brown eyes widened. He raised his trembling hands. "I did what you asked! Please, don't kill me! I have a son! I have a grandchild—"

Pike fired. At this range, he didn't need a two-handed grip. There was no way to miss.

The doctor stood there for a moment, shocked. He looked down at himself, at the red bloom spreading from the center of his paisley sweater. He gripped his chest and sank to his knees.

He might have uttered some last words, but Pike was no longer paying attention.

He shrugged on his long-sleeved undershirt, two sweaters, and his coat, a leather duster falling to his knees. He replaced his gloves, scarf, and hat. He snatched up the Oxycontin he'd stolen from the looters earlier and stuffed the pill bottle in his left pocket.

He'd lost his KA-BAR combat knife and his Sig Sauer P320 in the library. However, he'd collected the Beretta 92FS from the poor shmuck who'd brought him to the doctor. And of course, he'd regained the Winchester Model 70 Featherweight in .270 with a Nightforce SHV 3–10x42 mm scope.

The shmuck had also donated his old model Ski-Doo to Pike,

right about the moment Pike shot him between the eyes. The snowmobile was waiting for him just outside the clinic.

He tucked the Beretta in his coat pocket and slung the rifle over his shoulder. He left the doctor to die in his examination room and made his way through the medical clinic to the front door.

The door's glass was shattered. He stepped through the broken glass and paused for a moment beneath the awning. The sky was gray and dreary. Dusk was already descending. It had taken longer than he'd expected to find the doctor and receive the proper medical care.

It was cold. But it was always cold. It was the snow he was worried about. As long as it didn't snow, he was fine.

He pulled his Zippo lighter out of his coat pocket along with a pack of his favorite Djarum Black clove cigarettes purchased online from a store in Indonesia. Clove cigarettes were illegal in the United States. He would not be able to find them in stores in any state.

The thought made him furious. He hadn't cared about the loss of Amazon's Prime shipping or Netflix binging. These, though, he would miss dearly.

Irritated, he flicked the Zippo lid to settle his nerves. *Click, click, click.* It was a soothing, repetitive sound from his earliest childhood. A sound he'd once loathed but learned to love. Much like the *snap* and *crack* he craved.

The story was tedious and trite. A father who'd liked to drink and smoke too much. Who'd enjoyed a living punching bag when he drank and smoked.

He'd had a certain affinity for Zippo lighters, clove cigarettes, and violence. Three gifts he'd passed on to his son—before he took off for parts unknown when Pike was seven.

He'd never missed his father. He'd never missed anyone.

He lit the cigarette, inhaled deeply, and blew out a mouthful of smoke. The cold burned his nostrils as he breathed in the sweet scent. *Click, click, click.*

He studied the town as he smoked. A thick blanket of snow covered everything. Hunched, empty buildings. Trampled footprints everywhere. Streaks and splatters and puddles of blood in the snow told the tale of a hard, desperate night.

Other than the bodies, not a living soul dared to walk Main Street. The looters and thugs had disappeared with the dawn, crawling back to whatever caves they called home.

It would be years before the people of Branch recovered from last night, if they ever did.

Not that he cared.

The tiny blip of Branch was a wart on the ass of Manistee National Forest.

Pike dropped the stub to the snow, not bothering to grind it out with his boot. He slipped the lighter into his pocket as he strode to his newly acquired snowmobile. It was filled with fuel and ready to rumble.

He drove through town slowly, searching the trampled snow, reading the story it had to tell. It took him less than an hour to find it. The single set of snowmobile tracks that led south from the outskirts of town just past the library, the smoothed edges of a sled trailer's tracks behind it.

He'd found them. Or at least, the trail of breadcrumbs they'd left behind.

The girl, the soldier, the dog.

He longed to kill each of them, slowly and painfully, one by one.

As long as it didn't snow, he could follow their distinctive tracks. As long as it didn't snow, he would find them.

He knew their final destination. He wanted to destroy them long before they reached it.

Even if he never stepped foot in Fall Creek again, he needed his reputation to remain intact. Just in case. Gavin Pike always had plans, back-up plans, and contingencies. It was how he'd managed to remain hidden in plain sight all these years.

Besides, he enjoyed his mother's blind adoration. He enjoyed thinking of Noah Sheridan still mourning his little lost wife. A stupid and gullible fool, utterly ignorant of the truth.

As far as Fall Creek was concerned, he'd rather keep things as they were.

He restarted the engine and took off, tracking his prey. Hunting them.

The cold and the pain in his arm invigorated him. It throbbed dully in time with his pulse, reminding him of exactly what he owed, and to whom.

By this time tomorrow, the girl, the soldier, and the dog would all be dead. He'd make damn sure of that.

5

LIAM

DAY EIGHT

L iam didn't head straight into the town of Ashland. He drove the snowmobile through several fields surrounding the town, taking his time to assess things before heading in.

He paused every so often and glassed the area. The terrain was flat, and the buildings frequently blocked his line of sight. It was impossible to gain a good vantage point.

As far as he could tell, things were quiet. They had a working snowplow, since Main Street was cleared enough to allow a single thoroughfare. The stalled vehicles had been pushed to the curb among snowdrifts as tall as the cars themselves.

A few people struggled down the sidewalks through knee-high snow, coats pulled tight, hoods drawn over their heads, gloved hands shoved deep into pockets. A line had formed outside the grocery store. Another outside the pharmacy and hardware stores.

He didn't see broken windows or signs of looting. Nothing presented itself as an obvious risk.

They parked the snowmobile at the edge of the tree line along the outskirts of town. It meant a mile hike on snowshoes, but Liam couldn't risk the snowmobile getting stolen. He hacked off some pine boughs and concealed the machine as best he could.

Grudgingly, he left the AR-15 as well. He hid it carefully several yards from the snowmobile. He didn't want to attract undue attention. And the AR-15 attracted plenty.

Hannah checked on Ghost. He was still out of it, his pupils unfocused. She got him to lap up a bit of water from the camping pan, but that was it. He laid back in the trailer with a whimper. He watched them, his brown eyes beseeching.

"We aren't leaving you," Hannah whispered. "We're getting help. Stay here and we'll be right back, I promise."

He didn't like leaving Ghost behind, either, but carrying the massive dog meant he wouldn't have his hands free to wield a weapon. That was not an option.

"You should wait here with Ghost," he said to Hannah.

Hannah shook her head. "I'm going with you. You might need me."

"I won't."

"You don't know that."

"I do."

She jutted her chin stubbornly. "Liar. I helped with CiCi. She would've shot you if not for me."

Liam's chest went tight.

Hannah stiffened, as if realizing all over again that CiCi was gone—and how. Tears sprang into her eyes.

The memory of CiCi was painful for them both. The tough old broad had nearly gutted them with buckshot, but she'd taken them in instead. She'd been nothing but kind and generous.

Pike had repaid that kindness by tracking them to her home in the Manistee National Forest and murdering her.

When Liam finally found him, Pike was going to die a slow and incredibly painful death.

Liam had promised Hannah that. And he meant to deliver.

"Hannah—"

She waved him off. She looked west toward a distant cluster of trees, her mouth moving silently. She was doing her counting, the thing she did to get control of herself again.

After a moment, she breathed deeply, scrubbed at her eyes with the back of her forearm, and regained her composure. "I'm okay."

He didn't want to leave her behind. If she was with him, he could protect her.

They went together.

They hiked into town and circled behind the buildings along Main Street. They kept to themselves, kept away from the small pockets of people he'd noted earlier.

Every sense alert, he continuously scanned for trouble. He watched the alleys between buildings, windows and doorways, the rooftops.

He kept his right hand in his pocket, fingers curled around the grip of the Glock. He didn't want to appear as a threat to the townspeople, but there was no way in hell he was going anywhere without a weapon in hand.

Hannah panted breaths that steamed in the frigid air, one hand on her belly. She was getting tired easily, though she didn't complain.

He didn't like taking her into potentially hostile territory. He liked the thought of leaving her behind even less.

Pike had managed to get too damn close last time. Liam had thought he was protecting Hannah; instead, he'd allowed himself to be led astray by a diversion. The oldest damn trick in the book.

Was he getting soft? Losing his touch? Had his grief and numbness blinded him?

The first day of the EMP had stolen everything from him that he'd ever loved—his brother, Lincoln. His sister-in-law, Jessa. His nephew.

At least he'd been able to leave the boy with his maternal grandparents, but now he had nothing. Nothing but his honor. And his mission to get this pregnant woman safely home to Fall Creek—then kill the sadistic psychopath hunting her.

After that, nothing mattered. The whole damn world could collapse in on itself like a dying star for all he cared. It could burn itself to the ground.

His fingers brushed against the second object in his coat pocket nestled against the Glock. The tiny knit hat. Gray and green stripes, just the right size for a newborn.

He kept it with him as a reminder of what he'd lost, who he'd left behind.

Remorse and regret threatened to strangle him. He pushed those emotions down deep. He needed to focus.

He wanted to quicken his pace, but Hannah couldn't walk that fast. He slowed to match her gait, kept his eyes peeled.

They didn't see anything at first. They kept looking, moving deeper into town. He scanned the street again, peering into windows, studying the buildings.

The gas station was dark and deserted. So were the dry cleaners, the florist, the hair salon, and an autobody shop.

Hannah tugged his arm and pointed. A block from the autobody shop, nestled between a few office suites. Paws and Claws Pet Clinic. Whether the veterinarian would be in was another matter.

A few minutes later, they'd reached the rear of the clinic. Liam skirted an oversized dumpster blanketed in two feet of pristine snow. Hannah stepped into his footprints right behind him.

The rear door was propped open with a rock.

Liam stopped. Hannah stopped. She didn't say a word or ask

any questions. He couldn't even hear her breathing now. She knew when to be quiet.

Adrenaline spiking, he strained his ears, listening for any sounds inside the clinic.

Nothing.

Maybe whoever had forced their way inside was long gone. He studied the prints around the door. Several sets, leading in several different directions. Maybe the place had already been looted, or maybe these were the footprints of the clinic staff.

No way to tell, though he doubted the employees would leave the back door open.

Quickly, he removed his snowshoes and left them with Hannah. He gestured for her to stay put while he cleared the building. Thankfully, she obeyed.

Every muscle tensed, Liam adjusted his grip on the Glock 19 and pulled it out of his pocket. A round was already chambered, a full seventeen rounds in the magazine—eighteen total.

He had two full magazines left after confiscating rounds from the 9mm pistols he'd stolen from the thugs in Branch.

He crept inside. Shapes loomed in the darkness. Everything was draped in heavy shadows. He didn't want to use his flashlight until he'd cleared everything.

After giving his eyes and ears a minute to adjust, he entered a long hallway, the walls beige and papered with photos of beloved pets, the concrete floors covered in a shiny epoxy for easy cleanup.

Several doors led to small rooms with a stainless-steel examination table, a sink and counter, and a bench for the pet owners. Each room was empty. The air smelled like damp animal fur and antiseptic.

A couple of windows provided weak, watery light. He glanced through the rectangular pane of a swinging door that led to a reception area—two dozen chairs lined up along the wall, a receptionist counter with a bank of blank computer monitors.

A noise up ahead. A muffled scraping sound.

Liam raised the pistol, held it in a two-handed grip, and slunk silently down a second darkened hallway. His wet boots made soft squelching noises against the floor. He slowed his movements, placing each foot with tremendous care as he crept closer to the room.

He reached the opened door on his left. White light emanated from the room. He pressed against the wall, gun up, and turned swiftly into the doorway. He took everything in with a glance.

It was a surgical room—stainless steel table, a cart laid out with dozens of metal instruments, cabinets filled with bandages, medications, needles, and other supplies.

A few cabinet doors hung open. A couple of the shelves were already emptied, but most of the medications remained.

A man stood facing away from him. He was reaching into a cabinet. A flashlight pointed at the ceiling. A rifle rested on the counter in front of him next to a reusable shopping bag brimming with pill bottles.

A thief.

Liam aimed at the back of the man's head and moved his finger from the trigger guard to the trigger.

6

LIAM
DAY EIGHT

Liam's nerves were shot. Part of him wanted to pull the trigger and be done with it. The man was a thief, a scumbag. A hostile. Better off dead just like the three thugs he'd killed that morning.

Another part of him hesitated. His damn conscience again.

"Turn around nice and slow," Liam said.

The man whipped around, face contorting in surprise and fear. One hand hovered above the counter, inching toward the rifle butt.

"I wouldn't." If he even twitched, Liam was blasting him into next week. "I won't warn you again."

The man raised his arms in the air, a white bottle of pills clutched in his left hand. He was a skinny guy in his early forties, with a flimsy blond mustache and glasses sliding down the bridge of his nose. He wore a buttoned-up peacoat, underdressed for the freezing weather.

He licked his cracked, chapped lips. "Don't shoot! Please! Don't shoot me!"

"Give me one good reason not to."

"I c-can explain," Peacoat stuttered. "I—I just needed some antibiotics for my wife. She's got bronchitis from the cold, and we don't have a working car or a way to drive through all this snow to get to a hospital."

"You're stealing."

"Not from you!" Peacoat cried. "I know Dr. Laudé, okay? I know the secretary and Jane Smith, the vet tech, too. I work at the hardware store across the street."

"You know them so well you waited until they were gone to steal from them?"

The man's face went pale. Dark circles ringed his eyes. His nose was red. He looked cold, sick, and exhausted. "I'm sorry, okay. I'm sorry. I'm not—I'm not a thief. I don't even cheat on my taxes. But the pharmacy is only accepting cash, and we don't have any left. Used the last we had on a grocery run three days ago. That food's already gone, too. I don't know what we're going to do."

Footsteps to his six. The man's eyes shifted from Liam to something behind his shoulder. Liam tensed before recognizing the slow shuffling gait.

"Don't kill him," Hannah said.

"Thought I told you to stay," he said, never taking his eyes off the skittish thief.

Hannah shuffled up beside him. "I'm not a dog," she said mildly. "I heard voices. I came in. I was careful."

He shook his head in frustration. "You could've walked into a firefight."

"You clearly had it under control."

"That's not the point." He felt like a parent lecturing an unruly child—not that he knew what that was like, but he assumed it was equally irritating. "Get behind me."

She didn't. "You don't have to kill every person we meet. We talked about this."

Peacoat's wide, frantic eyes darted between them, confusion and fear giving way to terror at her words. His legs were shaking.

Liam rolled his eyes. "That's why he's not dead yet."

"We're not going to shoot you," Hannah said. "Not if you aren't a danger to us or others."

"Says who?" Liam muttered.

Peacoat glanced anxiously from Liam to Hannah and back again, not sure who to believe.

Liam didn't lower his gun or take his finger off the trigger.

"I'm not a danger, I promise," Peacoat begged. "My wife won't make it without me. She needs me. Please."

"Liam." Hannah placed her hand on Liam's bicep.

Part of him wanted to shake her off, to wave her away like a fly, but he restrained himself. "What?" he growled.

"He's an idiot, not a killer." Hannah walked to the counter, wisely skirting the thief in case he made a grab for her. She snagged the rifle with her good hand and came back to stand beside Liam.

She nestled the long gun in her arms, resting atop her rounded belly, and turned to the cowering man, her expression stern. "Tell us your name. Who are you?"

The man didn't lift his gaze. Shaking, he stared at Liam's boots. "My name is Dennis. Dennis Reynolds. I'm—I'm ashamed, okay? Never thought I'd be in this situation. So desperate I'd steal from people I know. But my wife—I don't know what else to do. Her cough, it's bad. And her fever . . . we've got every blanket in the house piled on top of us. We're wearing three or four layers of clothing, five pairs of socks, everything."

"You don't have a fireplace?" Hannah asked.

"It's electric." Peacoat—Hank—looked embarrassed. "We

didn't want to mess with a wood-burning fireplace. I thought it was too messy, too much work."

"Does your town have an emergency shelter? Somewhere you can go?" Hannah's voice was calm and reassuring. Almost soothing. The panicked, fear-crazed woman he'd forcibly wakened from her nightmares only this morning had disappeared.

Dennis shook his head miserably. "A few churches and a community center still have generators, but they're only accepting families with children. They're all full. It's been eight days. They're running out of fuel. At first, people were caring and helpful. The last couple of days, though . . . the grocery stores will be empty by tomorrow, people are saying. We haven't heard anything other than the emergency broadcasts. No one's come to help."

Hannah felt sorry for the shmuck. He could see it in her face, a softening around her eyes.

Dennis's shoulders sagged. "I'm just trying to save my wife."

Liam nodded his head at the bag of pills on the counter. "Seems like you're taking more than your share. How many sick wives you got?"

Dennis had the decency to blush. "People are trading things. The cash is gone, so what's left? Some people have liquor to trade, others bundles of firewood or a jerrycan of diesel. Flashlights and batteries. Rifles and ammunition. Nobody's thought of here yet. I was the first one. The smart one. Animals are a lot like people, right? How different can it be? Dr. Laudé's already visited a bunch of sick human patients. Our walk-in clinic doctor is MIA."

Hannah went still. "You happen to know where Dr. Laudé is right now?"

"This early? Probably at home. Though she's been making the rounds to visit sick people in their homes. She lives a few blocks from here." Peacoat eyed the muzzle of the Glock still pointed at his head. "You lower that thing and I'll tell you where."

Liam narrowed his eyes. "How about you escort us there, and maybe, if I'm feeling particularly generous, I might let you live."

Dennis's gaze skittered away. He was completely cowed. "Yeah, okay. Sure. That's a good deal."

Liam might have chuckled at the situation if he had a sense of humor. He didn't. It had been lost along with everything else.

7

QUINN
DAY EIGHT

Sixteen-year-old Quinn Riley stared straight ahead as she trudged through the snow toward Greenway Park and the gathering crowd.

The town council chose the small park in town along the riverbank just past the bridge over Fall Creek. In summer, the large open area was used for picnics, pickup football and soccer games, kite flying and tag, and live concerts from local bands in the evenings.

Now it was the site of a funeral.

It was warmer than it'd been in a while, the temperature in the low twenties. The sun shone weakly in the bowl of the blue sky. No wind stirred the barren branches of the trees lining the river.

Birds twittered happily, as if the world hadn't suddenly stopped turning, as if violence hadn't torn through their town less than forty-eight hours ago, leaving its trail of devastation, misery, and heartbreak.

Several hundred people were gathered in the wide-open space in front of a large performance platform with a roof and open sides. They wore coats, scarves, and gloves. Their faces were somber, horrified, grief-stricken. Many were weeping.

News of the atrocity had spread through the small town like wildfire. Everyone knew what had happened the night before last. Everyone knew who had died—and who had survived.

She felt hundreds of eyes on her as she passed. At least half the town was here. Half the town staring at her, a torrent of whispers like a wave following in her wake as they moved aside.

She brushed her Windex-blue bangs out of her eyes and tried her hardest not to scowl back at everyone who stared at her. She wore her eyebrow and lip piercings, but she hadn't applied her usual heavy kohl-black eye makeup today.

She hadn't felt like it. Hadn't felt like herself. The face staring back at her in the mirror was a stranger, in more ways than one.

Several of her classmates huddled together turned to watch her. So did their parents. No wonder Gran had claimed her hip was bothering her and sent Quinn in her stead. This was awful.

Did they hate her because of her mother? Did they know Octavia was there that night? Or were their macabre stares because she was one of only three survivors, the "last girl" of every dumb horror movie ever?

She tried not to flinch, tried not to let the anxiety show. She did her best to block them out, to put those tough walls right back up, to show them she didn't care what they thought.

Usually, she didn't. But today? Today everything was different. She was raw, every nerve ending exposed. And she hated it.

She stopped near the front of the open space, maybe ten yards back from the platform. There was no grave site at which to mourn. No coffins to lower into the loamy earth. Not even a pyre for burning.

The bodies were being stored in makeshift body bags in one of the farmer's big metal and concrete barns. It was temporary, until the ground thawed, or they figured something else out. For now, it was cold enough to keep them refrigerated and keep the scavengers at bay.

The corpses from the church massacre were all there. Little Juniper and Chloe. Their kind mother, Daphne. Gramps' body was there, too.

Noah Sheridan had taken the arduous trip back to the ski resort to retrieve his body. He'd done it for Quinn. He'd kept his promise.

Memories flooded in—the freezing ski lift, Gramps going cold and still beside her. And the church, the monsters in black ski masks and guns, the screaming and running and dying.

"Hey, honey," a voice said.

Quinn blinked, startled. For a moment, she'd forgotten where she was.

The principal of Fall Creek High School, Annette King, peered at her, a concerned look on her face. She was in her late forties with silver hair in a short pixie cut. "I just wanted to see how you're doing."

Quinn's chest tightened. Everything felt distant and disconnected, like she wasn't really here, like she was outside of herself somehow, watching everything happen.

It hadn't all hit her yet. She'd been so determined to escape, to survive. She had. She'd saved Milo. But not Juniper and Chloe.

Bravery hadn't been the problem. She would've torn Billy Carter's throat out with her teeth if she'd had a chance. She hadn't been strong enough. Tough enough.

"I'm fine," she forced out.

Principal King pursed her lips. She looked like she'd been through the wringer herself. She'd been manning the emergency shelter at the high school almost nonstop since the EMP.

She was the type of person who always put others' needs

before her own, was always trying to help people. First, her students. Now, the town.

"Are you sure—"

"I'm fine."

The principal patted her shoulder. "I'm here for you if you need to talk about anything. If you need anything at all."

Quinn nodded dully. She barely heard the woman. She scanned the crowd, desperate for a distraction. Her frenetic gaze darted here and there, unable to stop in any one place for long.

She recognized Mike Duncan, the gas station owner, and his college-aged nephew, Jamal. Near the front stood Shen Lee, the Chinese-American pediatric nurse who'd checked her over that night, next to Dave Farris, the owner of Fall Creek Inn, and Robert Vinson, the local pharmacist.

Noah, the cop, and Milo, his eight-year-old son, stood near them. She wanted to see Milo and even Noah, too, but she didn't feel like dealing with Noah asking her if she was okay a million times. It was how he showed he cared. It was still freaking annoying.

She glanced up at the platform. A row of chairs had been placed on the stage behind a skinny white podium. Several rectangular tables decorated with dozens of pictures of the victims stood at either end of the platform.

Now that the florist shops were all dark, no one had been able to find flowers in the middle of winter; they'd decorated with ribbon instead. Colorful ribbons of all sizes, colors, and lengths wrapped the platform beams. Hundreds of ribbons hung from the branches of nearby trees.

Superintendent Sinclair, Chief Briggs, and Atticus Bishop, the pastor of Crossway Church, stood on the stage, conversing quietly. The superintendent's police officer son, Julian Sinclair, and Darryl Wiggins, the owner of the local bank, huddled close to the superintendent.

Several men in gray camo uniforms she didn't recognize milled around the stage. They were armed with rifles and sidearms and looked like soldiers.

Superintendent Sinclair said something, and the people on the stage sat down in the chairs except for Bishop. The superintendent moved to the podium.

"Thank you for coming," she said into a battery-operated megaphone so everyone in the crowd could hear.

Her blonde hair was smoothed into a crisp bob at her chin. Beneath her winter coat, she wore a form-fitting plum-colored pencil skirt and jacket. Her makeup was perfectly applied, but her eyes were red, like she'd been crying recently.

The superintendent smoothed her hair and straightened her skirt. Her posture was perfect. "The pastor of Crossway Church, our own Atticus Bishop, will be conducting the ceremony today. Together, we grieve for the forty-seven innocent lives lost two nights ago—"

A wail splintered the air.

In front of Quinn, a woman dropped to her knees. Her shoulders quaked. "My sister! My sister is gone . . ."

Quinn stiffened. She recognized the woman's black curly hair, broad shoulders, and puffy silver coat. Maxine Bernstein worked at the hardware store.

Quinn knew her sister, had seen her in the sanctuary that night. The dental hygienist from Brite Smiles Dental. The woman she'd locked eyes with right before the monsters had opened fire.

Quinn had watched her die.

The woman let out another high, keening wail of grief. The sound knifed straight through Quinn's heart.

She sucked in a sharp breath. A wave of dizziness flushed

through her, terrible memories flooding her mind. She tried to push them out, to regain control.

"How can she be gone?" Mrs. Bernstein cried. "How can she be dead?"

Her husband bent over her and helped her to her feet. He put his arm around her waist and whispered into her hair. She rested her head on his shoulder, still weeping, and allowed him to lead her away.

People moved aside, their faces filled with compassion, pity, and shared sorrow. Several patted the Bernsteins' arms, shoulders, and backs as they passed. Several people were crying, men and women both.

"I'm so sorry for your loss," Superintendent Sinclair said softly, her voice cracking. "I'm so sorry." The superintendent kept talking, but Quinn barely heard her.

A tinny sound buzzed in her ears. Words were pointless. Words meant nothing.

They wouldn't ease that woman's anguish. They couldn't give anyone their loved ones back. Couldn't begin to replace what was lost. Couldn't bring back Chloe and Juniper either.

The sun on her face did nothing to warm her chilled skin. She felt cold from the inside out. Like something inside her had frozen solid but was threatening to shatter like ice.

After the superintendent said more stuff about community and grief and coming together—blah, blah, blah—she finally handed the megaphone to Atticus Bishop.

The crowd hushed into absolute silence. The only sounds were shifting bodies, quiet weeping, the birds chirping.

Atticus Bishop dwarfed the podium. Big and burly, he wore a black leather jacket over a Hawaiian shirt covered in pink flowers. His warm brown skin was ashen, his eyes red-rimmed. He gripped the megaphone in one hand, ran his hand through his afro with the other.

The crowd waited.

He cleared his throat. Cleared it again.

Quinn blinked back the sudden wetness in her eyes. She felt the absence of two squealing, energetic little girls like they were two holes in her own heart.

Her lungs constricted. It was hard to breathe. Her hands clenched into fists at her sides.

"Thank you, my friends and neighbors," Bishop said finally, his voice loud and booming but ragged with grief. "Thank you for gathering with me to mourn our great loss this morning. There are no words that can encompass the tragedy that has touched each one of us. We've lost friends, neighbors, sisters . . ." He closed his eyes briefly. "And daughters."

She couldn't listen. She couldn't hear this. Couldn't handle it.

She thought she'd wanted to be here, but it was a mistake.

She had to get the hell out.

8
_____

QUINN
DAY EIGHT

T he crowd pressed in too close. She was closed in, cut off. Helpless. Her pulse thudded in her ears. White spots danced in front of her vision.

She stumbled back, stepped on someone's toe.

"Ouch!"

Quinn whipped around.

It was Whitney Blair, a girl she went to high school with, and her father, Mr. Blair—the same guy Quinn had rammed with her cart in Friendly's only a week ago.

Whitney looked at her and covered her hand with her mouth. "Oh, I'm so sorry, Quinn."

Why in hell was *she* the one apologizing? Quinn was the one who'd stepped on her foot. Even uptight Mr. Blair was looking at her with pity.

"I'm really sorry about what happened to you, Quinn," Whitney continued, like she couldn't tell that Quinn just wanted her to shut up. "It must have been so awful. I'm so glad you're okay."

Quinn's heart beat harder. It didn't matter that Whitney's condolences seemed genuine. Quinn hated this. She hated all of them.

A hard knot of emotion tangled in her gut, pressed against the backs of her eyelids. She was seconds away from losing it.

"I'm fine," she snapped.

"But—"

"Just leave me alone."

Whitney's sympathetic gaze shifted from Quinn to the stage.

Bishop had stopped talking. The sudden silence burned Quinn's ears. She turned slowly, hot shame flooding her cheeks.

Atticus Bishop stared straight at her. Their eyes met. His eyes were haunted, his features hollowed out with sorrow. The loss of his children etched into every line and pore of his face.

Quinn went rigid. She couldn't move, couldn't breathe.

Bishop handed the megaphone to Chief Briggs and jumped off the platform to the ground. The crowd parted silently before him. He strode toward Quinn.

Everything else faded away but Bishop.

Quinn wanted to run. She wanted to be anywhere but here, facing the father of the kids she'd failed to save.

Stupid tears stung her eyes, but she couldn't hold them back. The memories seared her brain, the screams and shouts echoing inside her head. Juniper's terrified face. Chloe shrieking her name.

The words were like glass in her throat. "I—I couldn't—I tried—"

Before she could say anything else, Bishop enveloped her in a fierce hug. Her wet cheek pressed against his broad chest. His massive arms encircled her, shutting out the crowd, the murmurs and stares, the soft weeping—everything.

Instinctively, she stiffened. Tried to pull away.

He didn't let her go.

"My mother—"

"Isn't you. You aren't accountable for her. Aren't responsible for her."

"I'm sorry," she whispered, her voice muffled against his leather jacket. "I tried to get them out. I promise I tried . . ."

"My child." He lowered his head over hers and spoke softly so only she could hear. "You have nothing to be sorry for. Nothing."

"I . . . couldn't save them."

His strong body trembled. His baritone voice was raw with pain. "Neither could I."

Something released inside her chest. Her heart like a closed fist opening slowly. Something thawing deep inside her.

She gave in. She allowed herself to relax into him, allowed him to comfort her. She couldn't help it. Couldn't fight it anymore.

She'd been as strong as she could for as long as she could. Abruptly, she felt like a kid again, scared and overwhelmed and alone.

Milo had been there, but he was the little kid she needed to protect. She couldn't burden him with her own trauma.

Bishop knew what it was like, what she'd been through. She wasn't alone with this anymore. He knew exactly how she felt without her having to say a word. He understood her, knew what she'd done and what she hadn't, and forgave her anyway.

Bishop didn't blame her for failing to save the girls. He didn't blame her for her mother's role in all this.

And if he didn't, maybe the rest of them wouldn't, either.

She didn't know how long they held each other. It didn't matter. Nothing mattered but their shared grief and pain. His compassion was the solace she desperately needed. Despite his own suffering, he gave it freely.

Finally, Bishop pulled away. He cupped her face in his large hands. Tears leaked down his face. He made no attempt to brush them away. "Juniper and Chloe and Daphne are in God's hands now. They don't hurt anymore. They're not afraid anymore. 'He will wipe every tear from their eyes. There will be no more death or mourning or crying or pain, for these things have passed away.'"

Quinn found herself nodding. Gran believed in God, did all that church stuff that Quinn had never found much use for. But she saw how it comforted Bishop, how his faith sustained him after a tragedy that would fell any other man.

Something deep down in her soul longed for the same peace.

If Bishop had found it after all that had been taken from him, maybe it was real. Maybe it was something she, too, could find and hold onto.

"Thank you," she whispered.

Bishop squeezed her shoulder.

A distant shout drew her attention. Bishop stepped back and looked around, shielding his eyes with his hand.

Another shout. Someone yelling angrily from the back of the crowd.

Toward the rear, the crowd rippled and gave way, people hurrying to move aside as a group of six or seven men and women surged through them toward the front.

Their bodies were taut, hands clenched into fists, their expressions furious. They were staggering like they were drunk.

"This isn't the time for tears!" shouted the man leading the way. He shook his fist in the air. "It's time for justice!"

"What are you going to *do* about it, Superintendent Sinclair?" a woman shouted. Her name was Patsy Snyder, the owner of Friendly's Grocery. Her brother was one of the victims. "What about you, Chief Briggs? You gonna get off your fat ass and see justice done for once?"

"They're still out there!" the first man shouted. "You're stringing up ribbons while you should be stringing up the monsters that did this!"

"Where's justice for my brother? Kill those monsters!"

"They killed my neighbor and her kids. They deserve to die!"

Chief Briggs cleared his throat into the megaphone. "A plan is in place. We're organizing now. The procedures must be—"

"To hell with procedures!" someone else shouted.

"Justice now!" a woman in the crowd cried. "Justice for Crossway!"

Others picked up the cry. Dozens of people chanted, "Justice for Crossway!"

The mood of the crowd shifted from grief to outrage in only a few moments. Quinn could feel the dangerous, electric energy thrumming through them. Catching like a cold and spreading rapidly.

These were normal, boring, law-abiding people, friends and neighbors. But their fear and anger were controlling them now. They were unrecognizable.

"Calm down!" Chief Briggs shouted into the megaphone. "Everyone remain calm right now!"

The crowd didn't listen. They surged forward like a single coordinated organism. Fists raised and beat the air. Faces contorted in fury, demanding justice. They threatened to overwhelm the stage.

Chief Briggs stared at the belligerent crowd, aghast. Darryl Wiggins leapt from his seat and turned to the superintendent, gesturing wildly.

The strange uniformed men moved in front of the platform and started pushing people back. Several of the local cops joined in.

Bodies rushed around Quinn, bumping and jostling her. Bishop put himself between her and the worst of the crowd.

"You shouldn't be here," he said, his hands outstretched to shield her. "Things are going to get ugly."

Everything was ugly now. And it was only going to get worse.

"I'm not afraid of ugly," Quinn said.

9

HANNAH
DAY EIGHT

"Will Ghost be okay?" Hannah asked anxiously.

Liam stood beside her, stiff and stony-faced. He kept shifting from foot to foot, his free hand balled into a fist at his side, tapping the Glock against his thigh with the other. He didn't want to admit it, but she knew he was as tense and nervous as she was.

Ghost lay on the operating table in the center of the Paws and Claws operating room. On the way here, he'd vomited twice. He panted, tongue lolling, his big chest rising and falling rapidly. His intelligent brown eyes were dulled. He was conscious, but barely, like he'd fallen into some sort of stupor.

Hannah hated seeing him like this—such a powerful, regal creature reduced to something limp and helpless terrified her.

Dr. Beverly Laudé glanced up with a strained smile. "That depends."

The veterinarian was in her early sixties, with full cheeks and smile lines radiating from her kind eyes, her short gray hair curling beneath her winter hat. She was practical, intelligent, and instantly concerned for Ghost. They hadn't needed to coerce her at all.

Dr. Laudé was more than willing to help. They'd been lucky to reach her at home. Dennis Reynolds had scampered away as soon as he'd shown them the correct house, his bag of stolen goodies bulging beneath his coat.

Hannah didn't blame him for stealing. People did what they thought they had to when they were desperate to save their loved ones. Still, there was a line.

What Dennis had taken for himself meant less for others who were just as needy. It meant fewer meds for Dr. Laudé to use to save the animal and human patients in her care—meds Ghost might need right now.

Dr. Laudé looked down at Ghost with affection. "Great Pyrenees Mountain Dogs are wonderfully loyal and protective dogs. Smart, too."

"He's very smart," Hannah said, her voice breaking. "He's the smartest dog I've ever met. Please tell me you can save him."

"I need to examine him first. I can't make any promises."

Dr. Laudé had set up several battery-operated camping lanterns for light. She snapped on a pair of plastic gloves and donned a lab coat from a hook on the wall. The operating room smelled sterile, medicinal, and clean.

"What exactly happened?" the vet asked.

Hannah flinched. "He was shot."

Dr. Laudé glanced at Hannah, her expression curious. "May I ask how?"

Apprehension tangled in her gut. Her heart contracted.

She shook her head. She didn't want to talk about it, didn't want to say Pike's name aloud. Not here in this calm, quiet room. It was a ridiculous thought, but saying Pike's name here in front of Ghost felt like it might jinx everything.

Pike didn't belong here. He didn't belong in her head. She refused to give him any power.

"Someone came after us, wanted our supplies," Liam said into the silence. "The dog attacked him to protect Hannah."

He understood her reticence without her needing to say a word. Hannah shot him a grateful look.

Dr. Laudé frowned as she examined Ghost, her hands moving expertly over his body. She pulled out a penlight and checked his pupils. "I'm assessing for shock and trauma, checking his airway, breathing, heart rate, and presence of bleeding or fractures."

She straightened, her face grave. "You came at the right time. My generator is almost out of fuel. I've been conserving as much as possible. I'll turn on the power to take a radiograph—an X-ray—of his skull to look for potential skull fractures.

"It looks like the bullet might have just skimmed his skull, but I'm seeing concerning signs of increasing ICP—intracranial pressure. His level of responsiveness is deteriorating rapidly. Unequal pupils. The vomiting. His blood pressure and respiratory rate are both too high, and his pulse rate is decreasing. That's known as the Cushing triad, a late sign of increased ICP."

Hannah couldn't breathe. Her heart dropped into her stomach. "What does that mean?"

"The brain is swelling, and the resultant intracranial pressure is causing neurological deterioration. It's imperative to reduce the swelling of the brain tissue immediately."

"And if you can't?"

"I'm sorry."

Hannah shook her head fiercely. She wrapped her arms around her ribs and hugged herself. "No, no, no. That's not an option. He can't die. You have to save him."

"I'll do my best," Dr. Laudé said. "I can promise that much."

"How do you treat this?" Liam asked tersely. "Does he need surgery?"

"If he doesn't have a major skull fracture, then no. I can use hyperosmotic solutions to draw fluids from the tissues. Mannitol will decrease the production of spinal fluid. I can give him some oxygen as well. It's important to reduce his systolic blood pressure. For a Pyr his size, I want to see it around one twenty over sixty-six mm hg, give or take."

Hannah tried to feel relieved. Surgery now probably meant a death sentence. And she was incredibly thankful that the vet still had the meds Ghost needed in stock.

Dr. Laudé squeezed Hannah's shoulder. "The next several hours will tell us what we need to know."

Dr. Laudé turned back to Ghost. Hannah and Liam offered to help, but she shooed them out, telling them she'd check back in two hours with an update.

It would be the longest two hours of Hannah's life.

10

HANNAH
DAY EIGHT

L iam paced the long, narrow waiting room in front of the plate glass windows, prowling like an impatient lion. He kept his Glock in his hands and constantly checked outside, watching the parking lot, the street, and the hardware store across the road for signs of trouble.

Hannah tried to fold her legs in the chair, but her belly got in the way. Liam handed her his go-bag. She used it as a pillow, unzipping her coat and stretching out on the connected plastic seats. "Thank you."

She rubbed her tired eyes. Her lower back ached. Her ankles were swollen. The room was cold, but not as cold as it was outside. Her belly moved, and something poked against her bladder. She ignored it.

Dread and anxiety twisted her insides. Her mouth felt coated in something bitter and metallic, like she'd swallowed a copper penny. She was worried about Ghost. Worried about everything.

She tried counting the chairs, the animal posters on the walls, the cars in the parking lot, the tile squares of the floor. Nothing worked. She needed a distraction.

She glanced over at Liam. "Not everyone is bad, you know."

He kept pacing, kept glaring out the window like he wanted to fight something. "That thief was no hero."

"Maybe not, but he didn't deserve to die, either."

Liam only grunted.

"There are degrees of 'bad.' Dennis may not be an altruistic angel, but he wasn't a gangster warlord, either."

Liam snorted. "Give him time."

She rolled the words around on her tongue before she said them. "Some people are good."

CiCi had treated her with dignity and great kindness. Dr. Laudé was freely giving her energy, expertise, and precious limited supplies to help strangers and save the life of a dog she didn't even know.

Liam himself had risked hypothermia and more to rescue Hannah in the woods. Everything he did now was for her, not for himself.

"You really believe that?" His gaze was trained on the street, the dozens of cars hunched beneath shrouds of snow. "After everything you've been through?"

She stiffened. The idea of trusting other people was terrifying. She didn't deny that. But she had to fight against it. Had to overcome the toxic thinking, the way *he*'d trained her to think, to act.

To cower, to submit. To fear everything and everyone. To hate.

Otherwise, he won. Freedom from her physical cage meant little if she couldn't get him out of her head, if she still lived like she was trapped.

She said, "I do."

Liam's gaze landed on her again, sharp and penetrating. Everything in her wanted to look away, to lower her eyes to the floor, but she forced herself to meet his eyes.

"The world is full of greedy, hateful, violent people," he said. "Without the government to control them, without the police and the threat of prison to rein in their impulses, people will become the worst versions of themselves. People who will kidnap and rape and worse."

She wasn't naïve. Wasn't stupid, either. She knew evil. Had looked into its eyes.

The whole country was sliding into lawlessness and mayhem. Desperation bred fear, hatred, and violence. Within a few weeks, almost everyone would be that desperate. Many already were.

"You're right," she said softly. "I know what humans are capable of. I still don't believe they're all bad. No matter what happens. There is goodness in the world. There has to be. Otherwise, what's the point?"

He didn't answer her.

She bit her lower lip. "Look at Dr. Laudé. She's helping us with no benefit to herself, isn't she?"

He shook his head. "She'll help the wrong person. Give too much. Someone will either take all she has or kill her for it."

Neither said anything for a moment. They were both thinking of CiCi.

"You think the good ones will just end up dead."

"I do."

"Maybe they need a protector."

He looked at her.

"Someone who can teach them how to defend themselves. You can be a good person and a fighter."

"A good person and a killer?"

She didn't hesitate. "Yes. Absolutely. If it's the right person and for the right reasons."

He nodded but didn't say anything.

She slipped her good hand into her right coat pocket and felt the handle of the folding knife, the pistol nestled beside it. "You said you would teach me."

Liam turned and glanced back at her. The gray daylight streaming through the windows highlighted his rugged features, his eyes a fierce blue. "You want to start now?"

Her heartbeat quickened. "I need something to distract me. Please."

Liam nodded and took one more glance outside at the town, which looked completely abandoned, not a soul in sight. Their snowmobile with the trailer was parked out front, the only machine not smothered in snow.

He strode over to her, pocketed his own gun, and held out his hand for hers.

She fished the Ruger out of her pocket and handed it to him. He ejected the magazine, cleared the weapon, and checked to make sure the safety was on. Satisfied, he dry fired the weapon to check its functioning.

She heaved herself to her feet, hand on the chair back for balance. She felt more and more awkward with each passing day. She pressed her hand against her lower back with a wince. "What's first? Find a shooting range? Some empty pop bottles?"

"We don't have the extra ammo to expend at target practice. We need every round for self-defense. And we don't want to draw attention with gunshots."

Her face fell. "Oh."

"I can still teach you the correct stance, how to hold it, how to aim. And where the safety is."

Her cheeks flamed. She recalled the library, her terror, her fingers fumbling over the gun, forgetting the slide-mounted safety in her blind panic. "I remember."

He eyed her. She didn't like the way he was looking at her. Like he thought she was small and weak.

She hated that it was true. She'd done her best to stay healthy in her basement prison, but there was only so much a person could do. She'd always be small, but she didn't have to stay weak. "Show me."

He demonstrated. "You'll want to hold it in both hands, with your left hand braced beneath your right-handed grip."

A wave of shame swept over her. "I can't hold it like that."

"Sure, you can. You just—"

"My left hand. It's useless."

He hesitated. His expression darkened. A shadow she couldn't read passed over his face, then was gone. "Pull off your gloves."

She obeyed. In the harsh daylight, her bad hand looked even worse than usual. The broken fingers disfigured like claws, misshapen, like the warped and gnarled branches of an old tree.

She could move them, but only with great effort—and pain. Only her thumb still functioned relatively normally. It was ugly. Grotesque and repugnant.

She flushed with embarrassment and self-disgust.

She hated it exposed in the light, hated that Liam was the one seeing it. She didn't want him to think of her as ugly or hideous. It was a stupid thought, but she couldn't help it.

She tried to withdraw her deformed hand, to tuck it in her pocket, back in her glove, behind her back—anywhere—but Liam seized her wrist before she could pull away.

His features didn't contort with revulsion. He didn't look at her in disgust. He examined her disfigurement with a clinical detachment, his fingers tracing hers gently.

His touch jolted through her like a shot of electricity. Her stomach roiled, her heart drumming loud in her ears.

She cleared her throat, close to tears and hating herself for it.

How weak he must think she was. How pathetic. "I can't do anything with it. Like I said. Useless."

He frowned. A line appeared between his brows. He was still holding her hand. "Not entirely. Can you curl your fingers into a fist?"

She did. Slowly, awkwardly, painfully. She grimaced but didn't stop. Her pinkie and ring finger were too disfigured to move much at all. Her pointer finger could curl in slightly until it tucked into her curved thumb.

"Think of it like making a stand to brace your right hand. Balance the pistol grip in the divot right there between your thumb and finger."

She followed his instructions. The butt of the pistol fit. She concentrated on steadying her arms and managed to balance the Ruger well.

He gave her a grim smile. "There you go."

He showed her how to widen her stance, straighten her shoulders, hold her arms, and brace the gun as best she could. He showed her how to steady her breathing and squeeze—not pull—the trigger.

She bit her lower lip and studied the gun. "How do I rack it one-handed?"

He pointed to a magazine-covered end table between two sets of chairs. "Put the area near the front sight on the table edge and push down. You can do it with the edge of something hard—a counter, holster, or the heel of your boot."

She practiced racking the slide one-handed until she got the hang of it. Liam demonstrated how to reload by tucking the pistol between her knees while in a seated position or into the crook of a bent knee, though that seemed more difficult.

They practiced everything he'd taught her again and again, with Liam taking frequent breaks to check outside.

He showed her how to develop situational awareness. How to scan her surroundings, stay alert, and watch for anything out of place.

Hearing and smell were equally important. He taught her to recognize the normal scents and sounds of every building she was in. Buildings had their own rhythms, sounds, and smells. She needed to learn what was normal, so she would recognize it if something changed.

It was one thing to practice with Liam right beside her; quite another when she was on her own.

In the presence of a real threat, would she remember everything? Would her body betray her by freezing? Her mind going numb, disappearing on her when she most needed to think, to act? She couldn't let that happen.

She had to be stronger than she'd ever been. Smarter and braver.

"Do that every day," Liam said. "You'll get better."

"What about the knife?"

He raised his eyebrows. "You're not tired yet?"

She was, but she wouldn't admit it. Every day, she felt her energy draining from her, leeched by the parasite inside her womb. If she sat around doing nothing, she'd be just as tired but plagued with fretful worry for Ghost.

And who knew when Pike or another threat might emerge? Ghost was in intensive care because she hadn't known what to do. She didn't want to make that mistake again. Couldn't make that mistake again.

She chose to believe in good people, but she refused to be naïve. People would have to prove themselves trustworthy. And those that didn't, well, she needed to be ready.

She wouldn't let Ghost down again.

She straightened her shoulders. "I want to learn everything you know."

Liam let out a sudden, surprised bark of laughter. "That would take a while."

She stared back at him, unflinching. "Let's start with the knife, then."

11

HANNAH
DAY EIGHT

Anxious hours passed. The afternoon dragged by with agonizing slowness.

Liam paced. Hannah chewed her lower lip and worried constantly. And she prayed. She didn't know whether God was still listening to her, but she prayed anyway. Fervently, with all her heart. She didn't know what else to do.

She held the Ruger in her lap with her good hand and imagined herself aiming, exhaling, squeezing the trigger again and again. Practicing in her mind the way she'd done with her music back in her basement prison. The songs she'd written, memorizing each line, each chord, playing it over and over in her head, miming it with her fingers until it was almost real. Almost.

At one point, Liam dug some water and MREs out of his pack, but Hannah could do little more than drink. With every hour that passed, the knot in her belly grew tighter and tighter.

As the afternoon stretched toward evening, Dr. Laudé finally appeared in the reception area. She gestured at Hannah and Liam with a flashlight.

Hannah's heart leapt into her throat. "Is he okay?"

Dr. Laudé gave nothing away. "Come see for yourself."

She uncurled herself from the hard plastic chair nearest the door and slipped her pistol into her coat pocket. If Dr. Laudé saw it, she didn't say anything.

Hannah and Liam followed the vet down the darkened hallway, the flashlight beam sweeping eerily across the floor and walls. Hannah's limbs felt heavy, her stomach filled with lead.

She entered the operating room. A low woof greeted her. In the dim, wavering light, Ghost's body threw a huge shadow on the wall. He was lying on his belly, his head up, and his long, plumed tail thumping delicately against the stainless-steel table.

"Ghost!" She flung herself at him, her vision already blurring.

She leaned across the operating table, ignoring the sharp jab of a metal corner against her belly, and buried her hands in the soft scruff around his neck. "I was so worried. I thought I'd lost you."

Ghost snuffled happily into her ear. He pressed his dry, cool nose against her hair, her forehead, her closed eyes, her nose and chin. He licked her cheek and whined softly in greeting.

Dr. Laudé had cleaned him up good. His fur was shaved in a small section on his head near his right ear. The ragged wound from the bullet had been cleaned and sutured.

Her heart ached with love. She fought back the tears. If she started crying now, she might never stop.

Oh, screw it. She let the tears come. They were grateful, joyous tears.

She felt Liam's presence as he moved to the table beside her.

Ghost looked at Liam and let out a low woof that rumbled against Hannah's hands. Liam reached out hesitantly, as if half-afraid the dog might chomp down on his fingers.

Ghost sniffed him, didn't bite.

Liam relaxed a little and scratched beneath the dog's chin.

Ghost leaned into the scratch, half-closing his eyes in pleasure. His bushy tail *thump, thump, thumped* against the table.

Liam smiled. "Good to see you up and around."

Hannah watched them, trying to hide her surprise. First, that
Liam would be so openly affectionate toward Ghost, and second,
that Ghost was equally responsive.

Whatever distrust Ghost had reserved for Liam seemed to
have evaporated.

Maybe he remembered Liam carrying him through the snow
to the barn, lowering him gently into the hay. Maybe he understood that Liam had come back for them both.

"How is he doing, Doc?" Liam asked.

"Good news. The intracranial pressure has gone down. The
radiograph revealed no skull fractures or bone shards. If Ghost
experiences no additional nervous system deterioration over a
forty-eight-hour period, and if his blood pressure and blood sugar
levels remain within normal limits, the prognosis is quite
favorable."

Liam cocked his brows. "So that's a yes?"

"Yes," Dr. Laudé said, smiling. "Dogs, especially stoic breeds
like Pyrs, can recover remarkably quickly. I've seen them jump
down from a cage four feet off the floor a few hours after major
surgery. Ghost is young. He's extremely tough. And I can see that
he has a lot to live for. He's obviously much loved."

Hannah rubbed behind his floppy ears, careful to avoid the
sutures. Ghost's loose black jowls falling back in a self-satisfied,
Cheshire-cat grin. "He is."

"And spoiled rotten," Liam said wryly.

"I wouldn't have it any other way." Dr. Laudé removed her lab
coat and tossed it into an empty basket next to the counter. She
stripped off her gloves and tossed them into a nearby trashcan.

"That being said, we need to carefully monitor him for the next forty-eight hours. He needs rest and fluids."

Liam tensed. "We were planning to head out."

"Oh, no. Absolutely not. You aren't taking that dog anywhere. Not for a few days at least."

"We can't stay," Liam said.

"We're staying," Hannah said.

Liam shot her a hard look.

She raised her chin and shot him a look of her own.

"It's important," Dr. Laudé said quietly. "I know you have somewhere else you want to be. I know it's dangerous to be far from home right now. You love this dog? You want him to live? I need to monitor him."

Hannah didn't want to remain here any longer than they had to, either.

They'd been careful. There were a dozen towns they could have fled to. Pike was wounded. He'd be slow.

She wasn't stupid. Anyone they came across was at risk. Even Dr. Laudé, if Pike somehow managed to discover how she'd saved Ghost.

She remembered Pike leaning in close, smiling savagely, whispering in her ear as he told her what he'd done to CiCi, how he'd killed her for her kindness.

The longer they remained here, the more likely it was that Pike would follow their tracks and trace them right to her doorstep.

On the other hand, to leave now imperiled Ghost. Maybe some people wouldn't value this animal's life as she did. Maybe they wouldn't understand. But she wasn't accountable to those people.

She wasn't putting Ghost at risk, period.

They'd just have to make it work.

"Liam, we have to," Hannah said softly.

Ghost nosed Liam's hand insistently until he scratched beneath his chin again.

Liam looked down at the dog, shook his head, and let out a beleaguered sigh. "Fine."

"I'd normally suggest the two motels in town, but they're completely full. Their generators ran out three days ago, so I don't think anyone would choose to be there right now, if you know what I mean."

Hannah wrinkled her nose. "I do."

Dr. Laudé smiled wearily. "You're welcome to stay at my home, though I'm afraid I won't be a very good host. I have food and water, since I can trade my services for what I need. But I'm not home much. Lots of folks are sick and getting sicker. Some are already running out of their prescription meds. The local pharmacies are either out, or people can't pay the new exorbitant cost."

"We couldn't impose," Hannah said.

Dr. Laudé angled her chin at Liam. "I've got two dead trees on my property that I could sure use for firewood, if a young, strapping lad happened by to do the hard labor for me. I'm too old for chopping down trees."

Hannah tugged on Liam's coat sleeve. The corners of her mouth twitched. "I've got a strapping lad right here."

Liam gave a gruff sigh, but quickly gave in. "I see I'm outvoted here. That won't be a problem, Dr. Laudé. I can help."

"That's settled, then." Dr. Laudé ran her hands through her curly gray hair and tucked the short strands behind her ears. "How did things get so crazy so quickly? This isn't like any power outage we've ever experienced."

"Because it's not like anything anyone has ever experienced," Liam said.

"They're saying the power grid is down, that something—the

sun or a nuke or a meteor—fried it. That the president and congress are all hiding out in Mount Weather, and us little people have been left to our own devices."

Liam shrugged. "We've heard the same."

"It is what it is, I suppose. We'll just have to make the best of it, do what we can." Dr. Laudé sighed. She glanced at Hannah, then gave her a second, longer look. Her gaze dropped to Hannah's belly. "Since you're here . . . may I check you quickly, Hannah?"

Hannah flinched. Her coat was still unzipped. Without the oversized thing to hide her shape, her rounded belly was obvious.

She swallowed. A memory of Milo as a newborn flashed behind her eyelids—soft, downy scalp, huge brown eyes, wrinkled old man face nestled perfectly against her chest.

She pushed it away. This was different. Completely different.

She wanted to say no, but that would draw even more attention from the kind-hearted vet. Attention she didn't want.

She allowed the vet to poke and prod her belly. She looked away, her eyes suddenly stinging. She bit her lower lip, hard.

Dr. Laudé grunted in surprise.

"What?" Liam asked. "She growing a goat in there?"

Hannah rolled her eyes. "Anyone ever told you that you can be more than a little insensitive?"

He remained impassive. "Nope. Never."

"Somehow I doubt that."

Dr. Laudé shook her head. "You're showing small and you're underweight, but you're much further along than I first thought." She looked up at Hannah. "What's your due date, honey?"

Hannah swallowed. Her face flushed hot. "I . . . I don't know."

Dr. Laudé frowned. "Really? Okay, well. This baby is already head down. You feel that pressure on your bladder?"

Hannah felt it like a tremendous weight bearing down on her, like time running out. A tiny, ferocious thing inside her, stealing her nourishment, her energy.

She glanced nervously at Liam.

Liam's face had gone pale, his eyes narrowing in shock—and concern. He was as unprepared as she was.

"What does that mean?" he asked gruffly.

Dr. Laudé patted Hannah's stomach and straightened. "I can check to see how effaced you are. I'm no obstetrician, but I've birthed hundreds of calves, foals, puppies, you name it. I can check things for you."

All the blood rushed to her head. Trepidation filled her. The smart thing was to say yes. She was fully aware of that. It didn't matter.

She didn't want this stranger poking around where she didn't belong. Couldn't bear the thought of anyone touching her there. She gave a hard shake of her head. "No, thanks."

Dr. Laudé looked concerned, but she didn't argue. "Then it could be anytime. Nature has her own timetable." The vet squeezed her knee. "But soon, Hannah. It's coming soon."

12

OCTAVIA RILEY

DAY TEN

"I don't wanna die!" Octavia Riley wailed.

"No one's dying but the pigs." Ray Shultz glowered at her. "Now shut the hell up."

Ray, Tommy, and Billy were positioned at the windows of their junky trailer. A half-dozen other men settled in the kitchen and bedrooms or just sprawled in the living room in the armchairs or the floor. They were all armed to the teeth.

It was somewhere past three a.m. Or maybe it was four a.m. already. She'd been up for almost three nights straight. It was wearing on her.

Wearing on everyone. They were all haggard and twitchy. They couldn't sleep. The cops could attack at any moment.

Several of Tommy and Ray's friends were hunkered down in sniper nests around the property, including the roofs of the sheds and the second and third trailers behind the main one.

The ones stuck outside made their unhappiness known with constant bellyaching about their balls freezing off, coming through the kiddie walkie-talkies they'd scavenged from the trailer park.

They were lucky to find working radios after whatever it was had fried everything to bits.

All their guys were armed with AR-15s, AK-47s, shotguns, and other weapons she couldn't identify. A few of their girlfriends were armed with guns, too. Several women and children who normally lived at the compound had moved in with friends or relatives until this all blew over.

Octavia didn't bother with weapons. She lay sprawled on the couch in a dirty sweatshirt and two pairs of sweatpants she'd been wearing for far too long.

The fire burning in the fireplace kept the cramped living room warm enough. It also provided the only light in the room. Another flashlight had run out of batteries last night. She was down to only one that worked.

When the fire got low, she threw on more logs and crumpled up pieces of trash that littered the floor. They'd used up the last of the trash bags and dumped them down the ravine.

Dirty plates and cups covered the coffee table. The stench of rancid things wafted through the trailer—feces, urine, and rotting food.

It made her massive headache even worse. Dried blood still crusted the side of her head. She'd blacked out two nights ago. Ray said she was lucky as hell they'd found her and dragged her unconscious ass out of that storage room before the cops arrived.

She didn't want to think about that. She did her best to ignore it all. She pushed aside some of the mess, dug out a bump of white powder with her long pinkie nail, and sniffed deeply.

It burned her nostrils like a blowtorch. Her eyes watered as she tilted her head back and felt it drain down the back of her throat.

She waited for the crank to hit, the bliss of the high, the ride that would take away the cold, the hunger, and the stress of the last few days. What she really wanted was to fall into a coma and sleep all damn day.

Ray was ready to take out the town's entire police force. He wanted to take over Fall Creek, rule it with an iron fist. He was too stupid to do it, though.

Billy, on the other hand. He was a cunning S.O.B.

It had been his plan to shoot up the church in the first place; Ray had just wanted Bishop. A few hits of crank to pump them up, and the others were fully on board, riled up, greedy for violence, and ready to blast anything that moved.

Billy was the one who killed those kids. Shot those two little girls in cold blood.

Octavia never would've done that. Not Ray, either.

Billy scared the living crap out of Octavia, when she thought about it.

She tried not to think about it. She tried not to think about anything.

It didn't work. Not anymore. Not even high.

The images of that night wouldn't stop intruding inside her head. She'd been cranked then, too, so the memories were jagged and disjointed and came to her in pieces, too sharp and too bright.

They made her head hurt. They made her want to fry her own brain to forget.

"I'm not a killer," she mumbled. "I didn't kill nobody. Not like you."

"Shut up," Ray said again. He ran a hand over his balding salt-and-pepper hair. His deep-set eyes gleamed with malice. "Or I'll make you."

She knew to leave him alone when he got like this. But she couldn't help it. "I shouldn't even be here."

"You're not going anywhere," Ray said. "You're gonna be right here when we slaughter every last one of them."

"For Nickel!" Tommy said in his weird, drawn-out southern drawl. "We do them for Nickel!"

One of their friends from town had told them that the cops had killed one of the Carter brothers—Randy "Nickel" Carter— whom they'd accidentally left behind in their rush to escape the church.

Now Tommy, Billy, and Bucky wanted blood. Not just for Ray's sake or for a stash of food or gold, but for vengeance.

The men chimed in with grunts of approval. They were all in.

Kill the pigs. Take over the town. Live like kings.

Who wouldn't be on board with that plan? She was on board, wasn't she?

She'd had enough of this stupid town thumbing their noses at her. Let them see who she really was, what she was capable of.

She'd strut around like a queen. Take whatever house in Winter Haven she wanted. Whatever clothes and jewelry and the nicest working car she could find. Taking all the food.

She'd be the freaking queen and let those self-righteous yoga and soccer moms fear *her*, respect *her*. They could clean up her crap and cook her dinner.

They could wait on her, serve her, cower and tremble like little mice she could crush with her foot.

Yeah, she liked that plan. Liked it just fine.

Liked it almost enough to forget how she'd gotten to this place. The things they'd had to do to get here. The things she'd still have to do.

"It'd be nice if we had that kid you promised us," Billy said darkly. He was short, compact, and wiry, with that disturbing lazy eye that made it look like he was always watching her, even when he wasn't. "The cop's boy. We could've worked with that."

A shred of memory unfurled behind her eyelids. Quinn. Her daughter—angry and defiant, pushing that little kid behind her, protecting him, denying Octavia what she wanted. What she needed.

She ran her tongue over her crooked, yellowed teeth. They felt furry and gross. When was the last time she'd even bothered to brush her teeth?

One of the back molars was loose. She worked it with her tongue, wondering absently if it would hurt when it finally popped out. Her hair was greasy, her scalp itching like a thousand little bugs were crawling everywhere.

It was hard to keep her eyelids open. Everything was heavy, so heavy. "Wasn't my fault."

Billy sneered. "Nothing's ever your fault, is it Octavia?"

"I got hit on the head!" she whined.

"More like you *let* your daughter escape." He studied her in the firelight with those oily, beetle-black eyes she despised. "Shoulda known better than to trust a whore."

She opened her mouth to protest, but nothing came out. She *had* freed Quinn. She'd done it on purpose. Even high, she knew better than to let the likes of Billy Carter get a hold of Quinn.

She hadn't been the best mother. No one would debate that. Not even her.

There was always something else, more fun and more exciting and just *more*. Quinn was fine without her. She'd always been fine. Besides, Octavia's uptight mother was always around to take care of things.

So why not party? Why not enjoy life while you could? Before age and disappointment and responsibilities sucked you dry, like every single adult she knew.

Everyone hated their short, miserable lives, but they never did a damn thing about it. Not her. Not Octavia Riley. She wasn't gonna be tied down to anything. She was gonna live the high life. The best life.

Her eyes dimmed as she felt the loose tooth with her tongue again. Ray had punched her in the jaw last week. Maybe that was why it was loose.

Screw Ray. Screw Billy.

Even high, she'd done a good thing. The right thing. She'd protected her daughter from Billy and the rest of them. She'd do it again, too. Hell, she'd die for that girl if it came to it.

When this was over, she'd make things right with Quinn. She'd always meant to, but things just got in the way. She'd do better. She'd be better.

They'd be queens together, her and Quinn. Mother and daughter.

Octavia smiled to herself. Yeah, that was an even better plan.

She closed her eyes and let the high take her, let herself drift in a place that was far from here, from the stink of filth and trash and sweaty, unwashed bodies, from the promise of death that oozed from every molecule in the air.

The trailer grew quiet but for the snores of the men as they succumbed to sleep, too exhausted to fight it anymore, even with drugs.

Outside, Tommy Carter's pit bull started up a racket.

Octavia jerked herself awake. She didn't know how much time had passed. Ten minutes or an hour? Maybe more.

"What's that?" she mumbled sleepily.

The men stumbled to their feet, grunting, disoriented, scrambling for their guns in the dark. Tommy and Ray staggered to the living room window. Bucky racked his shotgun.

"They're here," Billy said with unrestrained relish. He was the only one who sounded wide awake. His lazy eye twitched in its socket. "Time to start killing."

13

NOAH

DAY TEN

Thirty-year-old Noah Sheridan adjusted his grip on his newly acquired AR-15 and steadied his breathing. Though he was half Venezuelan, he took after his Irish-American father, with dark brown hair, even features, a strong jaw, and a fair complexion.

He kept himself trim and reasonably fit. Still, scaling this steep ravine in two feet of snow was incredibly challenging. His thighs burned. His heart thudded against his ribs.

The frigid air stung his cheeks. His ears were freezing, his breath escaping in crystalized clouds. He worked his fingers to keep them from stiffening up.

The woods were almost completely silent but for the quiet crunch of his boots as he and his men crept toward the Carter property.

He squinted in the early morning darkness, concentrating on not snagging his clothes or weapons on twigs and branches, or running into a tree trunk.

A handful of the militia had night vision goggles, but he

didn't. Neither did Jose Reynoso or Julian Sinclair on either side of him.

They all wore ballistic vests. In addition to the AR-15, Noah wore his Glock 19 service pistol, sheathed tactical knife, and extra preloaded magazines for both the sidearm and rifle.

It would be dawn soon. The sky was already lightening from black to gray. Trees, branches, bushes, and fallen logs began to emerge from the shadows.

He paused every few steps, listening hard, searching the dim light, and catching his breath. The slog uphill had been a difficult one, but they were nearly to the top, nearly there.

A twig cracked. Noah whipped toward the sound, his adrenaline spiking. Sutter crouched several yards ahead of him. He motioned back toward Noah, Julian, and Reynoso, then pointed toward a break in the trees straight ahead.

A wide clearing stretched out before them. Noah glimpsed a low rectangular shape against the snow. Then another and another.

They'd reached the Carter place.

Noah's heartbeat quickened. This was it. The moment of truth.

The Fall Creek police department and the militia had spent the better part of the last two days gathering supplies, training together, and going over the logistics and assignments.

Everyone had their place. Everyone knew their role.

Rosamond Sinclair had invited Mattias Sutter and his Volunteer Militia Brigade of Southwest Michigan to move into the self-sustaining community of Winter Haven in exchange for the town's protection.

This was part of the deal.

Last night, they'd met in Superintendent Rosamond Sinclair's home to go over the final plan one last time. Noah, Daniel Hayes, and Jose Reynoso represented law enforcement, along with Julian Sinclair—a fellow police officer, the superintendent's son, and Noah's best friend.

Mattias Sutter brought three of his people. His second-in-command, Sebastian Desoto, a Hispanic man in his forties with a hard, flat face and a military buzz cut. A slim but fit white guy in his twenties named James Luther, who wore a grim, serious expression and didn't say much.

And lastly, Shauna Albertson, a plain-looking woman in her early thirties with her dun brown hair pulled into a tight ponytail. She wore a khaki shemagh bandana tied around her neck, a drop leg holster on her thigh, and an ex-military posture.

Mattias Sutter had spread out a topographical map of Fall Creek and the surrounding area. They'd found it in a filing cabinet in the old courthouse that had been requisitioned into the Fall Creek town hall. Without GPS and satellites, they were reduced to paper maps and memory.

Mattias Sutter was an imposing man. Six-foot-three and two hundred and fifty pounds, he was a bald white guy with a barrel chest, thick neck, and bulging biceps the size of footballs.

At first glance, he looked like a brute, a bouncer, all fists and violence and no cunning—but a hard intelligence shone from his pale blue eyes. He wasn't a man to underestimate.

"We go in hard and fast," Sutter had said grimly. "Kill anything that moves."

Noah glanced sharply at Sutter. He fiddled with his wedding ring, his trepidation growing.

This felt all kinds of wrong. He didn't like conducting a raid without their ducks in a row, without approval from the top. Especially a raid as crucial as this one. "Where's the chief?"

Sutter shrugged. "He doesn't appear to have the stomach to do what needs to be done. We'll let him sit this one out."

Sebastian Desoto snickered.

Officer Hayes' worried expression echoed Noah's. A heavy, middle-aged Caucasian man who loved pasta and pizza a little too much, he was a decent guy who cared about doing his job well. "We don't have a warrant—"

"Exigent circumstances," Julian said. "Remember?"

In order to enter the house without a search warrant, they needed credible grounds to believe that immediate action was necessary to save a person's life, prevent evidence from being destroyed, or keep a suspect from fleeing.

They had the grounds.

They knew Ray and his men were in there, knew they were guilty as sin.

"There's no way to reach the assistant district attorney," Jose Reynoso reminded him. A burly former Marine in his forties, Reynoso was built like a tank and knew how to fight like one. He was a good cop, but better friends with Julian than he was with Noah. "We're on our own here. We can't pussyfoot around. It's time to act."

Noah thought of his good friend Atticus Bishop, weeping and distraught. Thought of his wife Daphne cradled in his bloody arms. His little daughters laid out before him, devoid of life and so still.

So utterly still, like fragile, beautiful dolls.

All those bodies. The lives and futures stolen from mothers and fathers and children. And in the midst of it, his own son.

He saw Milo in his mind's eye—his olive-toned skin, black hair, and dark eyes. How much he resembled his mother in his mischievous expressions, his mannerisms, his stubbornness. How when he bit his lower lip just like Hannah, it made Noah's chest ache.

How close Noah had come to losing everything.

He'd already lost Hannah. He couldn't lose Milo, too.

Anger overtook his fear. This was the right thing. The necessary thing.

For Milo, who was safe in Fall Creek with Molly and Quinn. For Bishop and his dead family. For the forty-seven innocent victims gunned down in the Crossway massacre.

"We need to do this," Noah said. "We have to do this."

Hayes nodded reluctantly.

Satisfied everyone was on board, Sutter grunted and folded the map. He stuck it in a pocket of his fatigues. "We go in at dawn."

An unsettled feeling slithered through Noah's gut. He'd felt the same eerie unease at Crossway Church in the aftermath of the massacre. How wrong it had felt.

Not only because of the horrible crime committed within those walls, but because of what and who wasn't there—the detectives with their coffees and trench coats, the crime scene techs processing the scene in their Tyvek suits.

They didn't have drones for reconnaissance or choppers for air support. No dispatch to call for additional backup. No state cops or FBI grunts.

If they got pinned down, they were on their own.

He'd only drawn a weapon a half-dozen times in six years of service, half of them within the last week. He'd spent plenty of time at the range and in training exercises, but nothing could quite prepare you for aiming and firing at another human being. For shooting and being shot at in a fire fight.

The Fall Creek Police Department boasted four full-time officers, including Chief Briggs, and three part-time officers. The part-timers had moved to full-time and then some after the EMP attack, which some people had started calling Black Christmas, since the lights went dark on Christmas Eve.

Clint Moll had been injured in the line of fire when they'd first attempted to take the compound three days ago. Nurse Shen Lee had managed to salvage his right arm, but he'd be out of commission for months.

Over the last week, they'd collected another dozen or so volunteer and reserve officers from the community, folks with prior military or law enforcement/security experience.

It wasn't enough. Not for what they faced.

For what was coming—opportunist criminals, gangs, and desperate refugees fleeing from the cities would eventually make their way to small towns like Fall Creek. Sooner rather than later.

But now they had the militia. Fifty additional men with semi-automatic weapons, stun grenades, and even a grenade launcher. They had more goodies than a small-town police force without its own armory; that was for sure.

Fall Creek needed all the help it could get.

Noah felt his heart threatening to hammer right out of his chest. The cold froze his fingers, numbed his feet. He sniffled but didn't dare wipe his nose. He couldn't let his guard down for a second.

The four rickety old trucks outfitted with snow chains were on their way to the Carter compound, following the single-lane rutted dirt road that was the only way in or out by vehicle. A truck and several militia blocked each end of the road to prevent an escape attempt.

A mile-long overgrown gravel driveway led to the main clearing and forty-acre property located several miles outside the township of Fall Creek.

By the time the law enforcement vehicles roared up the driveway, the compound would already be surrounded by at least three dozen armed men and women.

Ray Shultz and the Carter brothers were waiting for them. But they had no idea of the merciless onslaught about to descend upon their heads.

14

NOAH
DAY TEN

Noah, Julian, and Reynoso crept to the edge of the clearing, weapons up and ready. Sutter squatted behind a large tree and motioned them forward.

Noah barely felt the cold anymore. He heard little over the roar of his own heartbeat.

The wooded property was located atop a hill that abutted the river to the north, with a steep ravine along the western perimeter. Several trailers littered the crown of the hill, along with barns, sheds, and other outbuildings. The main doublewide trailer was located in the center of the complex, sandwiched between several smaller singlewide trailers on either side.

The snowy shapes of gutted vehicles were scattered here and there. The rusted frame of a bed leaned against a cluster of large rain barrels a few yards from the house. A washing machine lay on its side between two slim pine trees on the eastern side of the property.

A mangy pit bull barked and snarled, straining on its rusty chain attached to one of the sheds. It was too cold for any domestic animal to be left outside. The thing looked miserable and half-frozen.

"Team One is a go," Samantha Perez, one of their officers, said through the radio.

Desoto led Team One, who was trekking in from the east. Noah, Julian, and Sutter were with Team Two, approaching from the steep ravine along the western perimeter. The river blocked access to the north. Luther's men were approaching via the single road from the south.

"Team Two is a go," Julian said.

"Team Three a go." The radio crackled. "Coming in fast," Luther said.

Four rickety old trucks with chained snow tires roared up the driveway and pulled in front of the property in a wide, flat area. A dozen snowmobiles barreled after them.

The vehicles squealed to a stop, parking parallel to the main trailers thirty or so yards away. Six officers emerged swiftly from the trucks, shotguns and rifles drawn.

Twenty militia slipped off their snowmobiles and bounded from the beds of the trucks, semi-automatic weapons in hand. They took up defensive positions behind the vehicles and nearby trees.

Sutter's men simultaneously opened fire from multiple sides.

A barrage of high-caliber rounds shredded all three trailers. Heavy rounds punched through the flimsy roofs, windows, and walls. Hot brass rattled into the snow at their feet, steam rising as they fell.

The sharp staccato of semi-automatic fire split the air. The suspects opened fire on them through the trailer windows. Glass shattered. Rounds pinged off the fenders and undercarriages of the vehicles.

The deafening *rat-a-tat* made his ears ring. Sound went tinny and distant.

Adrenaline icing his veins, Noah broke from the thinning line of trees, ran to the trucks, and ducked behind the engine mount of the nearest F250. He squatted, rested the rifle across the hood, aimed at the middle trailer's windows, and fired.

A shot whined past him. He ducked, pulse beating hard in his throat.

The militia shouted and yelled as they swept the grounds with deafening bursts of semi-automatic fire.

He forced his breathing to slow, swallowed the fear and anxiety, and focused. With the rifle butt pressed to his shoulder, he swung the optics left and then right in a slow grid pattern, scanning the shadows.

The sky had lightened, faint orange streaks peeking over the tops of the trees to the east.

He searched for a hint of movement or the gleam of reflected light. His tense gaze tracked over the field, the trailers, the gutted cars and barrels, the sheds.

There. Movement on the roof of the eastern trailer. Maybe thirty yards. The shoulders of a crouched figure, a lowered head. The gleam of a rifle barrel. A sniper.

Rounds struck all around Noah, splitting shards of bark, pinging off metal, and spitting dirt and snow. A soft thud, and a soldier moaned and went down three yards to his left.

He didn't have time to check on him. He had to take this shooter out.

He took careful aim, exhaled, and squeezed the trigger in a short burst. The rifle bucked in his hands. Rounds shredded the siding two feet below the sniper's location. He'd missed.

The sniper tried to get low, but he had nothing to use for cover. His head and shoulders were still visible.

Noah re-aimed, fired a second burst, and this time hit his target. The sniper jerked, then sagged. His body rolled off the pitched roof and tumbled to the snow. He didn't get up.

Noah shifted and caught movement as two suspects darted behind one of the gutted, rusted out cars. He waited for one of them to expose himself.

He did, and Noah aimed and fired at his unprotected head with two quick bursts. The first burst struck the suspect in the shoulder. He spun and staggered out from behind cover. The second burst ripped across his belly and ended his short, pathetic life.

Noah tried not to think about it. Tried not to think about the people dying all around him, right in front of him. Forced himself not to dwell on his role in it. Not now, not when they had a job to do.

Several rounds ricocheted off metal only a foot from his face, sparks flying.

A second man who'd been shooting at the trailers from behind the thick trunk of an oak tree screamed and fell.

Noah couldn't tell if it was a member of the militia or one of Fall Creek's own. He just kept shooting. He ran out of bullets and ducked down to reload, his stiff, nearly frozen hands fumbling with the magazine, adrenaline making him shaky.

Mattias Sutter crouched behind a nearby truck and hoisted a grenade launcher over his shoulder. He fired at one of the sheds on the western side of the clearing, where three or four shooters were attempting to hide.

The grenade exploded. A thunderous boom split the air.

Smoke billowed from the windows. Screams of terror and pain erupted. A ratty-looking woman and a man stumbled out, their clothes and hair on fire, their bodies already ravaged.

Desoto's team crept in close from the east while the suspects were occupied with attacks from the west and south. They snuck around the side of the trailers and hurled several stun grenades inside.

Groans and moaning mingled with the frantic barking of the pit bull. Within a matter of seconds, the return fire from the trailers went quiet.

"This is the police!" Noah shouted. "If you do not wish to be shot on sight, come out now, hands in the air!"

He waited, still crouching, heart hammering in his chest, his mouth as dry as a desert.

No sounds from the main trailer. No movement. He saw nothing on the rooftops.

Several bodies lay in the yard, fallen from their sniper positions or caught in the crossfire as they attempted to flee.

The remaining suspects had hunkered down. Or maybe they were already dead or dying.

"We're going in," Sutter's voice crackled over the radio.

"Copy," Julian said. "Let's nail these scumbags."

They fanned out around the property, some approaching the main trailer, others investigating the singlewide trailers and the sheds, all alert and cautious, weapons up and ready to fire.

A fresh burst of adrenaline spiked through Noah's veins. He rose quickly to his feet, skirted the truck, and joined his fellow officers at the main trailer.

His breathing came fast and shallow. His palms damp inside his gloves as he tightened his grip on his rifle.

The smells of gunpowder, hot brass, and drywall dust filled his nostrils. The boom and crack of the firefight still echoed in his ears, ringing inside his head.

Julian withdrew a flash-bang grenade from a pouch on his vest. Sutter had given him a few. Noah took up position on the left side of the back door. Reynoso pushed himself against the wall on the opposite side.

Team Three was in position to storm the front.

After a nod from Julian and the all-clear on the radio, Noah swung out, raised his leg, and slammed his foot into the door just below the handle.

He kicked hard a second time and wood splintered. The shoddy door crumpled and burst inward.

They were in.

15

NOAH
DAY TEN

Noah dropped to a crouch, rifle up. Julian came up behind him and hurled the grenade inside. They dodged out of the way as the concussive blast rocked the inside of the trailer.

The grenade exploded with a blinding light and deafening blast but no shrapnel. It was designed to cause disorientation and confusion. It worked as perfectly as it was designed.

Julian was first inside, barreling through the door with zero fear or hesitation. Julian was always the first one in. Brave, daring, and a little foolhardy. No one had ever called Julian Sinclair a coward.

Noah went after him, followed by Hayes and Reynoso. Reserve Officer Oren Truitt stood guard outside, making sure no one entered or exited behind them.

Inside, the trailer was dark and dingy.

The stench hit him first, nearly bowling him backward. Mold and something rancid—the stink of human feces from overflowing toilets.

Noah blinked to adjust his eyes and flicked on the weapon-mounted light. There was nothing he could do about the stink but endure it.

The kitchen and living room were one squished space separated by a dingy countertop. Dirty dishes piled in the dry sink: scummy plates, bowls, and silverware spilling across the counters.

A bloated black vinyl recliner sat across from an antique coffee table covered with drug paraphernalia. Stacks of DVDs were piled on the floor in front of a big-screen TV as wide as the trailer. Trash everywhere.

Three bullet-riddled bodies sprawled on the living room floor in front of the windows, their weapons next to them. Noah kicked them out of reach. Hayes moved in behind him to verify their lack of a pulse.

A thug leapt out from behind the leather recliner. An automatic weapon flailed in his hands, but he aimed wildly at the ceiling. Dressed only in black boxers and socks despite the cold, he shouted and staggered, still disoriented. His belly dribbled blood from a bullet hole in his gut.

Noah's heart kicked with adrenaline. Before he could re-aim and fire, Julian got a bead on him and squeezed off two rounds.

The thug dropped, dead.

Sutter and Luther subdued two more suspects in the kitchen, groggy and disoriented from the flashbang. Ray Shultz and Tommy Carter sagged on their knees, bawling like babies and shrieking insults.

Tommy Carter bled profusely from a bullet wound in the flesh of his shoulder. Shultz's face was pockmarked with cuts from glass shards.

Hayes and Reynoso spread left, covering the living room, while Noah and Julian went up the center toward the long hallway between the living room and the kitchen.

Two doors to the left, two to the right. Likely three bedrooms and a bathroom. They edged down the darkened hallway until they stood outside the first door on the left.

Julian reached down, turned the knob, and entered the room. Noah followed immediately after. He scanned the room clockwise, leading with his rifle. Julian did the same, scanning counterclockwise.

He crossed the scummy, matted carpet. Checked behind the dressers, beneath the bed.

Pulse thudding, finger on the trigger, he opened the sliding mirrored closet door with the toe of his foot—half-expecting a thug to leap out with a pistol pointed at his face.

Nothing but junk and a smelly tangle of clothing.

"Clear," he said.

"Clear," Julian said.

They slid along the wall before entering the next room. They repeated the same task, Noah and Julian stacked beside the next door, ready to rush in and clear it. Noah burst through the opening, Julian coming in right behind him, his weapon-mounted light piercing the dim shadows.

"Clear," he said.

The radio crackled. Desoto's team had cornered Bucky Carter in one of the dilapidated sheds. They had him in zip ties.

Noah and Julian cleared the third room—a scuzzy bathroom with mold growing in the bathtub, the shower curtain half pulled off its rings.

Noah elbowed the last bedroom's door open and lunged inside, weapon up. He swung left while Julian swung right, their movements like clockwork, teammates who trusted each other implicitly.

Noah took in the dim, dirty room in a single glance. A mattress with yellowed, soiled sheets and a pile of blankets in the middle of the floor. Cheap peeling particle-board dresser and nightstand. Drug paraphernalia strewn all over both.

Movement snagged the corner of his eye.

A woman was crawling out the window against the far wall. The blinds were knocked onto the floor. Her lower half was still inside, legs kicking wildly, her head and torso already outside.

Her coat had snagged on a protruding nail. She'd raised the window only enough to wriggle out. The top frame had slid down and was now pressing along her lower back, effectively trapping her.

Noah moved swiftly into the room, his rifle aimed at the woman. "Don't move!"

To his right, he sensed Julian checking the closet. There were no other doors or bathrooms. The rest of the room was clear.

"Go to hell!" the woman shouted.

Then Noah recognized her.

Octavia Riley.

16

NOAH
DAY TEN

Noah edged toward the trapped woman. "Back out of the window, nice and slow. You got a weapon? Toss it now."

She cursed furiously at him. "Does it look like I have a gun on me, you moron!"

He checked out the window.

Both her hands were empty. A backpack slumped in the snow beneath her, out of her reach. She wrenched her torso so she could glare up at him and flip him off with two fingers.

The radio crackled again. "This is Team Two. We've got an active shooter in the trees behind the third trailer. Requesting assistance."

"Copy that," Julian responded. "The main trailer is cleared. Team One can assist."

"Can you handle this all by your lonesome?" Julian asked.

Noah rolled his eyes. "Go ahead."

"Figured it was time to take the training wheels off." Julian shot him a grin—a real, genuine grin, just like old times—and trotted out of the room.

Noah leaned the rifle against the wall, lifted the window

frame, and unsnagged Octavia's coat. He wasn't gentle when he hauled her back into the room.

As the adrenaline and intensity of the battle faded, his anger returned.

Quinn had told him what had happened. Octavia had been at the church. Octavia had helped Billy take Juniper and Chloe. She'd saved her own daughter, and Milo by proxy, but that didn't erase an ounce of her culpability.

"Turn around. Hands on the wall. Now."

Octavia complied with a litany of lewd curses.

He frisked her, holding his breath at the stink emanating from her every pore. Her black hair hung in limp, greasy strands down her back. Her scrawny body was still thrumming with her latest high.

He shoved up her coat sleeves and slapped the cuffs tight on her wrists. He turned her around and recited her rights.

It was habit. They had no way of getting her a public defender right now. He wasn't even sure where they could hold her for the next few days, let alone the following weeks and months.

She glowered at him. "I didn't do nothin'. You people have it out for me. You've always had it out for me."

He remembered her from high school. She'd been one of the most beautiful girls in their small town, but always wild and rebellious. Never into the good guys. Only into the ones who would hurt her and that she could hurt back.

Her beauty had faded to a facsimile of what it once was. Her face was gaunt, her dark eyes like marbles, shining with the madness of crank or whatever the hell she was on.

He used to pity her. Now, he just pitied Quinn.

"Don't look at me like that!" she shrieked.

Her rancid breath assaulted his nostrils. He took a step back. "It's over for you, Octavia. This is the end of the line."

"I didn't shoot anyone! I didn't kill nobody! That wasn't me!"

He shook his head wearily. He was so cold, so tired. He just wanted a hot meal and a warm bed. And his son, safe and snuggled beside him.

Bishop would never have that. His family had been stolen from him. Stolen by this wasted excuse for a human being.

"You're an accomplice. You might as well have pulled the triggers yourself."

"No!" She shook her head frantically. Strands of dirty hair fell into her eyes. "We were set up! We were told what to do!"

He spun her around and herded her toward the door. The rantings of a mad woman. Scumbags like her would say anything to try to escape their fate. "Let's go."

"How do you think we got out of that crappy old jail cell you locked us up in, huh? Someone let us out!"

He froze. That got his attention. In the middle of the night, in between nightmares, it was the thought that niggled the back of his mind, which refused to let him go. "What did you say?"

"Some guy. He let us out."

"What guy?"

She turned to face him, twitchy and on edge.

His gut tightened. "Who, Octavia, who?"

She chewed on her lower lip. Her bloodshot eyes darted about the room. "He wore a hood. It shadowed his face. He lowered his voice. He sounded familiar, though. Not a stranger." She leered at him. "Someone you know, I bet."

"That's not very helpful."

"He said the Bishops were hiding gold with all that food. Gold that would be good in an apocalypse. We could buy whatever we wanted. All the drugs and food and gas we needed to set ourselves up for life. We would be kings." She smiled, revealing her crooked, yellowed teeth. "Queens."

Noah stiffened. Bishop had told him a similar story. "Atticus Bishop doesn't have money. He spends it all giving back to the community."

Her nostrils flared. "How should we know? This guy, he let us out. He told us what to do. It wasn't us. It was him. You gotta get him. He made us do it!"

"Pretty unbelievable story if you ask me, Octavia. No judge or jury is going to buy that."

"It's still true! You gotta investigate or whatever." She lurched toward him, nearly losing her balance.

He put out a hand to steady her. The problem was, maybe he did believe it. Only he had no idea what the hell to do with that information or how to investigate it in the middle of the apocalypse.

Channing Harris, one of their new volunteer officers, had fallen asleep while serving guard duty and awakened to the antique lock jimmied open and the prisoners gone. The ancient key had also gone missing.

In the chaos after the attack, they hadn't done much to investigate. There were no fingerprints to dust for or enter into the system, no camera footage to analyze. Even under intense interrogation, Harris insisted he'd simply fallen asleep.

Reynoso figured that one of the Carter brothers had managed to smuggle in a small knife or pocket multi-tool. Hayes had admitted that with everything going on, they'd also failed to conduct a thorough cavity search.

"You gotta help me!" she begged. "I saved your kid. I could've killed him, but I saved him! Billy was gonna shoot him and my daughter right there. But I didn't let him."

"Quinn saved my son's life. Not your sorry butt."

"I did!" she cried, weeping now. "It was me! I saved them both. I did that! You gotta do something! You owe me!"

The barest hint of sympathy mingled with the revulsion twisting his stomach. She'd had a mother and father who loved her and an amazing daughter in Quinn Riley. She'd thrown it all away. "It's too late now, Octavia."

Her restless gaze flicked past him. "Please!" she cried, her hoarse voice breaking. "Please, help me!"

Sutter stalked into the room. He took her in with a single look and shook his head in disgust. He flipped his rifle in his hands and cracked the butt against her temple.

Octavia crumpled without a sound and fell sideways onto the mattress, unconscious.

17

NOAH
DAY TEN

"What'd you do that for?" Noah asked, alarmed. "She was already subdued. She—"

Sutter glared at Noah. "She was irritating me. I could hear her screechy voice from the kitchen."

Noah stared down at her prone form, his brow furrowed. "There was no need for it."

"Need for it?" Sutter scoffed. "What's wrong with *you*? Your whole town is begging for these monsters' heads on spikes. And we're going to give it to them."

Sutter kicked at Octavia with the toe of his boot. Not savagely, but like he was kicking at a piece of trash or roadkill, something revolting he wanted to dispose of as soon as possible.

Noah gritted his teeth. "You don't have to do that."

Sutter shrugged. "What was she going on about? The damn woman wouldn't shut up."

"She said someone let them out. There's an accomplice out there."

"She's high and insane. They all are. They'll say anything if they think it'll save them. But that time is gone. There are no lawyers here."

"Only for now," Noah said. "Even if this grid-down situation lasts months or even years, things will eventually go back to normal. We can't just do anything we want."

Sutter only grinned. "Says who?"

For a second Noah didn't say anything, too taken aback to respond.

Things were changing too fast. He didn't like it, didn't like the unease slicking his insides.

"Superintendent Sinclair—" Noah started.

"The superintendent authorized us to do whatever we saw fit to end this and protect the town. That's exactly what we're doing."

"We still need to do things by the book where possible—"

Sutter just laughed. "There is no book. We burned the book."

"We're still responsible for doing the right thing. We're still the law."

"Wake up, man!" Sutter said. "That's all over with. No pencil-pusher from the government is gonna analyze everything you did here from the safety of his fancy desk, looking to find fault in the actions of brave soldiers going into battle. The government is falling apart as we speak. Society is collapsing like the house of cards it always was."

Sutter was enjoying this. He and his men, and people like him, had been waiting for something like this to happen for years. *Wanting* it to happen. So they could be the ones in control. So they could have the power.

"Have you seen the cities? Even traveled outside this little enclave?" He snorted in derision as Noah shook his head. "It took less than a week. It's chaos. Every man for himself. Warlord wannabes and gang warzones battling over the FEMA and Red

Cross aid supplies they're stealing because there aren't enough military personnel to protect regular people.

"We have two choices. Give in like meek little girls, and die at the hands of human waste like this, or we take the power ourselves. Your government bosses are gone. You heard from them? From anyone? They've abandoned you. The longer you believe in them, the weaker you are."

Noah couldn't argue with him. He'd ventured outside of Fall Creek to retrieve the bodies at the ski resort, but he'd avoided every town and city. He hadn't seen the state of things outside Fall Creek with his own eyes.

Even so, he'd seen plenty. More than he wanted in an entire lifetime.

"I hear you," he said. "But that doesn't mean we throw everything out the window and become warlords ourselves."

"Of course not. We're all men of reason here. We'll do a far better job than the P.O.S. governor ever did. You'll see."

This guy thought he was in charge. It radiated off him. The sense of power and authority. The arrogance.

Like Noah and the other police officers were the subordinates in this equation.

Noah's gaze slipped to the AK-47 in Sutter's hands. He'd heard Sutter tell Rosamond they had years' worth of ammunition stored. And plenty of high-powered weapons.

He was supposed to trust these guys with the safety of the town.

Trust me, Rosamond had asked of him. He did trust her. Rosamond was smart. She cared for this town, for him. She'd never let him down before. And yet . . .

Sebastian Desoto strode into the room. His rifle was slung across his chest. He carried a thick coil of rope. Noah didn't know if they'd brought it or found it here. It didn't really matter.

Sutter's pale eyes darkened. There was something disconcerting in the way he stared at Noah without blinking. "They're animals. Human waste. There's only one thing left for them."

"What are you doing?" Noah had that feeling again, that oily unease sliding beneath his skin. "What's that for?"

Desoto dropped it on top of Octavia's unconscious body. He smiled. His wide, white teeth shone in the morning light streaming through the window. "Justice."

Before Noah could ask him exactly what he planned to do with that rope, Julian entered the bedroom behind Desoto.

"Speaking of justice." He shifted his rifle to his left hand and hooked his thumb behind him. "I've got something for you, brother."

Noah glanced warily from Octavia to Julian. "What?"

"You'll just have to come and see." Julian grinned eagerly. For an instant, he looked like the Julian Sinclair Noah had known before the EMP—charismatic and convivial, confident and handsome with his short blond hair, even features, and that charming smile.

Lately, he'd been tense and on edge, his expression drawn, his eyes haunted. He'd probably lost at least five pounds, maybe more.

But then, hadn't most people changed? And not everyone for the better.

"Come on," Julian said, cajoling. "Trust me."

Noah turned to Sutter. "Don't hurt her."

Sutter grinned. "Wouldn't dream of it."

Noah followed Julian out of the trailer, down a trampled path through the snow to the singlewide closest to the river. It was even filthier, if that were possible. Bags of trash littered the place.

The rancid stink of human excrement mingling with the ammonia smell of urine burned his nostrils. He covered his nose and mouth with the collar of his coat and coughed, eyes watering. "How do people live like this?"

"Tell me about it." Samantha Perez stood guard at the door. She'd pulled her sweater up over her mouth and nose. She dropped it when they came in. "Sorry, I'm just feeling a bit lightheaded."

"It's a miracle you haven't passed out from the stench," Noah said.

Samantha—or Sam, as everyone called her—tucked her chin-length black hair behind one ear. "And I thought my nephew's diapers were bad. Ugh."

Full-figured and curvy, Sam was also incredibly strong. She'd built her broad shoulders and muscled arms at the gym. After a decade with the National Guard, she knew her way around a gun.

A part-time officer before the EMP, she'd really stepped up in the last week. She was tough and dependable. Even funny, if you got her in the right mood.

Julian angled his chin at her. "Give us a minute."

Her gaze flickered from Julian to Noah, hesitating. "You sure?"

"We're good," Julian said. "We'll take care of this. You're relieved of S.O.L duty."

"Oh, thank goodness." Sam practically threw herself through the front door. "Good luck!"

After she was gone and the trailer was silent, Julian moved further into the living room. Noah followed him. Julian pointed without a word.

Billy Carter knelt in the center of the stained, trashed carpet.

18

NOAH
DAY TEN

Billy's hands were zip-tied behind his back. His face was a mess, his lip split, his right eye already swollen and purple.

Blood leaked from a bullet wound in his left thigh above his knee. More blood dribbled from a cut on his forehead and his mouth.

"Here." Julian's voice was raw. His eyes were bright and glassy, almost feverish. "This is him. He's the one."

Billy glared up at them, one eye wandering off to the left. He spat a bloody tooth onto the carpet at their feet.

Noah leaned his rifle against the wall. His hands clenched into fists at his sides.

It all came back in a rush. What Quinn had told him. That it was Billy who took Bishop's little girls from the supply room in the church.

Billy Carter. Child-murderer.

Revulsion filled him. "You killed Juniper and Chloe Bishop."

Billy gave them a leering smile. His teeth were bloody. His missing tooth left a gaping hole. "Where's my lawyer?"

Noah took two long strides and punched Billy in the face.

He hadn't even known he was going to do it. He'd never hit anyone in his life, not even the low-life criminals he arrested and tossed into jail.

Billy's head rocked back from the blow. He nearly fell over backward but managed to regain his equilibrium. "That's police brutality!"

"I'll show you police brutality, you cockroach," Julian spat. "Who are you going to tell, hmm?" He spread his arms wide. "There's no one here."

Billy glowered at them. His lazy eye gave him a bizarre, crazed look. His entire face was swollen and bruised purple. The bridge of his nose was crooked, blood gushing from his nostrils.

The terrible memories from that night seared Noah's brain— the blinding fear, the nerve-shredding panic, the dread like a sinking stone in his gut, the sickening despair as he entered the sanctuary, bore witness to the bodies.

How terrified and utterly helpless he'd felt. He wasn't helpless now.

"You murdered little kids," Noah forced out through clenched teeth. "You killed my friend's family."

Billy cursed and spat more blood. "You broke my nose."

"You killed them. It was you."

For a long moment, Billy said nothing. Noah thought he would deny it, claim his innocence like every other guilty-as-hell criminal.

"I did it." Billy lifted his head and met Noah's gaze with his single good eye. A slow, satisfied smile spread across his deformed face. "That what you want to hear? I did them all. The wife. The girls. You want to hear how they cried? How Bishop begged us to kill him instead? How they looked—"

Noah punched him again. Smashed his fist into Billy's face.

His knuckles stung. Pain drummed up his arm from the impact. Blood splattered his gloved hand.

He stood back. His arms fell to his sides.

Julian's mouth thinned. His expression went flat and stony. "Shoot him."

Noah went still.

"Do it!"

Billy's oily black eyes were red with burst blood vessels. He smiled through the blood caking his face, his voice slurring. "I enjoyed it. That what you want me to say? I enjoyed every damn second of it."

Noah trembled with anger and hatred. He loathed Billy Carter with every fiber of his being. Every second he breathed the oxygen that Bishop's girls never would filled him with an unbearable fury.

"Don't you want vengeance?" Julian hissed. "I sent Perez away for this. For you. Look, after Crossway, no one will bat an eyelash. No one will ask any questions. As far as anyone is concerned, this scumbag is just another casualty of that first barrage of defensive fire. Perez won't care. We were defending ourselves. It's good. This is all good. Iron-clad."

Noah licked his chapped lips, shook his head. He could barely think through the red haze of anger, his pulse pounding in his skull.

Julian drew his service weapon and placed it in Noah's hand. He closed his own hands around Noah's, his expression hardened. "You do what you need to do. For Milo. For Bishop's family. Don't worry about anything else. I've got your back. I've always got your back."

Noah wanted him dead. He was a maggot. A monster. The worst of humanity. He deserved to die. He deserved to die a terrible, painful, agonizing death.

And yet. Noah was still a cop. His sense of justice, of order and rules and law—it hadn't disappeared. He was who he was.

Something inside him deflated. He lowered his arm. Shook his head.

Without a word, Julian took the gun.

"I knew it," Billy crowed. "Too much of a pu—"

Julian raised the gun, pointed it at him, sighted his purple swollen eye.

Billy's arrogant face blanched. He tried to clamber to his feet, but with his hands and feet zip-tied, he was helpless.

Helpless before Julian's gun.

You should stop him, a voice whispered in the back of Noah's mind.

He didn't. He stood frozen, like somehow time had stopped and he was helpless to change or alter the events unfolding before his eyes.

He didn't move. He didn't say a word.

Julian squeezed the trigger.

Crack! The sound of the gunshot exploded against his eardrums.

Billy jerked. Blood sprayed. The center of his face seemed to cave in. Almost in slow motion, he toppled sideways to the floor. A stunned expression frozen on his brutalized features.

Noah stared, blinking rapidly. A distant buzzing filled his head.

Rattled, he took a step back. Inhaled sharply to steady himself.

Julian wiped the gun on his shirt and holstered it. He spat on Billy's body. "One less scumbag in the world."

Noah swallowed. "You killed him."

"*We* killed him." Julian's expression softened. He was calm now, placid. He rested a sympathetic hand on Noah's shoulder.

Edge of Darkness

"Sutter was going to do it anyway. This monster deserved a special brand of justice."

Noah shook his head, trying to wrap his mind around it. He stared down at Billy Carter's mangled face until his eyes stung.

This didn't feel like justice. Everything about it felt wrong.

Noah believed in the law. He believed in order and consequences. A higher authority to answer to.

Julian and Sutter believed that the only authority they answered to now was themselves.

And Julian . . . how easily he'd just killed a man. Intentionally. On purpose, not in the heat of the moment, like back in the church.

Julian was a cop, too. He'd sworn to the same code of ethics as Noah, but Julian wasn't even rattled. He seemed fine.

Noah felt simultaneously sickened and justified. Relieved—glad—the man was dead. Dismayed at how it'd all gone down. Unsure if he should be furious with himself or with Julian.

Or if he should just accept this new brutal reality, the way Julian had.

"Time to see justice done for the rest of these animals." Julian stepped over Billy Carter and headed for the door. "We'll take care of this mess later. Or maybe we'll just leave him to rot."

He glanced back at Noah. "You coming or what?"

Noah thought of the oath he'd made on that wintry ski slope not four nights ago. A vow to do whatever it took to protect his son, and this town.

Still shaken, he turned away from the dead body, from the man his best friend had just murdered. He wanted to be as far from this dreary, putrid trailer as possible. "I'm coming."

III

19

QUINN
DAY TEN

"Hey, Small Fry," Quinn said. "What do you think?"

Milo spun around, his eyes wide. The solemn, skinny little boy with the olive-toned skin, dark curls, and darker eyes, who'd somehow managed to worm his way into her heart despite her best intentions.

She waved a hand at her walls. "I call it my masterpiece."

Quinn's room was painted in murals she'd done herself. When she wasn't climbing trees, reading sci-fi thrillers, or practicing with her slingshot, she was drawing or painting.

Paper and pencils were cheap. Canvas and paint supplies, not so much.

A few years ago, Gramps had given her an unused pint of sunflower-yellow house paint he'd bought on sale. A week later, he brought her a bright shade of apple-green and a cheap paintbrush.

Two years later, she had a collection of over thirty colors, and had painted every square inch of wall and ceiling, the closet doors, her bookcases, desk, and bed. She'd paint the floor if it wasn't carpeted.

This was the third day since that night. The night of the

massacre. The night Milo and Quinn had almost died together but didn't.

It was mid-morning. After Milo's morning dose of hydrocortisone pills, which he needed to take twice a day due to his Addison's disease, she'd made herself and Milo a breakfast of Cheerios, almond milk, and crackers and peanut butter.

Peanut butter was one of Milo's favorite foods. He practically begged for it at every meal.

His father, Noah Sheridan, had dropped him off at Gran's house early that morning, well before dawn. Noah was off doing cop duties with the other police officers, the newly deputized volunteers, and the militia guys.

He was busy trying to keep the town from falling apart and the residents from turning on each other before they froze or starved to death. It was an impossible task.

Right now, he was hunting Ray Shultz and his tweaker crew of low-life mass murderers. Including Octavia.

She closed her eyes against the wave of brutal memories. Her mother was an accomplice to the massacre. She was a murderer. And yet, her mother was also the one who had protected Quinn from Billy Carter that night.

The whole thing was a confused mess she couldn't hope to untangle.

"Will you paint my room just like this?" Milo wandered around, sidestepping the clothes and junk strewn all over the floor, and examined her walls. They were covered in murals of monsters. King Kong, Alien, Godzilla, and the Minotaur, along with dragons, gremlins, and harpies.

She liked science fiction. Worlds of monsters and mayhem and magic where anything could happen. Where the dull and dreary and ugly didn't exist. Anything by Octavia E. Butler,

Robert Heinlein, Philip K. Dick, or Ursula K. La Guin, with some Stephen King thrown in.

"This took a long time. You can't just paint the Sistine Chapel overnight, you know."

Quinn shivered. Her bedroom felt as cold as an icebox. Gran's woodstove kept the kitchen warm and cozy, but the rest of the house was freezing.

She and Milo still wore their winter gear—long johns beneath sweatpants beneath snow pants, sweatshirts and winter coats, hats, gloves, and scarves wrapped tight around their necks.

At least it wasn't so cold that they could see their breath. Not like outside, which was a brisk five degrees.

Milo stopped at the crazy orange and red jungle scene she'd painted across the double closet doors. He pointed at the white unicorn in the center with the fiery red eyes and gleaming, pointed horn. "Who is that?"

She sat down on the edge of her bed. "Jeff the unicorn."

"He doesn't fit."

"Sure, he does. He's a bad unicorn."

"No such thing."

"He's bad-tempered and mean. He'll insult you and uses the foulest language. And if you really irritate him, he'll stab you with his horn."

"Jeff the stabby unicorn?"

She liked that. A smile twitched at the corner of her mouth. "Sure."

"Unicorns are supposed to be nice."

"Lots of things are supposed to be nice but aren't. Appearances are deceiving."

He considered that, chewed on his lower lip. "Why's he so angry?"

"Why do you think he's angry?"

Milo reached up and traced Jeff's graceful neck. "Maybe his mom left him."

Quinn gave him a sharp look. "You think so?"

He shrugged. "I dunno."

"Maybe. Maybe people—and unicorns—are allowed to have bad days sometimes."

"Maybe he's mean because he's sad and lonely."

Her chest tightened. All her usual sarcastic barbs and snarky quips failed her. She spread her palms across the black with blue polka dot bedspread Gran and Gramps had gotten her for her twelfth birthday. One of many birthdays her mother had completely forgotten.

She gathered a handful of fabric in each hand as her fingers clenched into fists. "Do you remember your mom?"

"Not really. There's lots of pictures of her everywhere." He turned back around and looked at Quinn almost shyly. "She sang to me. Every night before bed, Dad says. I can hear her sometimes, if I think about it really hard. She was super awesome at it. Dad says she sounded like an angel."

Quinn had no idea what to say to that, so she didn't say anything.

A memory flashed through her mind—her face pressed to the living room window, watching Hannah jogging down their street with toddler Milo in a jogging stroller, her chestnut ponytail bobbing as she bent her head to check on him. Her saying something in a high, musical voice, him laughing and laughing, giggles pouring out of him like water.

Why did she remember crap like that? Why had she watched Hannah with a lonely little girl's hunger, as if Hannah's motherly affection could ever be transferred to herself?

Hannah had barely known she existed, and yet, she'd known about Hannah, noticed her over and over, even before the

Christmas Eve when she'd vanished, fading into nothing like a ribbon of winter fog—here and then gone.

"Where is *your* mom?" Milo asked after a minute.

She flopped down on the bed and squished the pillow under her head. "She's an astronaut. Really busy up there in space."

Milo crawled into bed next to her and snuggled against her for warmth. He didn't ask, just assumed he belonged there. She didn't push him away.

"You think the power is on up there in space?"

"I'm sure it is."

"Everything is normal up there, the way it was before?"

"Probably."

"Will it ever be normal down here?"

"No. I think there's no such thing as normal. I think things just looked that way on the outside. Everybody pretending things were good and okay, but they never were. Everybody was barely holding on. Balancing on ice that was thin and cracking, but no one wanted to admit it. Now everything looks the way it really does—ugly."

"Your mom was in the church," Milo said in a small voice.

Quinn's heart constricted. "Yes."

"She . . . wanted to hurt us. With that bad man with the weird eyes."

"She didn't, though." She swallowed. "I made sure she didn't."

He slipped his tiny mittened hand inside hers. "I know."

They hadn't really talked about that awful night. Everyone else had asked them so many questions. Noah always looking at them both with that anxious, concerned expression of his.

She was sick of it, figured Milo was, too.

But it was different between them. They'd experienced it together, survived together.

She was the only person in the whole world who could under-

stand him. Her and Atticus Bishop. But Bishop had his ov.
family to mourn.

So it was up to her. To do something. To get him to be okay. It
was a feeling she could hardly understand or articulate, but she
needed him to be okay.

After a few more minutes, Milo asked, "Do you think your
mom will ever come back to you?"

She closed her eyes. Wanted to lie and make up some other
stupid story but she was too tired, and he was too sweet and
earnest, and her heart hurt too much. "I don't think so. I don't
think she's ever coming back."

"Mine either."

They lay there in silence for a long time.

"Will you sing to me?" Milo asked.

She thought of her dead phone, her dead computer, and radio.
All the music she loved, lost in a heartbeat. "I can't sing. I sound
like a dying frog stuck in a hot toaster."

Milo let out a sound halfway between a snort and a giggle.
"Cool."

"Not so much."

"Just a couple of songs? Please?"

Just one more? Puh-lease? Juniper's voice echoed painfully in
her head. She squeezed her eyes shut, pushed it out. She couldn't
let herself think about Juniper and Chloe. Couldn't let her mind
go back to the church.

She was even willing to sing to distract herself. She sighed,
fiddled with her eyebrow piercing for a minute. "Oh, fine. Whatever. It's your damaged eardrums. What song?"

"Do you like rock songs?"

"Like classic rock? Aerosmith. U2. Pink Floyd. Journey. The
Beatles."

ɔ's face brightened. "Those are the ones I remem-
Iom liked to sing."

n wasn't heartless, much as she tried to pretend she
was. It was ɔ̣ much easier to act like nothing could hurt you than
to face the truth that everything hurt.

That the things that hurt the most came at you from the most
unexpected directions, from the people and places you should've
been able to trust.

Like churches. Like mothers.

She sang to him. Started with U2's "With or Without You"
and "One" and moved on to Tears for Fears' "Everybody Wants to
Rule the World." She only remembered half the words, and she
was ridiculously out of tune, but that didn't matter.

By the time she got to The Beatles' "Here Comes the Sun,"
Milo started singing with her.

He had his mom's voice. High and clear and pure. So beautiful it made your heart hurt. A part of her was still here,
inside him.

She wasn't sure when she first started to cry. Maybe during
"Blackbird" or Simon and Garfunkel's "The Sound of Silence."
Hello darkness, my old friend . . .

The tears dripped down her cheeks. She couldn't help it.

Milo squeezed her hand. She squeezed back. He kept her
here, kept her connected to this room, this bed, this place.

They lay like that for a long time, side by side like brother and
sister, seeking warmth and finding comfort and solace in each
other.

The bedroom door flung open. Gran stood in the doorway,
leaning on her cane. Odin and Thor rubbed against her ankles,
mewling softly. "There you are."

Cane or no, Gran was no frail old lady. She was tough and
weathered. Gran had grown up on a farm. She still cooked every-

thing from scratch on the woodstove, cultivated a winter garden, and had chopped her own wood before her stroke.

You didn't want to get on Gran's bad side.

Quinn sat up fast. She swiped her wet face with the back of her arm. She didn't like people to see her cry, not even Gran.

Loki jumped on the bed and shoved his head beneath Milo's arms, begging for a good petting. Milo squeezed him tight.

The strained expression on Gran's face sent a chill racing up her spine. Quinn rose quickly to her feet. "What is it? What's wrong?"

20

QUINN
DAY TEN

Milo slipped off the bed. Quinn clambered after him. "What's happening?"

"Jared Taylor's boy just came by, knocking on all the doors." Gran's hazel eyes glittered. "They caught them. The monsters who did it."

Quinn went still.

"The superintendent ordered a public execution."

"What?" Quinn swallowed. Dread tangled in her gut. She couldn't wrap her mind around it, couldn't get her frantic jumble of thoughts to piece together Gran's words. "No jail? No arrest and trial?"

"The townspeople are demanding vengeance. I reckon they're finally waking up to the new way of things." Gran's face was pale and haggard. A network of wrinkles spanned her taut features. "Can't say I blame them. Not one bit."

Memories seared Quinn's mind. Screaming and bullets. Blood everywhere. A little girl shrieking her name. Her mother's tortured expression, her wild, desperate eyes.

Her mouth went dry. "I have to go. I have to go see."

"Then go."

"What about me?" Milo asked. "I wanna go."

Quinn squatted down so she was level with him. Her chest was so tight, it was hard to breathe. Her pulse roared in her ears. She needed to be there. She needed to be there *right now*.

"You'll be safe with Gran. I'll come back, I promise. I'll come back."

Milo stepped back and gave Quinn a forlorn look, like a little lost puppy.

"Your Jedi mind tricks don't work on me, Small Fry." She stood and pulled her gloves out of her coat pockets. Her hands were shaking. "You'll be fine."

"I'm making poop buckets," Gran said matter-of-factly. "You'd be surprised what a fine toilet you can make with a bucket, some sawdust, a pair of scissors and duct tape, and a few pool noodles scrounged up from summer storage in the basement. Believe it or not, we're gonna get a good price for these buggers. I could use some help, boy. No sense lying around being lazy when there's so much to do."

"*Poop* buckets, Milo," Quinn said with forced cheer. "Think about how much gross fun that could be."

He nodded, a tremulous smile twitching the corners of his mouth. "Okay. Maybe."

"No maybes about it!" Gran said sternly. "I wasn't joking when I said I needed your help. I also pay my helpers with peanut butter cookie sandwiches. Two cookies slathered with creamy peanut butter pressed together. Not sure you can handle that level of peanut buttery goodness, though."

His small grin widened. "I can handle that."

Fat Odin wound himself around Milo's legs, his tail sticking straight up. Milo picked him up, and the cat rubbed his head beneath Milo's chin.

"His fanny pack with his meds is in the kitchen. If I'm not back—"

Gran waved her off. "Milo and I will figure it out. Get your butt outta here."

Quinn hugged Milo quickly, mouthed a "thank you" to Gran, and hurried into the kitchen. She seized the truck keys from the hook by the back door and dashed out of the house, trying not to slam the door behind her.

The crisp, cold air hit her like a slap in the face. The afternoon sun barely added any warmth. The barren trees were still and silent, thick piles of snow clinging to their naked branches. A crow cawed from somewhere.

She didn't bother to cover her face with her scarf as she clambered into the Orange Julius. She'd scraped the ice and snow off the windshield earlier. The engine coughed to life and she cranked the heat to max.

She tried not to think about what might await her. She tried not to think about anything at all.

Less than ten minutes later, she was there. Distant shouts and shrieks echoing outside over the rumble of the Julius's engine. Dozens of voices. Maybe hundreds. They sounded angry. Like a mob or riot.

The crowd appeared ahead of her.

Hundreds of people blocked the center of Main Street. Instead, she took one of the back roads through a neighborhood to reach the alley behind the block of businesses.

Crossway Church was located toward the northern end of Main Street. She didn't want to see it. Knew she couldn't handle the tsunami of horrible memories. Not now.

She slowed as she passed behind the laundromat and the Asian bistro. She maintained the presence of mind to park the

Orange Julius behind the huge green dumpster in the laundro-mat's employee parking lot.

No reason to leave it out in the open as a temptation for anyone who needed transportation—which was almost everyone in town.

The sounds of the mob grew louder.

Quickly, she exited the truck, locked it, and pocketed the keys. She stomped through the snow toward Main Street. The snow between the buildings was already trampled by dozens of footprints.

The hardware store's windows were boarded up. Glass shards glinted in the snow beneath each window. Someone had broken in. Crass graffiti scrawled across the brick walls of the bank —"Screw FEMA," "Pigs Should Die," "Kill Everyone."

The mass of bodies obscured her view of Main Street. Every-one's backs were to her.

Her blood buzzed, her skin hot and tingly. She didn't even feel the cold anymore.

She drew a deep breath and entered the crowd. The cold air stank of sweat, unwashed bodies, and exhaust fumes. Several people had poured on the cologne and perfume to disguise their body odor. The heavy chemical stench burned her nostrils and stung her throat.

Quinn coughed, pinched her nose, and squeezed forward. Pushing and elbowing, she fought her way through to the front until she was positioned directly across from town hall.

The snowplow had cleared the road two days ago. Four inches of snow blanketed the street, but snowdrifts several feet high swamped the sidewalks.

A few hundred people lined both sides of the street in front of town hall. People crammed in front of the snowdrifts along the curb or stood on the packed mounds.

The crowd had whipped themselves into a frenzy. Everyone angry, shouting, and wild-eyed. Some gripped rocks and empty beer bottles. Others shook their fists.

"Justice!" dozens of people shouted. "Justice for Crossway!"

"We demand justice!"

"Kill the monsters!"

They were furious, grief-stricken, crazed with a desire for vengeance. Hungry to make the guilty pay. Desperate to keep it from happening again.

Superintendent Sinclair stood at the top of the old courthouse steps, the Greek revival white pillars rising on either side of her. Several armed men in gray camo uniforms—the militia—flanked her.

A dozen more lined the base of the stairs. Quinn glimpsed a few interspersed through the crowd. They didn't make a move to calm the mob, but they looked ready to intervene the second things got out of hand.

Chief Briggs leaned in next to the superintendent. His expression was tense and unhappy. He was gesturing fiercely, saying something that Quinn couldn't hear, but the superintendent appeared to ignore him.

The superintendent's son, Julian Sinclair, stood a few steps down on her left. Noah Sheridan stood beside him, his weapon holstered but his hand resting on his hip. He looked anxious and wary, his gaze continually darting over the unruly throng.

The rumble of snowmobiles filled the air. The shouts and cries for vengeance rose to a fever pitch. She could barely hear over the rabble.

She peered through jostling bodies until she could get a clear view to the north.

Four snowmobiles drove slowly toward the courthouse. Each

dragged a large, long shape behind it. She couldn't make out the shapes clearly. The hairs on the back of her neck rose.

As they drew closer, her brain finally clarified what her eyes didn't want to see. A splayed leg. An oval of a face.

People. The snowmobiles were dragging people behind them. People tied up with ropes. People still alive.

The mob roared in vicious delight. They hurled chunks of hardened snow at the bodies. Several people—men and women both—threw rocks and glass bottles.

Someone pushed against Quinn's back. "Move out of the way! I can't see!"

She ignored them.

The crowd kept jeering. The dark thrumming energy from the funeral had been amped up to a thousand. These were the people who waved to each other on the streets, who cheered politely for the other team at their kids' soccer games. They weren't violent by nature.

Or maybe they hadn't been violent before this because they'd never had to be.

But now? The country was in chaos. Everything had changed. No one knew what was expected of them. No one knew the rules.

Maybe no one knew what they were truly capable of—not until they were pushed past a certain point, an arbitrary limit that didn't really exist. Now everyone was being pushed. Everyone.

Who would they become after?

The men on the snowmobiles parked along the side of the street just before the courthouse. They wore matching gray camo uniforms with long black rifles slung across their backs. More militia. They were everywhere.

The militia eased off the snowmobiles, removed their helmets, and strode back to the four bound people lying on the road, struggling and cursing.

She couldn't call them victims. She knew who they were.

Six militia soldiers yanked each of them to their feet and sliced the ropes tied around their waists and chests. Their hands were still zip tied behind their backs.

The militia marched them toward the steps. They were all ragged, beaten, their faces bruised, scratched, and bloodied, but Quinn still recognized them. The bulging frog-eyes of Ray Shultz. Tommy Carter's tall, slim frame. Bucky Carter's flat, dull features.

And one more. The one with stringy black hair and a ragged, hollowed-out face that had once been beautiful. A face that, once upon a time, had occasionally been kind.

Octavia Riley.

21

QUINN
DAY TEN

Quinn's blood ran cold. Her stomach was a snarl of shame and disgust, but also fear—and love. Octavia was deplorable and pathetic, but she was still her mother.

Quinn didn't know what to feel, what she was supposed to feel.

The militia lined up the three men and one woman in the center of the street perpendicular to the bottom of the steps. Soldiers pushed them to their knees.

Tommy and Ray hurled curses and insults. One of the soldiers yelled at them to shut up. A second soldier punched both in the side of the head with the butt of his rifle. Not enough to knock them unconscious, just enough to hurt. They finally quieted.

The superintendent, Officer Sinclair, Chief Briggs, Noah, and the militia guards remained on the top step, staring down at everyone with grim faces.

The angry mob started to surge forward, but several militia spun toward them and raised their rifles. Not directly at the crowd, but just enough to make their point.

"Stay back!" one of them shouted. "Let us do our jobs!"

Superintendent Sinclair raised a megaphone to her lips. She waited for the throng's shouting to subside. "Men and women of Fall Creek. I never thought I'd be standing before you like this. Never would I want this or choose this. In the last two weeks, we've endured disasters and traumas we never thought we'd have to endure. We believe things will go back to normal eventually, but we now understand that it won't be soon. We're on our own. And since we're on our own, it is our job to protect ourselves.

"As all of you know, two nights ago, seven low-life thugs entered the Crossway Church and opened fire, gunning down forty-seven innocent men, women, and children. Our family. Our neighbors. Our friends."

Someone near Quinn began to cry. The occasional sniffle and choked sob rippled through the crowd. A low murmur of sorrow mingled with anger.

"This is an unprecedented atrocity. Before, these criminals would be arrested, jailed, given court dates, and sent to trial. They would be sentenced and imprisoned for the rest of their lives. But we can't do that now. With no power and few supplies, the nearest jails and prisons are already overwhelmed and barely holding things together. They can't take any more inmates. We do not have the facilities to house them here."

"We're not giving these animals a single slice of bread from our children's mouths!" a man screamed.

"FEMA feeds rapists and child molesters before taking care of their own people!" someone else shouted.

Superintendent Sinclair raised her hand to restore order. "You don't have to convince me. I hear you. I agree with you. And trust me, I will not allow a single Fall Creek child to starve while we give our precious supplies to these monsters. I won't do it!"

Tension thrummed through the crowd. The mob didn't cheer. They waited to hear what she would do. Their expressions and body language said everything. They wanted blood. And if the superintendent wouldn't give it to them, they'd take it themselves.

A militia soldier stomped up the steps. He was a big guy, muscular and straight-backed, built like a rhinoceros. He looked like the type who'd rather shoot first and never ask questions at all.

He held his hand out for the bullhorn.

Chief Briggs glared at him. "Rosamond, what are you doing? You can't—"

The superintendent shot Chief Briggs a sharp look to silence him. Two of the armed militia stepped closer to Briggs.

Superintendent Sinclair handed the megaphone to the soldier.

"My name is Mattias Sutter," the man said in a clear, stern voice that brooked no nonsense. "My men and I are here at the behest of your superintendent. Our one and only job is to protect the town. We are not the government. We are not the police. We are not constricted by laws or policies or politics.

"This is a reset. The only government you have is the government you see right here before you. The Feds have bigger fish to fry. They aren't coming here to help you. They aren't coming to protect you from the refugees flooding from Detroit, Grand Rapids, and Kalamazoo. Whatever thoughts you had about them swooping in to save you, get them out of your head now. Unless you want to spend the next several years trapped in a FEMA camp with only a cot and a blanket to your name, you better get with the program."

Some people cheered. Others were silent. The woman on Quinn's left shifted uneasily. "Don't got a good feeling about this," she muttered under her breath.

"Anyone who threatens the safety of this town will be put down," Sutter shouted. "No mercy, no hesitation. What happens now is justice! Your justice. Justice for Crossway!"

The mob roared in approval.

"You can't do this!" Chief Briggs cried. His face purpled with anger. "This isn't justice! This is murder!"

The crowd hissed and booed at him.

"This is against the law—"

"Shut up!" Julian Sinclair whirled on him. "You're disturbing the proceedings, *Chief*."

Chief Briggs gaped for a moment, like he was shocked that this was even happening, and wasn't sure how to respond. Finally, he pointed a shaking finger at the superintendent. "I'm not the only one who disagrees with your methods!"

The superintendent stiffened. "The chief is clearly overcome with emotion. Please escort him inside so he can rest for a few minutes and regain his faculties."

She motioned to Sutter, who nodded at his men. The two soldiers who stood only feet from Briggs took hold of his arms. The chief tried to shake them off, but he was in his late sixties, and they were young and strong.

The soldiers were gentle but firm. "Please, come with us, sir."

"You won't get away with this!" Briggs snarled.

"We're all on edge right now," the superintendent said, still calm, though her expression was tight, her mouth pressed into a thin line. "I'm sure we'll all feel better once this is over."

Quinn glanced at Noah. He looked miserable. He didn't say a word as they carted Briggs from the steps. What did he think of all this? She still didn't know what to think—or feel—herself.

Superintendent Sinclair turned back to the crowd like the scuffle behind her wasn't even happening. She waited for the doors to close and the quiet to return.

She smoothed her blonde hair, tucked a stray strand behind her ear, and cleared her throat. "Ray Shultz. Tommy Carter. Buck Carter. Octavia Riley. By the power invested in me by the township of Fall Creek, I hereby sentence you to death by firing squad for forty-seven counts of murder in the first degree. The sentencing shall commence without delay."

The crowd went quiet. An eerie silence settled over the town. No engines. No buzz of machinery. Not even a bird chirped.

Quinn watched, her limbs heavy, her veins filled with cement. The frigid air seared her throat with every rapid, shallow breath.

Her mother was about to die.

She should feel dread and horror and grief.

She closed her eyes against a flash of blood and screaming, the scent of gunpowder singeing her nostrils. She should feel vindication, relief, a vengeful desire for retribution. The thugs who'd slaughtered men, women, and children in front of her were about to receive their just desserts.

She didn't feel any of those things.

A hollow emptiness spread through her chest. A cold, detached numbness. She was draining somehow, her insides leaking out of her onto the cold, snow-packed ground.

Mattias Sutter marched down the steps and squared off fifteen or twenty feet from the four mass murderers. A half-dozen soldiers cleared the area of stragglers and pushed the crowds back from the street.

Sutter shouldered his rifle and aimed at Ray Shultz's head.

"I'm sorry!" Ray cried. Tears and snot streamed down his torn up face. "Mercy! Please! I'll do anything, just don't kill me—"

Sutter fired two shots. The explosive gunshots splintered the air. *Boom! Boom!*

Ray's body twitched. He toppled sideways.

The man next to Quinn flinched.

Quinn didn't flinch. Dazed, she simply watched as Sutter shifted, his lethal weapon moving another step closer to her mother.

Sutter aimed at Tommy Carter and fired twice. Tommy jittered. His head snapped back. He collapsed and didn't move.

The fifth gunshot struck Bucky Carter in his right eye. The sixth in his mouth. Blood splattered the snow. He fell backward. His legs kicked a few times before he stopped moving.

Sutter shifted to Octavia Riley.

Octavia didn't blubber or cry or beg for mercy. She didn't say a word. Her narrow shoulders were rigid, her gaunt jaw set. Her eyes empty.

Her gaze didn't find Quinn in the crowd. There was no last-second reprieve. No final desperate moment of connection, of remorse. No *I love you* that Quinn could hold onto passed between them.

There was nothing. Nothing but the resounding *cracks* of the gunshots. Nothing but her mother jerking like a doll, the blood and the blank face and the body dropping to the snow.

And then it was done.

Quinn didn't remember much of what happened after.

Every cell in her body screamed at her to leave, to run, to get as far from the town hall steps as she could. But she didn't. She couldn't.

She stood there, her arms hanging at her sides, hands empty, her heart in her throat. Detached from herself. Anesthetized.

The militia brought out body bags and disposed of the corpses.

Not her mother. Not anymore.

Noah and the other cops followed the superintendent and Mattias Sutter into the courthouse. Chief Briggs slammed through the front doors and stalked down the steps, rubbing his forearms and muttering angrily to himself. No one followed him.

The crowd dispersed. Drifted away in clumps and clusters.

Their vengeance and anger slaked. They didn't look at Quinn. Didn't even seem to see her.

Maybe the horror of what they'd just seen—what they'd been a part of—was slowly seeping in. Or maybe they felt vindicated, justified.

Maybe it was some of both.

Quinn didn't care what the townspeople thought. She'd never given a damn about any of them or their gossip and judgement. She didn't care. She hated them all.

And yet, she'd never felt so utterly alone.

Her mother was dead.

Quinn Riley was officially an orphan.

22

LIAM
DAY ELEVEN

Liam gripped the Jeep's steering wheel so hard his hands ached. His thighs and butt were sore, his muscles straining with tension.

Since they'd gotten a late start, Liam had planned to drive as far as he could. Maybe even all the way to Fall Creek.

But the snow was deep, with heavy drifts everywhere. Stalled vehicles presented the obstacle course from hell. They'd taken M-37 South to M-46 West, before heading south. They crossed the Grand River and squeezed between Holland and Grand Rapids.

He skirted Holland on I-196 and kept south. It was a two-lane road and rural. The backroads here were a convoluted mess he couldn't untangle, but as long as they gave the cities a wide berth, they should be okay.

It was slow-going, only ten miles an hour in some spots, sometimes less. He carefully maneuvered around several car pileups or an overturned truck in the middle of the road. In four hours, they'd only passed two other working vehicles.

Hannah sat stiffly in the passenger seat beside him, her hands on her belly, her gaze set straight ahead. Poor Ghost was squeezed into the narrow rear storage area behind the front seats.

He curled into a tight ball, his head on his paws, looking dejected and miserable. Hannah fed him occasional pieces of beef jerky to pacify him. It worked. The dog loved jerky like cats loved catnip.

Storm clouds completely covered the sky. There was no moonlight or starlight, nothing to pierce the darkness but the Jeep's headlights. Snowflakes spiraled into the narrow cones of light.

It was ridiculously dark. His eyes couldn't make sense of all this blackness. He kept looking for the far-off glow of lights from towns and cities, but there was nothing.

Only darkness and more darkness. He knew towns and villages were out there, but it was like they'd been erased from existence.

They'd set out from Ashland on the afternoon of the third day —exactly forty-eight hours of close monitoring before Dr. Laudé allowed them to depart with her blessing.

Ghost's blood pressure had spiked a couple of times, but she'd been able to bring it down. He'd also gotten a little woozy the first night, and she'd hooked up an IV and given him some fluids. It helped.

It was good that they'd stayed.

The two days they'd spent at the veterinarian's house had been quiet. Liam had kept careful watch. Things were getting tense and rowdy in town, but no one approached the veterinarian's house with ill intent. The townspeople needed her.

Ghost improved each day. By the time they were ready to leave, he was nearly back to his old self. Still calm, reserved, and watchful—though he'd dashed around in the backyard, chuffing and barking, gleefully kicking up powder, and basically making a happy nuisance of himself.

Dr. Laudé said Great Pyrs loved snow. They were solemn, dignified dogs who took their responsibilities seriously, but winter often brought out the puppy in them.

Watching him prance around the yard, regal head held high, plumed tail fluttering behind him—Liam couldn't help but think that Ghost understood he'd been given a second lease on life. The dog didn't look like he planned to waste a second of it.

Neither did Hannah. She struggled into her winter gear and waddled outside after him. Liam leaned against the doorframe and watched them, arms crossed over his chest.

She tossed snowballs across the yard, and Ghost went after them with gusto. He leapt high and snatched the snowball right out of the air. When the snowball disintegrated in his jaws, powder spraying his nose, he snorted and shook his head, then trotted right back to Hannah for more.

Hannah glanced over her shoulder at Liam and smiled. A real, genuine smile that lit up her entire face. Her green eyes shining, chocolate-brown hair pushed behind her ears, her expression warm and open. She looked like a different person when she was happy.

Liam's chest squeezed. He found himself smiling back at her without thinking about it, without a conscious choice. He couldn't take his eyes off her.

When she wasn't playing with Ghost, Hannah spent the two days recovering herself, catching up on sleep and cooking meals for the vet when she stopped by in between house-calls and came home late, hungry and exhausted.

Dr. Laudé didn't have electricity, but she had a fireplace, a propane camping stove, portable propane heater, and several battery-operated camping lanterns. Plus dozens—hundreds—of candles. The woman collected Yankee Candles. The entire house smelled of balsam and cedar and apple pumpkin.

One of Dr. Laudé's customers had a well with a hand pump and had exchanged as many buckets and containers of water that they could fill for another month of heartworm treatment for their dogs.

They hand-scrubbed their clothes in a five-gallon bucket with detergent and hung them near the fire to dry. They washed themselves in private, then filled the kitchen sink and took turns washing their hair with shampoo. Liam refilled all their water bottles.

First thing in the morning, Liam brushed off Dr. Laudé's old chainsaw and cut down the two dead trees as promised. He chopped them into firewood and kindling and stacked everything on a tarp in the garage.

Once he'd finished with that job, he'd set off to explore the town and surrounding area. First, he'd instructed Hannah to stay alert and watchful, to keep the Ruger with her at all times.

He didn't like leaving her anywhere without him, but the house was warm, quiet, and safe. And she had Ghost. The dog seemed to sense that he needed to step up his game and refused to leave her side.

Liam had a list of items he needed before they left. A hundred and forty miles didn't seem all that difficult. But after the EMP, any number of obstacles could easily derail them. He wanted to be prepared.

Plus, neither Hannah nor Ghost could handle more hours in the freezing temperature and brutal wind on the snowmobile. He needed to find a vehicle. And fuel.

The snowmobile was faster and more versatile—they could stay off the roads and go anywhere. A car was warm and protected from the elements but slower and confined to the roads.

With a heavily pregnant woman and a recovering dog, Liam was forced to consider choices he didn't want to make.

Late on the second day, he'd found what he needed. Five miles outside of town along an old country road, he came across an abandoned farmhouse with a large steel outbuilding in back.

He'd picked the padlock and discovered a dusty hunter green 1978 Jeep outfitted with a lift kit and oversized tires. The Jeep was unlocked, the keys tucked in the glovebox. It even had a half tank of gas. Liam added some snow chains he found hanging on a hook next to a large rolling toolbox.

The Jeep rattled a bit, but the engine purred like a kitten.

He'd felt a little bad about taking the Jeep. The owners clearly weren't home and hadn't been since Black Christmas. Their farmhouse had already been looted, though there were still some goodies left in the back of the pantry.

He'd managed to procure several cans of fruit, a box of crackers and fruit snacks, and a bag of beef jerky. The beef jerky didn't even make it into his go-bag before Hannah promptly stole it and fed the entire bag to Ghost, who inhaled it ravenously, like he hadn't eaten in a month.

He still needed fuel. He'd borrowed three jerrycans from Dr. Laudé and lashed them to the back of the snowmobile. The local gas stations were already out of gas. A handwritten sign on the window stated, "No gas. No food. Looters will be shot."

No matter. He could get gas from the hundreds of vehicles stalled all over town. Newer cars had an anti-rollover valve on the gas tank that also acted as a siphon prevention system.

Maybe fifty percent of the cars had already been emptied, many of them by a screwdriver to the gas tank. A lot of gas was lost that way. Liam didn't like wasting resources.

He also wasn't interested in mouth siphoning. It was

disgusting as well as dangerous. It was easy to accidentally swallow the gas or breathe in fumes.

He'd scavenged two tubes—one long, one shorter—from Dr. Laudé's shed. Once he'd found a car with gas in its tank, an older Toyota, he inserted the longer tube into the gas tank until it was submerged and shoved the other end into the empty jerrycan on the ground. He inserted the shorter tube into the tank and used a damp rag to make a seal around the plastic tubes and the tank opening.

He blew into the short tube to create high air pressure inside the gas tank, forcing the gasoline through the longer tube and into the waiting canister. In this way, he filled the jerrycans, transferred the gas to the Jeep until its tank was full, then filled the jerrycans again.

He left the first two jerrycans with Dr. Laudé for her generator in repayment for her kindness. She was thrilled. The third, he kept in the Jeep as an emergency backup.

Now, Liam shifted in his seat, stretching his shoulders while keeping his hands on the wheel. He leaned forward, kept his attention on the road ahead, on possible obstacles and threats.

The blackness was thick and heavy, like an immense depthless ocean. It went on forever and ever with no end, no light—no one else on the entire bleak planet but himself, Hannah, and Ghost.

That wouldn't be so bad. Most people hated isolation. To him, it was both a bane and a solace. But right now, he felt his separation from the world more acutely than ever.

He thought of the solitude at his homestead in northern Michigan, his rural five acres abutting miles of forest that gave him the isolation he'd craved. After Chicago, he was sure that was all he wanted. To escape. To shut out the world, turn his back on humanity.

Did he still feel the same way?

You know the answer to that, Jessa's voice whispered in his mind.

One hand still on the steering wheel, he stuck his other hand in his coat pocket and felt the tiny scrap of gray and green knitting. His chest tightened.

He kept driving. An hour passed. Then another. More darkness. The headlights occasionally skimmed the looming shapes of hunched houses, a gas station, a convenience store.

"How far are we?" Hannah asked.

"We just passed the sign for South Haven. It's up ahead a few miles."

Hannah sat up straighter. "That's less than fifty miles from Fall Creek."

"I need to exit and figure out a back way to avoid the city."

"I'll help you with the map—" Hannah flinched. She sucked in a sharp breath.

He glanced at her, concerned. "You okay?"

She pressed her hands to her temples. "Just a really bad headache. It came on fast. I feel kind of sick."

"I have ibuprofen in my go-bag." The bag was stuffed between her feet since Ghost took up all the room and then some in the back. Liam's rifle leaned against the passenger seat.

She touched his arm briefly. "Thank you."

Instinctively, Liam stiffened. He swallowed hard. Her closeness—her very presence—was disconcerting.

He tried not to think of the last time he was this physically close to a woman.

Jessa. He felt her in his arms again, her hands wrapped around his neck, her head resting against his chest, her body limp and heavy.

He heard her rasping gasps, felt her life slipping away in his arms, his own grief and helplessness to stop any of it.

Less than two weeks ago. Already a lifetime.

His heart wrenched in his chest. He shoved the memory away. What good did dwelling on it do? Nothing. Still, it haunted him, no matter what he did.

Hannah twisted around to check on Ghost. He whined, clearly unhappy with his seating arrangement in the cramped rear storage compartment. "Not too much longer."

Ghost gave a disappointed chuff.

"I know, I'm sorry—" Hannah stopped suddenly. When she spoke again, her voice was tense. "What is that?"

Liam looked in the rearview mirror. The road was long and straight with clusters of forest interspersed with fields and farmland on either side.

Behind them, appearing over the rise of a hill, a pair of headlights punctured the dense darkness.

23

PIKE
DAY ELEVEN

P ike had spent three days hunting them.

It hadn't snowed since before New Year's Eve. The tracks were clear. Almost perfect. With that trailer on the back of their sled and hardly any vehicles marring the pristine snow, it hadn't been difficult to trace them to the barn just north of Newaygo.

He'd found footprints on the dusty floor. Droplets of blood in the matted-down sections of hay. They'd spent the night here.

He'd followed them from the barn south to Mason Drive and Highway 37. From there, things got a little muddied with a snow-plow and a few truck tracks messing everything up.

He figured they would try to save the damn dog. It wasn't what he would do, but he'd spent a lifetime studying and mimicking human emotions and behaviors.

He'd stepped in their shoes, moved in their skin. He'd learned their hang-ups, their illogical assumptions and feelings-based decisions.

And he knew Hannah. She would save the dog.

That meant a veterinarian. They'd look for a town close by.

The area south of Manistee National Forest was rural. There were only a few towns to choose from, most of them only clusters of a few hundred people, villages and townships with a gas station and a grocery store, if they were lucky.

Ashland was a bit larger and only a few miles further south. It didn't take a genius to figure out that was where they'd likely gone.

And it didn't take him long to find the Paws and Claws Clinic and discover their tracks again. He'd hung around for a day, using his badge to gain the townspeople's trust and get them to talk, finding out the information he needed.

A man and a pregnant woman with a dog. Where they'd stayed. What vehicle they'd left with.

He hurt no one. He hadn't needed to.

He'd confiscated a paper map from a gas station and studied it, smoking a clove cigarette down to the nub. Thinking like they did.

He figured the soldier would be careful to avoid Grand Rapids, Holland, and Kalamazoo. Grand Rapids to the east and Lake Michigan to the west sandwiched them into a narrow range of possible roads.

From there, it was a matter of elimination.

With his snowmobile, Pike had the advantage. He could go anywhere, and much faster than these cars trundling through the deep snow.

Crisscrossing the roads, searching the towns, doggedly chasing the green Jeep with ruthless, single-minded determination.

24

LIAM

DAY ELEVEN

The headlights were red and close together—not a truck or a car, and not a motorcycle.

A snowmobile, then.

Liam eased around a stalled sedan and slowed to a stop, making sure he had a clear stretch of road to accelerate quickly if needed. He shifted into park and waited.

The only sounds the groan of the engine, the dull buzz of the heater, and their own breathing. The cab smelled like artificial pine freshener and dog fur.

The headlights didn't grow any closer.

He glanced at Hannah. She shivered though the heater was on full blast, her shoulders hunched inward, as if she were instinctively attempting to make herself as small a target as possible.

He shifted into gear and kept driving.

The headlights followed. They didn't draw closer or pull further away.

He sped up. Slowed down.

The headlights followed them.

A few miles later, Liam pulled over again, this time several yards in front of a station wagon on the side of the road. It would block the snowmobile's view and offer some concealment.

"It's him," she whispered.

"Could be anyone."

She shook her head. "It's him."

From the back, Ghost emitted a low, throaty growl.

Liam looked in the rearview mirror again. The lights glowed red like demon eyes in the darkness.

He didn't believe in demons or monsters or ghosts. He didn't fear much. Still, a deep, unsettled feeling took hold deep in the lizard part of his brain. An icy prickle trickled down his spine.

He scanned their surroundings, taking in everything he could see—the two-lane rural road scattered with snow-smothered vehicles, the black bony trees on either side, the high snowdrifts, the driving flakes thickening the darkness.

The snowmobile was approximately a hundred and fifty yards behind them. The trees were mostly pine, tall and slim and wouldn't provide much cover. Lots of scrub and fields.

He needed to know if this was just a garden-variety asshole or a bigger problem.

He needed to know if it was Pike.

"I'm going to find out."

She leaned forward for a moment, clutching her belly and breathing hard through her mouth. "Don't shoot unless it's him."

"I won't kill unless it's him," Liam said, the only concession he was willing to make.

He switched off the engine. The headlights dimmed. Silence and darkness enveloped them. They would be okay without heat for a few minutes. "Stay here. Keep that gun in your hand."

Hannah exhaled a deep breath and nodded. Her features were pinched and white.

He grabbed the rifle from the floorboard at Hannah's feet,

opened the door, and stepped out into the night. The cold blasted his exposed skin, the wind buffeting him.

He jogged back ten yards to the station wagon—or what he thought was a station wagon—angled at a forty-five-degree angle in the southbound lane. He quickly swiped the snow from the hood.

He crouched behind the engine block, brought up the AR-15, and braced the barrel against the hood. He fitted the stock firmly against his shoulder and peered through the scope.

He found the twin red beams in his sights. His body went tense, his senses on high alert, every muscle thrumming with adrenaline.

He felt the cold all the way to his bones. His nose and throat instantly raw from inhaling the freezing air. Snow swirled into his face, burning his cheeks and nose and making it difficult to see.

The snowmobile was still parked. Still waiting. He glanced up, confirmed the distance, and peered through the scope again. The dimmest shadow materialized above the red glow, hardly visible through the snowy darkness.

Liam aimed a few feet above the target and to the right, toward the trees. Stilled himself, settled his heartbeat, steadied his hands. He let out his breath slowly, squeezed the trigger.

The rifle bucked against his shoulder. The loud report boomed like thunder.

Liam moved the barrel slightly to the left and fired again. He waited.

Anyone would flee at the first shot. Certainly at the second. Anyone but Pike.

The wind howled mournfully through the trees. Branches creaked and scraped against each other. The red beams didn't move.

Liam cursed under his breath. He had his confirmation. It was him.

What was Pike playing at? He didn't retreat, and he didn't attack.

He was a coward. A psychopath, but one too gutless to fight like a man. He fled at the first sight of an antagonist strong enough to fight back. He preferred to skulk in the shadows, kidnapping defenseless girls to dominate and control.

Hatred burned in Liam's chest. Not just for Hannah's sake, though that was part of it. He wanted to end this pathetic excuse for a man for his own reasons.

He adjusted his stance, shifting as the wet snow dampened his kneecaps. He peered through the scope again. He could make this shot. He could end this asshole right now.

The glowing red lights switched off. The world went black.

His pulse thudding in his throat, Liam glassed the area. He could see little but darkness. He'd never missed his night vision goggles so acutely.

He was tempted to fire a few shots in frustration, but they were pointless without a clear target. He needed to conserve his ammo.

Staying low, he crouched and dashed back to the Jeep. Opened the door and hurled himself inside the cab. He shivered and wiped the snow from his face, eyes, and hair.

"It's him," Hannah said. Not a question.

"It's him."

A beat of silence. "What's he doing?"

"He thinks he's playing games."

"He likes to do that." Her voice was so soft he could barely hear her. "That's exactly what he's like."

"I don't play games."

Hannah's voice was strained. "What do we do?"

"You and Ghost stay inside the Jeep. You have your gun. I'm going after him. I'm ending this right now."

"Liam . . ."

His hand was already on the door handle. He glanced at her. "What is it?"

She collapsed against her seat, gasping. Hands clutching her belly. "Contractions."

He froze. "What?"

"I think . . . I think I'm in labor."

25

LIAM
DAY ELEVEN

Liam's mind raced, cycling through calculations, all the worst-case scenarios.

The snow was falling harder, big fat snowflakes swirling in the twin glow of the headlights. The wind buffeted the Jeep.

"Are you sure?"

"I thought at first it was Braxton Hicks—false contractions. That's why I didn't say anything. But this is—" Hannah's voice broke off abruptly. She went rigid, the tendons standing out in her neck. When she could speak again, it was through clenched teeth. "I'm sure."

"Damn it!" he growled. "This isn't a good time."

"I know." She twisted around in her seat to face him. Damp strands of hair stuck to her cheeks.

Her skin was too pale. Her eyes were too bright, her pupils huge. She looked terrified—and unwell. "Something's not right."

"What do you mean?"

She rubbed her deformed hand. "My hands are tingling. Both hands. My feet, too. My head is throbbing." She swallowed. "And —and my vision keeps going blurry."

Fear lanced through him. Even he understood that this wasn't a normal part of labor and childbirth. They should have remained with the veterinarian until Hannah had given birth. They both had wanted to move on. He should have made them stay.

"I think . . . I think it's preeclampsia. With Milo, the OB office had posters about it up on the walls. High blood pressure, nausea, headaches. That's what I remember."

He didn't know a thing about preeclampsia. Jessa would've known. She would know what to do. But she wasn't here. She wasn't anywhere. They were on their own. "This . . . preeclampsia. It's dangerous?"

Hannah looked at him with naked fear in her eyes. "If you're asking whether it can kill me, the answer is yes."

He wanted to do or say something to ease Hannah's fear, to comfort her. But he was crap at that sort of thing. He was a man of action. "What do I do?"

She raised her delicate chin, the smallest act of defiance against the thing about to take over her body, nature exerting her will no matter how ill-timed or inconvenient—or what threat it posed to the mother. "I need to get it out. Whatever's happening to me, it'll stop once it's out."

Behind them, the snowmobile lights flickered on.

Liam watched them. They didn't move. They were stationary, waiting. *Waiting for what?*

He wanted to go after him. Everything in him wanted to—

She's in danger. Jessa's voice in his head. *You know that.*

"I need . . . somewhere to . . . rest." Hannah didn't say, *give birth.* Neither of them wanted to say it aloud.

But it was coming, whether they wanted it to or not. In the middle of a blizzard. A killer at their backs.

This was happening, and there wasn't a thing they could do to stop it.

Liam clenched his fists and swallowed a frustrated scream.

Everything he would do as a lone operator to nail this guy, he couldn't do with Hannah in his care. He was responsible for keeping her alive.

He couldn't leave a woman in labor alone while he hunted a killer. They'd have to outrun Pike, get rid of him somehow in all these back-country roads. They had to run.

Much as Liam hated it, it was their only choice.

"I'll lose him. We find a place to hole up and outlast this storm. If he shows up again, I'll kill him."

Hannah stiffened and clutched at her belly, sucking in several ragged breaths. She clenched her teeth and let out a low moan.

Ghost whined and tried to scramble to his feet, his claws scrabbling in the back, his head and shoulders too tall for the vehicle.

"You okay?" Liam asked her.

"Let's just get out of here." Her jaw clenched. "I'm okay, Ghost. Settle down."

Ghost gave her a dissatisfied chuff, like he believed her about as much as Liam did, but he flopped to his belly and laid back down.

Liam started the engine. They drove through the dark and the snow. The snow whirred from the sky, harder and harder, flinging bits of ice into the headlights. It grew harder and harder to see.

He exited onto M-140 and kept south. He glimpsed trees, bushes, and small, hunched houses in the sweep of headlights. He checked the rearview mirrors constantly.

It took less than ten minutes. The red lights reappeared.

Anxiety sprouted in his gut. Their stalker was relentless. He kept within a hundred yards of them, sometimes closer, but never too close.

When Liam slowed, he slowed. When Liam sped up, the glowing lights sped up, too.

Liam stopped suddenly, slamming the brakes. The chained tires slid before catching, the Jeep nearly fishtailing into a stalled truck. He yanked open the driver's side door. Leaned out and aimed back at the piercing red lights. Fired off a quick three-burst shot.

The machine's headlights switched off.

He couldn't get a bead on the guy in the dark. And he couldn't shoot and drive at the same time. Hannah was in no condition to help, even if she knew how to shoot a rifle with decent accuracy, which she didn't.

She hunched in her seat, curling in on herself. Every six or seven minutes, a contraction ripped through her. She stiffened and shuddered through the pain.

He felt the seconds ticking away in his blood, felt them running out of time.

Liam drove again.

The red lights reappeared and followed them.

He increased his speed, but he couldn't accelerate too much. There were too many obstacles in his way; it was too difficult to see more than twenty feet in front of him. If he crashed the Jeep, they'd all freeze to death in the blizzard.

He searched for any breaks in the trees, any paths to disappear into the forest, but the Jeep was far too large, the trees packed too tightly together.

Whatever he did, it didn't seem to matter.

The lights were like glowing red eyes. They searched them out again and again.

It was unnerving as hell. Mostly, it just made him furious.

Hannah moaned softly beside him. His fear ratcheted up

another notch. Not for himself, but for her. His pulse thudded in his throat.

Drive faster. Drive harder. Don't crash.

The headlights drew closer. The snowmobile abruptly accelerated. It ate up the yards between them with incredible speed. Red light filled the back of the cab.

"What's he doing?" Hannah asked.

Liam stepped on the gas. The Jeep bounced and jostled, the snow chains slipping, then catching. The engine gave a grinding protest. The wheel vibrated beneath Liam's hands. He felt it in his legs, his back.

Pike pushed forward. Bumped the Jeep's rear fender. Fell back and roared forward again, this time clipping the Jeep's right flank.

The snowmobile wasn't nearly powerful enough to push the Jeep off the road. It could harass them though, nipping at their heels, throwing them off their game, trying to force a mistake.

An error now would be costly. Pike knew it. Liam knew it.

Ghost let out an angry bark. The sound boomed through the small interior, loud as a gunshot. Ghost attempted to climb to his feet, but he was too tall in the narrow space. He blocked the rearview mirror.

Liam needed to see. "Hannah!"

"Got it." Hannah twisted around awkwardly, wheezing heavily, and shushed the dog, soothing him. Liam couldn't see what she did, but within a few seconds, she had Ghost lying down. He didn't stop his furious barking, though.

Pike rammed them from behind again. The Jeep lurched.

The forest gave way to an open field. Liam had no idea how big it was. He could see little but the yellow headlight beams bouncing ahead of him, everything to either side just walls of darkness and snow.

He banked right and veered off the road into the bumpy field. The tires spun and caught, grinding and tumbling through the thick snow.

The snowmobile followed right on their tail. Pike revved his engine and came up on their right side, parallel to the Jeep.

Maneuvering the steering wheel with one hand, Liam seized his Glock from the center console and pointed it toward the snowmobile.

Without being told, Hannah reached for the hand crank and started rolling down the passenger side window. Frigid air streamed into the cab.

The headlight beams washed over a two-story barn looming fifteen yards directly ahead.

Hannah gasped. Ghost let out an alarmed bark.

Heart thumping, Liam dropped the pistol, grabbed the steering wheel with both hands, and swung a hard left. He narrowly missed the side of the barn and plowed into a snowdrift instead.

Luckily, it was only a few feet high. Chunks of snow slammed into the front fender. Snow sprayed beneath the churning tires.

Pike swerved around the barn and came at him from the right.

Out of the corner of his eye, he caught a muzzle flash.

26

LIAM
DAY ELEVEN

Instinctively, Liam jerked the wheel, his fingers gripping the steering wheel like claws.

Adrenaline dumped into his bloodstream. "Get down!"

Hannah fumbled for her seatbelt but couldn't get it undone. She ducked, covering her head with her hands, but she couldn't get low with her belly in the way.

Liam gunned the engine and sped south across the field. The Jeep jolted and jostled them.

Little puffs of snow sprayed ahead of them to the left. The explosions of snow froze in the eerie yellow beam of the headlights.

Pike was firing at them.

Not at them, at their tires. Trying to incapacitate them.

Liam veered right.

A swell of darkness reared ahead of him. The snow suddenly dropped away into nothing. The front fender of the Jeep lurched sharply downward. Fifteen to twenty feet below them glimmered the pale shine of ice.

A lake.

Liam let up on the gas and attempted to correct their trajectory. Too late.

Time slowed. It happened in a second. Liam saw every detail, every flake of snow smashing against the windshield, every barren branch reaching for him with gnarled fingers.

The steering wheel spun uselessly in his hands. The whole world seemed to spin with it—the snow angling weirdly in the headlights, the trees, the snowy ground, the black sky.

The Jeep slipped, wheels sliding and skidding. The snowbank crumbled beneath the tires. The front right wheel spun over empty air. The Jeep lurched hard to the right, dipping dangerously.

Hannah was flung against the passenger door. She turned her shoulder into the impact, smacking her upper arm instead of her belly or head.

Ghost slammed against the back of Hannah's seat with an aggrieved bark.

The Jeep came to a sudden, jarring stop. Liam stiff-arming the wheel, his heart banging, mouth bone-dry. He stared into empty space, aghast.

The Jeep balanced on the crest of the high bank.

Snow drove through the coned beams of their headlights. Nothing below them but ice.

Hannah gasped.

Liam went absolutely still. "Don't move."

"Not planning to."

Ghost started to rise.

The vehicle swayed.

"Ghost!" they both cried.

Hannah sucked in a breath. "Lie down, boy."

Ghost let out a displeased whine.

"Please. Do it for me. Trust me."

With a huff, he flopped back down.

"Good boy."

The Jeep groaned, dropped a little.

Liam's heart bucked in his chest, his stomach a knot.

"No, no, no!" Hannah muttered.

Without moving, Liam gazed in the rearview mirrors, searching for Pike, already bracing himself for the impact when the snowmobile pushed them right over the edge.

"He won't," Hannah said through gritted teeth, as if reading his mind. "He doesn't want the lake to kill us. He wants to do it himself. He'll wait."

He trusted her judgement. "If we're not careful, the lake will kill us anyway."

"I know."

Liam turned his head slowly to look at her.

Her eyes were terrified, her face a rictus of pain. Another contraction shuddered through her. She remained as still as possible, but he could see the tremendous effort it required. How much it was taking from her.

"I'm going to try to reverse."

"Okay."

Every movement slow and cautious, Liam very carefully shifted into reverse. He turned the wheel. He pumped the gas, praying and cursing, willing the chained tires to catch, to dig in deep and find solid ground beneath all that soft snow.

Come on, come on!

The front fender dropped a few inches over the edge. The world pitched.

He felt his weight rolling forward, felt the lurch low in his belly like at the top of a roller coaster just before the drop.

If they plunged over the edge, they would smash through the

ice into freezing water that would suck the heat and the life from them in minutes.

Hannah would die on his watch. Just like Jessa had died on his watch.

NO. He couldn't allow that. Wouldn't allow it.

He wrenched the wheel, pulsing the gas, his muscles straining, willing the Jeep to reverse with every fiber of his being.

Finally, the tires caught.

Snow sprayed beneath the wheels. They inched backward, the right front tire spinning in empty air. The three remaining tires churned, the Jeep bouncing and jolting.

All four wheels settled back safely on earth.

For a frozen second, no one moved, neither of them quite believing they weren't pitching head-first into the icy lake.

Liam took several deep, steadying breaths. His shoulders were so tense they ached. Relief flooded his veins, but it was short-lived.

Pike was still out there.

Behind them, Ghost let out a low growl.

"I can't see him anymore." Hannah leaned toward Liam and peered through the driver's side window. "The storm's getting bad. He could be anywhere."

"He must have driven past. He's coming around for another pass. Missed the tires last time. Probably won't again."

Liam shifted into drive and gunned the engine. He nearly hit a birch tree, but managed to avoid it and rumbled back into the field.

Hannah pointed. "There."

The red lights appeared, dim through the driving snow. Directly ahead of them now, maybe seventy-five yards. Not moving. Waiting for their next move.

The frozen lake lay below them to the right. The field

stretched ahead and behind them, with M-140 somewhere a few hundred yards to their left.

Liam jerked the wheel, spun, and headed left toward the road. They bumped and jostled over the uneven ground.

"He's still coming." Hannah collected Liam's pistol and set it in the center console. She leaned forward, wincing, and dug for something in the go-bag at her feet.

"He's faster than we are," Liam said. "More agile."

She pulled out the paper map and unfolded it. She clicked on the flashlight resting in the cup holder and traced a line with her finger. "We passed the town sign a half mile back. We're outside of Watervliet, which makes this Paw Paw Lake. We're close to Paw Paw River. It's steep in some places."

"I don't know. I don't know this area."

"I do." She turned to face him, the paper map in her good hand. "I remember."

He glanced at her.

Her face was a pale oval in the dim light. Her eyes were clear. Filled with pain and fear, but steady. "I have an idea."

27

NOAH
DAY ELEVEN

N oah flipped the pancake and watched the batter bubble.

He stood before the stove, making pancakes for him and Milo with the last of the powdered eggs. He had half a container of whipped cream left to go with the peanut butter—Milo's all-time favorite meal.

They were having a late breakfast for once. This meal was a treat Noah usually reserved for special occasions, but after the last few days, he and Milo both needed something special, something just for the two of them.

The house Rosamond had given them in Winter Haven was a large four-bedroom log cabin with walnut plank flooring, vaulted ceilings with thick logs spanning the ceiling, and a white kitchen with an oversized granite-topped island.

Outside the large picture windows, he could see Darryl Wiggins' house fifty yards to the left. A thin line of trees spanned the gentle slope leading to the river a hundred yards back.

A cardinal perched on the branch of a maple tree. Several squirrels chased each other through the snow, darting from tree to tree.

Anxiety snarled in Noah's gut. It had been a long couple of days. Too long. The raid at the Carters, the thing with Billy, and the execution had all taken their toll. He was exhausted, weary to the bone in body and soul.

He didn't want to think about what had happened. The Carters were dead. That's what mattered. The town had received its justice. The monsters wouldn't hurt anyone else ever again.

Thoughts of Julian kept niggling in the back of his mind like irritating gnats he couldn't brush away. And the guilt. He tried not to think about that. Tried not to think about any of it.

He wanted to throw himself into bed and forget about everything for six hours of blessed sleep, but he couldn't. He had a responsibility to Milo.

Milo had his Lego figurines lined up on the counter, shooting each other with laser beams and whispering, "Pew, pew!" under his breath. His medical bracelet clinked against the countertop.

Noah flipped another pancake and studied him with an anxious frown. "Hey, buddy. Can we talk for a few minutes?"

"Sure, Dad."

The aftermath of the massacre had been a blur. The last few days, he'd left early and come home late. He'd been with his son, but he hadn't yet sat him down and talked to him about what happened. Not like he needed to.

Milo had been quieter than usual. Somber, a little clingy. But he hadn't acted nearly as traumatized as Noah had expected.

"How are you feeling?"

"Okay."

"Your stomach's good? You feeling tired or dizzy at all?"

Milo wrinkled his nose in exasperation. "I'm *fine*, Dad."

"Okay, okay. I hear you."

Noah flexed his fingers, stared at his wedding ring. He dreaded the conversation, but he couldn't put it off anymore.

Hannah was great at this kind of thing. She had a natural empathy and way with people. She knew what to say and how to say it. Noah felt awkward and tongue-tied, like he might say the wrong thing and scar his kid forever. "What about . . . other stuff?"

Milo didn't say anything, just waited for Noah to explain.

Noah blew out a breath. "I wanted to talk to you about what happened in the church. How you feel about what you saw."

Milo broke his gaze and looked down at the counter. He bit his lower lip, just like Hannah used to. "Quinn told me not to look."

"What do you mean?"

"She said it was a game."

"What kind of game?"

"She said not to look at the bad things that were happening. If I was the best at not looking, I would win."

Noah forgot to breathe. He forgot about the pancakes. "And you didn't? You didn't see anything bad or scary?"

Milo picked up one of the Lego figurines—Darth Vader wielding two lightsabers. He took both lightsabers out of Darth Vader's plastic hands and set them on the counter. "I like to win games, Dad. I think I beat her, too."

He looked at Noah and smiled. He'd never looked so much like his mother. Delicate, vulnerable, but a hidden strength behind those big dark eyes.

Noah could have wept with relief. "That's—that's so good, son."

"That man with the weird eyes was scary. And Quinn's mom. They were mean."

"Yeah, they were," Noah said, his loathing for Billy Carter filling him all over again. Guilt stabbed him. He pushed it away.

"Quinn fought them, though. Just like a superhero." Adoration shone in Milo's eyes. The kid hero-worshipped the girl. And who wouldn't, after what she'd done?

She could have saved herself and abandoned Milo. She didn't. Somehow, amid all that horror, a sixteen-year-old girl had had the presence of mind to protect a little boy's psychological health, too.

Prickly, blue-haired Quinn—sarcastic and smart-mouthed but fierce and brave. His and Milo's very own angel of mercy.

Milo seemed okay. He'd been through a lot, but considering how bad it might have been, he'd come out relatively unscathed. The next time, he wouldn't be so lucky.

Noah had to make sure there was never a next time.

"The pancakes," Milo said.

"What?"

"I think they're burning."

Noah cursed. An acrid smell filled his nostrils. He flipped the Mickey Mouse pancake he'd been working on. It was burned black. He used the spatula to flip it onto an empty plate and switched off the burner. "Sorry, no Mickey this time."

"It's okay, Dad. We've got plenty. It all ends up in the same place, Miss Molly says."

"We should listen to her." Noah fixed Milo's plate. He slathered a thick layer of peanut butter on two huge pancakes almost as large as the plate, swirled whipped cream on one, and slapped the second one over the first like a sandwich. He slid the plate across the counter. "Eat up."

"What happened to the bad guys?" Milo asked.

"They can't hurt you anymore."

"But what happened to them?"

He closed his eyes, saw Julian shooting Billy, Billy's face crumpling, collapsing in on itself. He forced his eyes open, forced the image down deep. "They're . . . dead."

Milo hesitated, seeming to consider that fact.

"You don't have to worry about them. None of them. You don't have to worry about any bad guys. It's my job to keep you safe."

"And Quinn."

"Her, too. The point is, you're safe. I promise I'll take care of you, no matter what. Okay?"

"Okay." Milo picked up the floppy pancake sandwich and took a huge bite. "Mmmm, dewishious!"

Noah's heart filled with an intense aching love for his son, for this child who meant the entire world to him. He blinked away the sudden wetness in his eyes.

He wouldn't break down in front of Milo. He'd save it for later, when he was alone in his bedroom—staring up at the dark ceiling, plagued by worry and unable to sleep.

He leaned across the island and ruffled Milo's black curls. "Anyone ever tell you how handsome you are?"

Milo grinned around his mouthful of pancake. "All the time."

28

NOAH

DAY ELEVEN

"**G**ood news!" Julian's voice came through the staticky radio.

"What is it?" Noah's grip tightened on the radio.

They needed good news. While the rioting had died down after the public executions of the Crossway murderers, things were still far from under control.

Every night, there were more lootings and break-ins. More dead bodies discovered—mostly the elderly, but a few young children as well. Hypothermia. Weakened hearts under massive stress.

A few dozen people in the shelter had come down with serious cases of pneumonia. More were likely to follow. Everyone was scared.

"Come to the middle school," Julian said. "It's the new designated community distribution center."

"What are we distributing?"

"Sutter came through, man! Just come and see!"

Noah was in the middle of dealing with an altercation over on Dogwood Lane in one of the neighborhoods behind Crossway

Church. Neighbors fighting with each other, accusing the other of stealing their precious and dwindling supplies.

He wrote the probable offender a ticket for a court he'd never attend and drove the black 1978 Ford F250 4x4 the police department had confiscated. One of the reserve officers had spray-painted "Fall Creek Police" on both sides in white paint.

They'd plowed the main roads three days ago, but the town fuel was extremely low, and they were waiting until the streets were impassable before plowing again. The weather was cold and gray, typical of Southwest Michigan, where the sun refused to make an appearance for six months.

Even with snow tires, the old truck struggled in several places. Noah got stuck once and had to stop and shovel his way out. He made a mental note to himself to stick with a snowmobile instead. The ride was colder but faster.

The middle school was located beside the high school. They shared the same property and football field. In the school's rear parking lot, three rugged trucks had backed up to the entrance, their beds crammed with supplies tied down with tarps.

A dozen volunteers were unloading boxes and crates of food, sanitary supplies, over-the-counter medications, and bottled water into the cafeteria.

A ragged line of hungry people was already beginning to form as the word spread. They crowded near the doors, barely able to stop themselves from seizing a box as soon as it was off-loaded.

Sam Perez and Reynoso were helping unload, lifting huge boxes with ease. They were smiling and joking with a few of the volunteers.

Funny how quickly some food and water lifted everyone's spirits. How quickly everyone's priorities changed from Facebook likes and keeping up with the Joneses to simple survival.

Mike Duncan and his physicist nephew, Jamal, were also volunteering, along with Tina Gundy, the mechanic's daughter.

Noah raised his radio and saluted Tina. "Hey, thanks for this!"

Mike, Jamal, and Tina had spent the past week at the auto repair shop, fixing whatever they could. They'd repaired ten more radios and finessed two additional trucks into working order.

They'd also set up repeaters to greatly extend the range of the handheld radios. Key personnel could now communicate throughout Fall Creek and beyond the town limits.

Tina grinned and waved back. "Whatever we can do to help."

"Just keep doing what you're doing."

Several people stood near the trucks in a loose semi-circle—Julian, the superintendent, Darryl Wiggins, and Chief Briggs. And Mattias Sutter.

Noah strode up and motioned at the trucks. "Where'd you get all this?"

Sutter grinned broadly. "We found a few stranded delivery trucks off I-94 near Bridgeman. Those semis weren't going anywhere. We had to unload it all by hand."

"Fantastic!" Wiggins rubbed his hands together. "I'm so hungry I could eat a horse."

"We'll bring in more. We've got a few wholesaler supply places we can hit up. And a pharmaceutical wholesaler that supplies nursing homes. It's out of the way—and the public eye—which means it's ours for the taking."

Chief Briggs scowled.

Sutter's smile didn't falter. "Only if it's abandoned, of course. Poor choice of words."

He turned to Rosamond and Noah. "We've got your list of medications the townspeople need. We found some insulin for Patty Snyder's mother. And more of your hydrocortisone, Noah."

Noah's pulse quickened. "Really?"

Sutter hooked his thumb at the nearest truck. "I've got it set aside in a bag up in the cab for you. At least two years' worth. Maybe three."

Gratitude surged through him. For a moment, he was speechless. It felt like he'd been holding his breath for the last two weeks and could finally breathe again.

Milo would be okay. They would get through this. He touched his wedding ring beneath his gloves. *I'm keeping him safe, Hannah. Like I promised.*

"Thank you. If you find any glucocorticoid vials—"

"Got it." Sutter patted his pocket. "It's on the list."

"We're running low on diesel and gas," Julian said.

"We found enough fuel to keep the shelter generators running for a few more days," Sutter said. "Don't worry. We'll take care of everyone."

"You just 'found' it? Fat chance." Chief Briggs pointed at Rosamond. "This is wrong. You know it is."

Rosamond smiled, but the corner of her eye twitched. "It's wrong that our children are warm and fed? Look around you. See all those happy faces? I appreciate your . . . morality, Chief, I do. But what was right two weeks ago isn't necessarily right today."

The chief didn't relent. His scowl deepened. "I won't be a part of this! I won't!"

Wiggins' features twisted into a barely repressed sneer. "You are welcome to leave at any time. In fact, we will happily escort you wherever you need to go."

Sutter took a step toward Chief Briggs. "If you're not with us, you're against us."

Briggs jabbed his finger at Sutter. "You! You don't even belong here! Your men are a blight on this town! Your 'vengeance' has already stained our hands with blood!"

Noah flinched.

Sutter didn't. "Your town asked us to do it. They wanted justice. Real justice."

"And we got it," Julian added.

"You'll pay for what you've done." The chief's voice rose. "I'll see that you go to prison for it!"

Sutter patted the AR-15 slung across his chest. "Somehow, I don't think so."

Briggs's face purpled with anger. He balled his hands into fists like he might actually take a shot at Sutter. Sutter was built like a tank—or a rhinoceros. The chief was in his sixties, his burly frame slowly giving way to fat. It wouldn't be a fair fight.

"We shouldn't be wasting our energy with arguing." Noah stepped between them. The public execution had left him unsettled, too. The whole thing did. But admitting that in front of Briggs would just add fuel to the fire, not put it out. "We all need to work together in this."

"Listen to Noah," Rosamond said. "Gentlemen, it's clear you both have strong feelings on the matter. Everyone here is trying to do the best they can for the town and everyone in it. If we don't work together, we'll fall apart. Just like what's happening in the cities right now. We cannot let that happen to us." She directed her sharp gaze at Briggs. "If that means we have to make some hard choices, then so be it."

Without a word, the chief turned on his heel and stalked off. A moment later, his 1970's Jeep roared out of the parking lot, the rear tires fishtailing in the snow before he regained control.

Then he was gone.

"Good riddance," Wiggins spat. A stiff, sour-faced man in his fifties, Wiggins was the rotary club president and the manager of Community Trust Bank.

Julian shot him a look, dislike clear on his face. Wiggins was also a brownnoser, always trying to get in Rosamond's good graces and garner himself more influence. Noah knew that Julian hated it.

Rosamond shivered and drew her scarf tighter around her throat. "He'll come around."

"And if he doesn't?" Sutter said darkly.

"Don't worry about Briggs," Wiggins said. "He won't be a problem much longer."

Noah shot him a questioning look. Wiggins gave a noncommittal shrug and smirked.

He muttered something about checking out the organization of the supplies but was probably skulking off to grab the best of whatever the militia had brought in for himself.

"My men have work to do," Sutter said. "Gotta get that tax collected."

He nodded to the superintendent and strode into the middle school, already on his radio.

"They won't bother Bishop," Noah said. A statement, not a question.

Rosamond touched his arm. "Atticus Bishop has earned his grief. And his solitude. No one will bother him. You have my word."

He was relieved, but anxiety still twisted in his gut. "Can I talk to you for a minute?"

"Of course. You know I always make time for you. Come with me to the shelter. I need to check in and show my face."

Julian stiffened. "I guess I'll check on the communication volunteers," he said, a hint of bitterness in his voice. "They were supposed to pass out the sanitation and trash instructions for each neighborhood by now, but I haven't heard anything."

"Good idea," Rosamond said as she twined her arm in Noah's. They headed for the shelter, leaving Julian standing alone.

29

NOAH
DAY ELEVEN

Several hundred townspeople were crammed inside the high school. It was far more crowded than when he'd visited only a week ago.

Cots and sleeping bags covered nearly every available inch of space. Families and couples slumped in clusters here and there. Stuffed suitcases and duffel bags were crammed in every corner.

The gym echoed with voices, all tight with strain and worry. Coughing and sniffling. Babies and children crying.

Rosamond stopped and smiled and bestowed sympathy and compassion, kindness and concern. She didn't shake anyone's hand.

People stared at her with haunted, hollowed eyes. Several of them looked shivery and pale. Beneath the smell of bleach, the stink of vomit hung in the stale air of the gym.

"What's wrong with them?" Noah asked.

"You cram so many people together, passing bugs around is bound to happen," Rosamond said under her breath as they hurried across the gym. They waved to Annette and Lee, who were setting up puzzles for a half-dozen kids in the corner.

They passed through a set of metal double doors and down a hallway lined with lockers. Cots and sleeping bags filled the hallways. It was colder out here, the coughing more pronounced.

Most classrooms were in use. The staff room and principal's office had been overtaken with desperate people seeking warmth.

They found an empty classroom. Rosamond took the comfortable chair behind the teacher's desk. Noah took a metal chair from one of the student desks and pulled it closer.

Rosamond leaned forward and rested her forearms on the desk. She steepled her fingers beneath her chin. "Noah Sheridan. What would I do without you?"

"Carry on like you always do, I suppose."

She laughed. It was a tired laugh, but still filled with warmth.

She was working herself to the bone to keep this town together. It showed in the shadows beneath her eyes, her perfectly coifed hair slightly unkempt, her suit a little rumpled.

"Don't forget to take care of yourself, superintendent. We need you."

"People need you, too, Noah. They need to see you. They need to know that law and order is still present here. In a different form now, but still here." She sighed, smoothed her hair. "How is Milo doing?"

"Milo is doing well. Better than I ever expected."

"Good. Let's keep it that way." Rosamond considered him carefully, her head tilted. "Something is bothering you."

He took a deep breath. "The militia. They seem so . . . aggressive."

Rosamond blinked. Her eyes went shiny. A tiny crack appeared in her armor. She looked away from him and wiped her eyes, drew in a deep breath. "We do what we have to. We can never allow such horror again. I won't allow it. Not on my watch. Do you understand?"

He nodded. He knew exactly how she felt. Guilt pricked him. He pushed it away.

The superintendent composed herself and looked at him. "What else?"

"The food tax. Folks aren't going to like it."

The fine lines around her eyes tightened. Her mouth thinned. "Ten percent isn't too much to ask, is it? To keep our friends and neighbors alive? People paid their taxes to the federal and state governments. I don't imagine people will be paying monetary taxes in the near future. Should they just stop? Or do they still owe something to the people fighting to protect them and keep them safe, healthy, and alive?"

"It makes sense when you put it like that."

"Will you make sure that the people understand that? I need your help in this to make it work, Noah. Otherwise, everything just falls apart."

He nodded heavily. The community needed to come together to help each other survive, but he still didn't like the idea of force. Neither would Molly and Quinn. "I'll do my best."

"I'm sure you will." She narrowed her eyes at him. "There's something else."

She always could read him well. He sat up straighter and told her about Octavia Riley's claims and Bishop's suspicions from the night of the massacre. "Honestly, this whole thing disturbs me. I don't like it."

"None of us like it. The Crossway Massacre is the worst thing that's happened in this town, in this county, hell in the entire state of Michigan. No one saw that coming. No one. But it proves the critical importance of law and order. We have to hold on until the governor or the feds get things under control and some semblance of civilization returns again. That's our job here. Our only job."

"And if someone did let them out?"

Rosamond rubbed her temples. "The human psyche wants a reason, an explanation. Sometimes there's nothing more than an old lock that broke and a good but exhausted man who fell asleep during a crisis. It happens. Human error is human error."

"But—"

"Octavia Riley is—was—a drug-addicted whore who shacked up with a psychopath. She knew she'd finally reached the end of the line. She saw a chance with you, an opening. Criminals will say anything to save their own worthless necks."

"I know."

"We don't have the manpower right now. You know this. We're all exhausted. We're all burning the candle at both ends just trying to keep this town safe and its people from starving and freezing to death. We've endured one blizzard. According to the emergency radio broadcasts, another is coming right on its heels."

He started to say something, but she raised a hand. "Ray Shultz and his cohorts are dead. You caught them. We got the bad guys, Noah. We did it. You did it."

Noah stiffened. The memory of Billy Carter flashed through his mind. His bloody smile, his lazy eye. His disconcerting, accusatory gaze.

That's what troubled him most. What haunted his nightmares. Not that Billy Carter and the others were dead, but how brutal and ugly it was. How quickly—how easily—it had happened.

Noah might not have pulled the trigger, but he'd stood by and allowed it to happen. It was a line he wasn't sure if he could come back from. If any of them could.

"The townspeople are satisfied," Rosamond said. "They need to mourn their loved ones in peace. Dredging this whole mess up again will only demoralize people and create divisions and mistrust. It puts our community at risk, Noah. Think about that for a minute."

He hated that niggling feeling in the back of his mind, but he also understood the necessity of solidarity, of community.

Dave had shared the ham radio reports—dozens of small towns already collapsing, overrun by gangs, marauders, and hungry refugees fleeing the cities.

Fall Creek was still standing. That meant something.

The tension in his shoulders eased. Rosamond had a way of helping him to see the bigger picture. He wasn't letting this go, just setting it aside for now. "When this is all over—"

The superintendent stood and held out her hand. "Of course. I will personally request a task force to investigate the Crossway Massacre. Enough bloodshed has been spilled. It is an ugly thing. A dangerous thing. The quicker it's put to rest, the better it will be for everyone."

He stood across the desk from her. They shook hands. "Thank you, Rosamond."

"We're family," Rosamond said. "Remember that."

The radio at Noah's hip stuttered static. "This is Luther at the Old 31 North roadblock. We've got a guy here who says he's from FEMA. You want us to let him in?"

30

NOAH

DAY ELEVEN

The FEMA guy was named Aaron Andrews. He was a short, overweight black man in a blue FEMA-emblazoned jacket and cap, clutching a clipboard and pen.

He'd arrived with a military escort. Four soldiers in ACUs stood around two armored Humvees, M4s slung across their shoulders.

Rosamond, Annette, Julian, and Wiggins surrounded Andrews in the small foyer just inside the entrance. No one made a move to head deeper inside with the crowd of restless refugees.

"What happened to us?" Julian asked. "Who did this to us, and have we nuked them into the next century, yet?"

"I can only confirm that we were indeed attacked," Andrews said, a pinched expression on his face.

"Surely, you've heard rumors at least," Annette said. "Rumors with a bit of oomph behind them? An educated opinion?"

His gaze shifted briefly to the soldiers before returning to Rosamond. "The scuttlebutt pins it on China. They're denying it, and their nuclear warheads are accounted for. But that doesn't mean jack squat."

"The White House knows," Wiggins said. "You can bet your ass on it. They're dragging their feet. Congress doesn't know their head from their tail end on a good day. They don't have the balls to do what needs to be done."

Andrews shrugged. "Not my department."

"When can we expect FEMA aid trucks to arrive?" Annette asked.

The man squeezed the bridge of his nose between his fingers. "I'm not here for that."

Everyone stared at him blankly.

Noah cleared his throat. "What?"

"We're alerting towns, townships, and villages in the region. FEMA emergency centers have been erected south of Kalamazoo in Portage and outside of St. Joseph off Old 31, along with Red Cross tent hospitals. FEMA busses will be escorting citizens to the appropriate regional centers, dependent upon the National Guard clearing the roads and keeping them clear. I'll provide you with a schedule to disseminate to your citizens."

"Not many folks here want to spend months trapped in a crowded, stinking FEMA camp," Julian said, scowling.

The man went rigid. "They're not camps—"

"We'll pass on the information," Rosamond said quickly to smooth over the tension. "Thank you so much for letting us know."

"What about food?" Noah asked. That was the most pressing concern. Even with the militia's supply run, what they had wouldn't last several hundred people more than a week. "When will the FEMA distribution trucks start coming?"

The man shifted from foot to foot and sighed, his obvious discomfort increasing. "They're not."

"Come again?" Rosamond asked.

"I'm not the decision-maker here," Andrews said dourly. "If

folks are hungry or need shelter, they can come to one of the official emergency centers."

"No aid is coming?" Annette said, dismayed. "Nothing at all?"

The guy shrugged helplessly. "I'm just trying to do my job. I'm sorry."

A sinking sensation took hold of Noah's stomach.

"That is unacceptable." Rosamond's voice was calm but sharp-edged with fury. She gestured behind her. "Look at these people. They're not getting enough as it is."

"Look, I'm sorry." Andrews wrung his hands and glanced back at his armed escort like he was wishing they'd come rescue him from another irate town. "Twelve trucks were attacked in Berrien and Cass Counties alone over the last two days. Every distribution truck requires a military escort. The National Guard has other priorities, so the number of relief convoys had to be reduced. We were forced to prioritize."

"What about air drops?" Noah asked, scrambling for ideas, for anything better than *nothing*. Molly had warned him, but he hadn't wanted to believe it. "Can't you use cargo or military planes or whatever to drop supplies?"

"We have. Most of the military's planes were hardened and still fly. As do most of the older plane and helicopter models. But that's incredibly expensive and a drain on resources. Not to mention the violent gangs, cartels, and militia already springing up and stealing and robbing whatever they can. In Detroit, none of the air-dropped goods are going to the people. They're stolen by gangs with high-powered weapons."

"We don't have that problem," Noah said. "You could air drop aid to any of the small towns around here."

"Let me be clear. Fall Creek's population is what? A thousand on a good day? We have seventy-five thousand starving families in

Kalamazoo. Two hundred thousand in Grand Rapids. A hundred and twenty thousand in Lansing. Detroit is seven to eight hundred thousand, not even counting the suburban spread."

Andrews frowned. "We're doing our best to reach every community, but some of you are just going to have to fend for yourselves."

Noah's insides twisted with trepidation—and mounting anger. "So you're just abandoning us?"

"You're country folk. You have farms and resources the cities don't."

"Are you freaking kidding me?" Julian's expression darkened like a storm cloud. "You're gonna stand here and spout that crap? It's *winter*. You see any crops ready to harvest?"

Andrews took a step back and raised his hands defensively. "You need to calm down, sir."

"We're calm." Rosamond placed her hand on her son's arm, a gentle restraint. She smoothed her features, though the corner of her right eye kept twitching. "We know this isn't your fault, Mr. Andrews. But is there anyone you could talk to? The regional director? We need aid as much as the big cities."

Andrews' expression softened. He was just a paper-pushing bureaucrat with no power to do anything even if he wanted to. He looked more tired than anything. Worn out.

"We have ten million people in Michigan. The challenges are overwhelming. Mass power outages, loss of water and heat, no communications, and no transportation . . . emergency services are doing the best we can, but we can't take care of everyone . . . we just can't."

Noah felt his anger leak out of him. He felt deflated. Even suspecting as much, hearing it said out loud was frustrating, alarming, and disheartening in equal measure.

"My hands are tied." Andrews wiped his brow. His face was sallow, circles beneath his eyes. "I'm sorry. I really am."

No one said anything after that. There was nothing left to say.

It was as they'd feared.

Fall Creek was completely on its own.

31

QUINN
DAY ELEVEN

Grief was a hard thing. Especially when you were grieving for something you'd lost, but also never really had.

A mother's love was a nebulous thing for Quinn Riley. Something she read about in books or watched in movies. Always an idea, a longing, rather than the real thing.

Now it was gone forever. She'd never have the mother who kissed her head before bed, who cuddled up for a story or a song, who listened while she complained about school, boys, and homework, who was there for her.

Neither she nor Gran talked about it when she returned to the house after the public execution, stricken and still reeling from shock. Besides, Milo was there. As much as she cared for him, he wasn't a part of this.

Gran stepped in and picked up the slack. She showed Milo how to can meat with the pressure canner. They made meatloaf together for dinner. When it got dark, Gran brought out the Aladdin lamps and showed Milo how to light and handle them.

Quinn went through the motions, barely present. She slumped at the table and fiddled with her lip ring, her mind a thousand miles away. She couldn't eat. The cats kept jumping into her lap and rubbing against her legs, but she ignored them.

After dinner, they listened to the emergency alerts on the hand-crank radio. The government had finally switched to a new stock message they repeated ad nauseum. The National Guard was partnering with FEMA and the Red Cross to distribute aid and establish shelters throughout the Eastern seaboard.

They still wouldn't state the cause of the blackout or mention the word EMP. They asked people to remain calm and orderly and assured the public that the power would be restored within weeks.

"Hogwash," Gran said. "They obviously don't know their heads from their tail ends."

Milo laughed at that.

Quinn kept seeing her mother's dead body falling into the snow and couldn't muster the energy to do anything, let alone smile or laugh.

Noah picked up Milo after six. When they were finally alone, Gran added a few pieces of firewood to the woodstove to keep it hot before settling in at the kitchen table. She leaned her cane against the nearest cabinet and rested her head in her veiny, age-spotted hands.

"She's dead, isn't she?" Gran asked without preamble.

Quinn nodded.

They sat there in the small, warm kitchen, the flames crackling cozily behind them. The Mossberg 500 leaned against the kitchen cabinet next to Gran's cane. Quinn's .22 was laid out across an opened newspaper on the table, waiting to be cleaned and oiled.

Valkyrie and Loki got into a spat—likely Loki pestering Valkyrie, as usual—and chased each other across the back of the sofa in the living room and around the La-Z-Boy. Odin meowed for more food even though he'd already licked his dinner bowl clean.

Thor climbed into Gran's lap and settled in for another nap, and Hel perched on top of the fridge, looking down on them all with his fluffy, twitching tail.

The cold wind howled. It creaked the shutters and shook a few loose shingles on the roof. Outside the kitchen windows, the darkness was absolute.

Quinn didn't cry. She'd vowed long ago that she would never cry over her mother. She didn't plan to break that vow now.

That didn't stop the fierce ache in her chest. That didn't stop the pain pulsing through her whole body like a living thing.

As crappy as Octavia had been, she was still Quinn's mother. And now she wasn't. Now Quinn didn't have a mother at all, crappy or otherwise.

She felt numb. And empty. The emptiness had a heaviness to it, like the spot where her mother belonged had taken on a weight and shape, an iron lump of grief and resentment and loss.

After several minutes, Gran heaved a grim sigh. "Sometimes you can love a person, and it's like sending all that love into a black hole. Doesn't mean your love wasn't good enough. Doesn't mean you weren't good enough. You hear me, girl?"

Quinn's throat went tight. She managed to nod.

"Every human being on this planet has free will. God gave us that free will. It's a gift and it's a curse. We each make our own decisions. And once we reach a certain age, we are responsible for those decisions.

"Sometimes it doesn't matter how much they were loved or how right they were raised; the decisions a person makes are selfish and wicked to the core. They choose to hurt other people. Sometimes there's a reason, and sometimes there isn't."

Quinn blinked back the sudden wetness in her eyes.

"The thing you need to remember is the fault lies with the person who made those choices and took those actions. Octavia did what she wanted to do, and that had nothing to do with you. There was nothing you could have done to make her different. To make her love you. Believe me, girl, I tried."

Gran had never said so much about Octavia in all of Quinn's memory. Gran had kept her feelings on the matter to herself. Like she kept a lot of things to herself.

Gran was a mother, too. She'd given Octavia all the love she had to give, and Octavia had rejected her, just like she'd rejected Quinn.

Quinn reached out and covered Gran's frail hand with her own. "How do *you* feel?"

"What do feelings have to do with it?" Gran said gruffly. She didn't pull her hand away.

"Octavia is—was—your daughter."

Gran gave a small shake of her head. Her eyes were shiny. "I grieved for Octavia long ago."

"Did you still love her? Even when she didn't love you back?"

Gran covered Quinn's hand with her own. Her voice was rough as gravel. "Every damn second of every damn day."

Quinn blinked, swallowed hard. Gran had still found it in her heart to love her daughter even when she didn't deserve it. Was the last person who deserved it.

Maybe it was okay for Quinn to feel the same. Resentment and anger and love and longing, all tangled together, side by side.

Maybe you didn't have to have it all figured out. It just was.

Gran cleared her throat. "This is your home, you know."

Quinn glanced at Gran.

Her face was as stern and solemn and fierce as always. Her sharp blue eyes were wet and filled with heaviness, like the night Gramps had died. "You belong here. With me."

Quinn swallowed the lump in her throat. "I wasn't planning on going anywhere else."

Gran set Odin gently on the floor and rose to her feet. She grabbed her cane from its spot against the cabinet along with the shotgun, which she slung over her shoulder. "Well, good. That's settled, then."

"Okay," Quinn mumbled.

"You should get ready for bed. Long day tomorrow." As Gran passed her, she hesitated. She squeezed Quinn's shoulder with surprising strength. "Love doesn't always get sucked into a black hole. Sometimes, it sticks around. Does some good."

Emotion rose in her chest. If she tried to speak, she'd start bawling like a stupid baby. She couldn't do anything but nod.

Gran gave her a knowing smile and shuffled out of the kitchen, headed for her bedroom. Quinn remained in the kitchen.

A memory flitted through her mind. Quinn was maybe five and groggy with sleep, Octavia leaning over her in the middle of the night, drunken and flushed and beautiful, eyes shining so bright as she laughed. *I missed you so much, baby girl. I just needed to tell you, to see your pretty face. I just couldn't go to sleep without seeing you. I love you to the moon and back, baby girl. You know that? The damn freaking moon.*

Quinn didn't move. The logs crackled and popped. The wind sighed and moaned.

She stared at the tongues of fire dancing behind the glass in the woodstove door for a long time. Until her vision blurred with tears.

32

HANNAH
DAY ELEVEN

A wave of pain seized Hannah's torso. She sucked in a sharp breath, every muscle in her body going tense. A fierce cramping in her lower back and belly, as familiar and primal as life itself.

She waited, trying to breathe through it, but it wasn't working. Her contractions were closer together. She fought through them each time, but she felt herself growing weaker, felt the pain and the exhaustion sucking at her last reserves.

It wasn't just the contractions, as if that weren't bad enough.

A white-hot pain like she'd never felt throbbed at her temples, the base of her neck. An intense pressure steadily building against her skull. Her hands and feet tingled like pins and needles, going numb and cold despite the heater.

It was preeclampsia. She knew it was. Knew what could come next—seizures, coma, death. This thing inside her wasn't just a parasite sucking the life out of her. It was a time bomb waiting to go off.

She had to get it out.

Black gnarled trees whipped by on either side. Their headlights washed over snow-glutted roads.

The Jeep lurched and fishtailed in the deep snow. Liam grunted as he struggled to regain control. He hunched over the steering wheel, single-minded in his determination. Visibility was twenty feet, maybe thirty. It was getting worse with each passing minute.

Hannah's heart slammed in her chest. She hated her helplessness more than ever. She had few if any useful skills to add. She couldn't even drive with these awful cramps, with her deformed hand.

She felt useless, a weight holding Liam down, keeping him from releasing his badassery. Putting them all in danger.

She gritted her teeth. She was determined to do whatever she could to pull her own weight. She would do whatever she could to help.

She held the map awkwardly in her lap. They'd passed Paw Paw Lake to the west and the municipal airport to the east. They couldn't see it in the snowstorm, just the sign. From here, 140 would take them twenty-five miles south to Fall Creek. They were so close. So close but it still felt like a thousand miles.

Despite the pain, she'd managed to find the road they needed and gave Liam instructions while he drove them into a sea of absolute darkness.

The woods fell away, and she sensed open space on either side; imagined farmhouses, farmer's markets, and small businesses scattered somewhere beyond the snow-driven darkness. They could see nothing other than what lay directly in front of them.

And Pike, always in the rearview mirror. Just a dim red blur nearly blotted out by the storm of white whirling flakes. Almost, but not quite.

He followed them. Unstoppable. Relentless. Ruthless.

She could feel him, could feel his sinister presence. Stalking through the dark, circling them like a shark circles its prey, relentlessly closer, closer, until he was ready to strike.

"There!" She pointed ahead. The small green road sign on their left read "Roberts Road." The storm was so bad she couldn't even read it until they were mere feet away.

Liam slammed on his brakes, nearly fishtailing, did a wide snow-spraying arc, and knocked the road sign clean over as he turned. He kept going.

"It should be up ahead two miles." She glanced in the mirror on the passenger side. Counted in her head, watched for the red headlights to appear. "Pike turned with us. He looks closer."

"Keep an eye on him."

She nodded, though Liam had eyes only for the road.

She breathed through another contraction, her teeth gritted, her muscles taut. It seemed to last forever before the pain released her. She sank back against the seat, spent and exhausted.

The snow spiraled into the lights, dashing against the glass. Millions and millions of flakes. No matter how quickly the wipers swept them away, they wouldn't stop coming.

The cab filled with the click and squeak of the wipers, the tick of the heater, Ghost's loud panting.

"Half a mile," she said.

Liam hit the brakes, but slowly, jerkily. The Jeep slewed sideways in the snow. Liam corrected, and they slid to a stop—mostly facing forward but a little skewed. Liam switched off the engine. The lights died. The heater went silent.

Like maybe their engine had stalled. Or a tire had popped. Or they were out of gas.

It was a calculated risk. Pike might not take the bait. He might just sit there and wait for the cold to infiltrate the cab and let hypothermia take them.

She doubted it. That same hypothermia was a threat to him, too.

Besides, it wasn't his way. He liked to do the killing personally.

They sat there, hearts pounding, hardly daring to breathe, both their gazes locked on the rearview mirrors. The red lights were barely visible. Close enough for them to see him and him to see them, but far enough away that an accurate shot was difficult.

Liam's hand remained on the keys in the ignition. His Glock was tucked beneath his right thigh for easy access. The AR-15 leaned against the seat beside her legs and the go-bag.

"Get your gun," he said. "Be ready."

She let the map slip off her lap. She pulled the Ruger from her pocket and flicked off the safety. She curled her bad hand into an awkward twisted fist and braced the butt of the weapon the way Liam had shown her.

Her hands were trembling. Fear clutched at her, riding each wave of pain. She counted the uncountable snowflakes, struggling to keep the mind-numbing panic at bay.

She wouldn't let fear get the better of her. She refused to let him win.

She glanced back at Ghost. He raised his head and growled, his tail stiff, his hackles raised. He knew danger was present, could sense their anxiety. Even barely recovered from being shot, he was alert, ready to defend his family.

"Good boy," she whispered. "Good boy."

She turned back around, kept her gaze on the side mirror.

The red eyes watched them.

The minutes ticked by. The snowmobile didn't move.

The cabin grew colder. The freezing air found cracks around doors and windows and pushed its way inside.

The contractions came in waves, growing stronger. Her head throbbing like someone had driven a rail spike through her temples. Her vision blurring, darkness threading the edges, as she stared unblinking into the rearview mirror.

Those two red lights, locked in, unwavering.

33

HANNAH
DAY ELEVEN

"I'm taking a shot." Liam gave her a long look. "You ready?"

She could barely meet the intensity of his gaze. His expression was stony, his mouth set in a firm line. His whole body tensed and coiled, like a panther preparing to pounce.

She couldn't let him down. She couldn't fail.

She tightened her grip on the pistol. "You can trust me."

Liam gave a terse nod. He released his seatbelt, rolled down his window, then leaned over her and rolled hers down. Snow whipped into the cab. The wind rushed in, reaching for her with icy fingers.

He shifted so his back pressed against the steering wheel. He slid the barrel outside the window. Liam aimed and popped off two short bursts of three rounds.

The cacophonous boom of the gunshots exploded inside the small cab. She wanted to clap her hands over her ringing ears, but she couldn't let go of the Ruger.

The red lights appeared to move. White spots behind her eyelids mingled with the swirling snow. She blinked to clear her vision.

The headlights grew larger and larger. The dull roar of the machine's engine emerged over the wind.

"He's coming!" she said.

"I see him."

The red lights kept coming. Closer, closer.

Liam fired again.

Pike swerved to the right, toward the passenger side, out of Liam's sight.

"Go! Go!" she cried.

Liam spun in his seat, the rifle dropping to his thighs as he went for the keys and started the ignition. He slammed the gas pedal. The Jeep growled and leapt forward.

Pike was already pulling up along the truck's rear flank on Hannah's side. Red light filled the cab. Ghost barked furiously. He was on his feet, slip-sliding around in the back.

"Shoot!" Liam cried.

She barely heard him over the ringing in her ears. A contraction hit her. The agony washed her vision with red. She struggled to brace herself against the seat and the door, to raise the Ruger.

Wind and snow whipped through the cab, streaming through the windows into her face. Snowflakes clustered in her eyelashes, smashed into her cheeks, her nose, her opened mouth as she sucked in searing mouthfuls of air.

Nerve-shredding fear tore at her, pulling her down. Blackness hovering at the edges of her vision. Outside the window, only more snow and endless darkness. The devil himself right at her heels.

"Use your gun, Hannah!"

This was the plan. This was what she was supposed to do.

The snowmobile pulled alongside the passenger side of the Jeep. Driving parallel, not five feet away from her.

Pike silhouetted against the red glow of the headlights, a dark shadow crouched over the machine's handlebars, his helmeted head turned toward her, only one hand on the handle, the other holding the gun.

He wasn't pointing the gun at her. He wouldn't shoot her. Not like this.

She had no such hang-ups.

This was it. Her chance to do something. To make it count.

Wind blasted through the unrolled window. She fumbled clumsily with the pistol. Her hands tingling with an excruciating numbness.

She didn't have time to aim or breathe properly. Barely knew what she was doing other than brace her hands and point and shoot.

She squeezed the trigger. The gun bucked wildly in her hands, the retort deafening.

The snowmobile jerked and swerved. He didn't flinch, didn't react. She'd missed him.

She pointed the gun. Fired again.

The machine slowed and hung a sharp right before swinging back again.

She squeezed the trigger. Shot at him a third time.

Missed again. Hitting him wasn't the point. Distracting him, getting him focused on her, that was the goal. And that was working like a charm.

She fired. Four shots.

Pike ducked, straightened, fired back. *Boom!* Not at her, but the Jeep. A second round followed the first, then another. *Boom! Boom!*

The Jeep slewed. Hannah felt herself thrown backward. She slammed against the seat, whiplash twinging her neck. The pulsing in her head agonizing.

Almost there. They had to be nearly there.

Another gunshot split the air. She ducked low. The seatbelt scraped against her belly. The next contraction radiated through her entire body, so powerful it stole her breath.

Liam cursed, wrenching the steering wheel, desperate to regain control of the Jeep. The reek of gasoline filled her nostrils. She gagged, nearly vomited.

She pushed herself up again, forcing herself to take another shot, to do her job and distract Pike as long as necessary. She squinted against the driving snow and wind, against the white spots dancing in front of her vision.

The snowmobile roared beside them. Pike's head turned their way, his weapon lifted.

They reached the bridge.

34

HANNAH
DAY ELEVEN

Everything seemed to move in slow motion. The Jeep and snowmobile roared side by side. The stretch of road and the river straight ahead, high steep banks sheering off down to the river on both sides.

Just before they hit the bridge, Liam spun the wheel and swerved to the right and struck the snowmobile hard.

The Jeep veered sharply and smashed into Pike's snowmobile. The jolt cracked through Hannah's spine, reverberated through her skull.

Pike wasn't expecting it, still had only one hand on the handlebar, one holding his weapon. He was so focused on avoiding Hannah's gunfire while simultaneously trying to take out the Jeep's tires that he never saw the river—or the steep embankment hurtling toward him.

Pike's snowmobile careened out of control. The machine's front skis struck the snowbank blanketing the short guardrail just before the bridge and snapped clean off.

The snowmobile's forward momentum flipped it end-over-end and pitched it over the precipice into the Paw Paw River.

. . .

Hannah felt herself splinter. Time stopped. She felt the Jeep following the snowmobile over the edge, so fast and easy in the snow, smooth as sledding.

Hannah trapped in her seat as she tipped over and headed down, down, down. The black glistening river rushing up to meet her. Nothing in the windshield but that black ice gaping large and dark and wide as a universe swallowing her whole. Free falling, her stomach in her throat, her heart too stunned to beat. No reversing it, no calling for help, no changing the unalterable physics of the world.

The front fender striking first, then the hood crumpling like a soda can, the rest of the Jeep slamming full-speed into the ice, the jarring, bone-rattling force of the crash, that abrupt *stop*.

Maybe they would teeter there for a moment, balancing on the knife's edge as the force of the blow reverberated through the frozen slab, spidering cracks spreading, spreading through the fracturing ice. Maybe they would look at each other and hold hands in those last awful seconds, the last two humans in the universe. Hannah and Liam. Liam and Hannah.

And then the great groaning *pop* as the surface gave way beneath them and it was terrifying, plunging into that black cold nothing that will swallow her and never spit her back up. She would be gone, will disappear, sucked down into endless frozen darkness—

"Hannah!"

She was gasping, sobbing, clawing her way up from cold black nothing and she wasn't drowning, wasn't dead, wasn't even in the water.

Liam shook her shoulders. "Hannah! Wake up!"

His voice distant, dim and far away beneath the high-pitched ringing in her ears. She blinked. He came slowly into focus. That grim, rugged face. Those gray-blue eyes.

The only light came from Liam's flashlight lying in the center console. She didn't remember where it had come from.

The Jeep was quiet and still. No rumbling engine, no heat, no headlights. Snow gathered thickly on the windshield. Flakes swirled inside the cab through the side windows. They gathered on her arms, her belly, her hair. It was cold. So cold.

"What—what happened?"

"We did it. He went over the edge. Into the water."

"We didn't go over."

He smiled at her. It was a nice smile, completely transforming the hard planes of his face. "Close. But no, we didn't."

Her whole body tingled. Her head felt like it was about to split open. She was tired. So tired.

Liam shook her again. "Don't do that. Don't go away on me. Pike shot the Jeep. He got the engine, the gas tank. It's dead. We have to get out of this blizzard, or we'll die here."

"I don't want to die," she mumbled.

"Neither do I."

Ghost pushed himself between the seats, placed his big paws on the console, and shoved Liam out of the way.

Liam raised his hands and leaned back. "Woah, boy!"

Ghost's tail thumped the seats as he nuzzled Hannah's face, woofing in concern. His hot, stinky dog breath filled her nostrils, but warmed her frozen cheeks. She leaned into him, wrapped her arms around his neck, and pressed her face into his broad, fluffy chest.

"You sure he went over?" she mumbled into Ghost's fur.

"I checked myself. There's a huge hole in the ice. The Ski-Doo went right through. That asshole went with it."

"Okay." It didn't seem real yet. She was too cold, too stunned, in too much pain. It would sink in later. "Okay."

Liam reached down at her feet, grabbed his go-bag, and set it in his lap. He ejected the magazine from the AR-15, slid it into a side compartment of his pack, pulled out a fresh one, and slapped it on. He buckled the rifle to his sling.

She was still clutching the pistol grip so hard her fingers were stiff and numb. She held it out to him. "Here."

He shook his head. "It's yours. You did good. You did exactly what you were supposed to do."

She tucked it into her coat pocket. She might have blushed if she didn't feel like vomiting.

She shoved open the passenger door and clambered out. Ghost scrambled across the front seats and leapt after her. She patted her coat pockets, made sure she had the knife and the pistol.

The wind beat at her, tugging at her clothes, her scarf, her hair, intent on knocking her right off her feet. Snow drove into her face and eyes. She shielded her face with her arms, wishing for a pair of snow goggles. A contraction wracked her. She nearly stumbled from the pain.

She was twenty miles from home. But in this blizzard, that didn't matter. All that mattered was finding shelter.

An intense desire came over her. An instinct. Something deep down and primal, like a mother wolf searching for a den—she needed somewhere warm and safe to hole up, to bed down, to do this thing her body was making her do. She had no power over it, no choice.

Ghost pressed against her thigh and walked alongside her. She buried her good hand into the scruff of his neck. He was the only thing keeping her on her feet.

Liam came around the Jeep, his pack slung over his shoulders, the flashlight in his hand. He handed her a length of paracord and leaned in close so she could hear him over the wind. "Tie this around your arm. We have to stay connected, or we'll lose each other."

She nodded dully. A contraction hit her, and she sagged, nearly falling. Liam took the opposite side to Ghost and put his arm around her. Gratefully, she leaned into him.

They started off. Each step was exhausting, the snow pulling at her legs. She slogged on, head down, teeth clenched, willing herself to put one leg in front of the other, willing herself to keep moving.

She couldn't fight, couldn't shoot, couldn't do much of anything. But she knew how to endure. She knew how to keep going, to keep living even in the face of insurmountable odds.

That had to count for something.

35

HANNAH
DAY ELEVEN

Liam's figure was a shadowy blur beside Hannah. The flashlight beam barely penetrated past three or four feet.

Everything disappeared in driving sheets of white snow. Outside that circle could've been anything. A city of skyscrapers. An arctic ocean. The end of the world.

The cold was a predator itself, a living thing, malicious and merciless.

Her eyelashes were so crusted with snow she could barely open her eyes. Her face and ears burned. She held Ghost's fur tighter, her fingers going stiff and numb.

Her feet were numb, too. From the preeclampsia or the cold, she didn't know.

The pain was a ravenous beast gnawing at her insides. A demon, an alien. A parasite. It would kill her to get out.

Maybe Pike would have his revenge in the end after all.

Liam stopped abruptly. She stumbled, tripping on a thick crust of snow. He tightened his grip around her waist, steadying her, then pointed to a chest-high object in front of them.

Hannah stared at it blearily, not understanding what it was for a second.

Mailbox, her muddled mind whispered. A mailbox meant a house. Four walls and a roof to shelter them from the storm. A bed with a mattress. Maybe even a kindly old grandma to make her soup, start a warm bath, and wrap heaps of blankets around her shivering shoulders.

"Almost there," he shouted into her ear. Liam turned at a ninety-degree angle and strode through the heavy snow. She shuffled beside him, trying to keep up.

An intense cramp radiated through her entire body, hot and pulsing. Her head throbbed, her thoughts spiraling. It was harder and harder to think clearly, to force herself to focus.

Ghost barked, dashing ahead of them. Leading the way. A huge shape reared out of the swirling darkness. They'd reached the house. A porch. Snow-covered rocking chairs.

Liam helped her up the steps and banged his fist on the door. "Hello!" he shouted. The wind stole his voice and whipped it away into darkness.

No sound came from the house. No candles or lanterns glowing in the windows. No one appeared to be home. Maybe they'd never made it back. Or maybe they'd already moved on to an emergency shelter.

"We'll try the back," Liam shouted.

She was shivering so badly she could hardly walk by the time she and Liam circled the house and found the rear sliding glass door. Liam used a decorative landscaping rock he'd found beneath the snow to break the glass.

He scraped the jagged shards from the frame with the brick, reached inside, and unlocked the door. He wrestled it open. Mounds of snow spilled across the tile. Finally, they were inside.

Liam swept the flashlight beam across the interior. They were in a kitchen—round wooden table covered in a lace tablecloth, squat white cabinets, yellowing linoleum floor. A pink ceramic pig cookie jar on the counter. Old and out of date, but clean.

The house smelled faintly of chemical cleaners. There was no stench of rotting food or unemptied trash cans. Whoever lived here must have gone somewhere for Christmas vacation and hadn't returned.

Ghost stood in the center of the kitchen and shook out his wet fur, spraying globs of snow everywhere, including on Liam.

Liam glared at the dog. "Really? Right next to me?"

Ghost looked up at them and tilted his head, an overly pleased expression on his face.

"Even dogs have a sense of humor," she mumbled.

Liam shook his head in resignation. He placed the flashlight beneath his Glock and held them both in a two-handed grip. "I'm going to clear the house, just in case. Stay here."

Ghost followed Liam through the archway into the living room, probably eager to shake more snow at him. Hannah sagged into the nearest kitchen chair. She rested her elbows on the table and let her head fall into her hands.

She waited, dreading the next pulse of agony. It was only going to get worse.

A few minutes later, Liam was back, a handful of firewood balanced in his arms. "Found this stored under a tarp in the garage. No one's been here for a while. No one's looted the place yet, either. Don't open the fridge, though."

Within several minutes, Liam had a healthy fire crackling in the fireplace. A warm, flickering glow filled the cozy living room. She breathed in the comforting smell of wood smoke and charcoal, the heat slowly melting her frozen skin.

Liam hauled down two twin mattresses from bedrooms upstairs—little girls' rooms, judging by the purple princess and pink and teal unicorn sheets. He pushed them in front of the fireplace, shoving aside a coffee table stacked with National Geographic magazines and moving the plaid couch against the far wall.

He went upstairs again and returned with several candles, which he lit and set on the mantle, on a bookcase across the room, and on the kitchen table. On his next trip upstairs, he came back with an armful of blankets and pillows piled higher than his head. He tossed them on the mattresses.

Ghost gave a pleased yip and pounced on the nearest mattress. He turned in a tight circle like a cat and flopped down right in the center of the blanket pile.

Liam grunted. "Thinks he's king of the castle."

"He is."

Liam cocked his brows. "You gonna give up your mattress, then? I'm certainly not."

She hissed a pained breath. "In my book, that dog can sleep anywhere he wants."

"Fair enough."

Liam helped her to the mattress. She sank down gratefully beside Ghost. The dog crept forward on his belly, leaned into her side, and rested his head on his paws.

Liam knelt beside her. He gestured at her snow-crusted clothes. "Can I help you?"

She nodded through the pain.

He removed her hat, gloves, scarf, and coat. He unlaced her boots and pulled them off one by one. He stripped off her layers of damp wool socks, then draped a *My Little Pony* blanket over her.

Gratitude filled her. "Liam—"

"Just rest." He stood. "I'm going to use some plywood from the garage to block the sliding glass door. Then I'll get water from the hot water heater and search the cupboards for some supper."

Ghost raised his head, ears perked.

"Yes, for you, too." Liam headed for the kitchen.

The contraction that rolled through her was worse than any that had come before. White spots flashed behind her eyelids, her head pounding. She groaned.

Liam stiffened. He turned slowly, dread contorting his features.

She breathed through it, teeth clenched, and forced herself to meet his gaze. "It's coming. The baby is coming."

36

PIKE

DAY ELEVEN

Pike felt no fear, only a stunned sort of surprise as the Jeep plowed into him and the snowmobile skidded wildly. It careened into the guardrail, striking it with such force that it upended and pitched over the edge.

Pike was thrown from the machine, his hands ripping free, legs losing their hold. He was falling, tumbling end over end, plunging twenty-five feet to the ice below the bridge.

He landed hard on his right side. White-hot pain exploded in his shoulder, his hip, his ribs. His head struck the ice with a solid *thunk*. White stars spun dizzily behind his eyelids.

He moved cautiously, gingerly. First his left arm, then his right. Hands, wrists, elbows. His foot, ankle, knee. Left, then right. He rolled his shoulders.

His whole body ached. He was probably bruised and scraped all over, but nothing seemed broken. His left forearm burned—the maimed flesh from the dog bite ripping open again.

He clenched his teeth and rolled into a sitting position, his legs stretched out in front of him. The back of his head pulsed dully. He'd have a killer headache.

Snow swirled thick and heavy. Icy flakes stung his face. The wind tugged and pulled at his coat, threatening to tear his scarf loose. His head was bare. He'd lost his helmet in the fall. And his Beretta. He wasn't holding it in his hand anymore.

He blinked, rubbed snow from his eyes.

The far bank of the river lay thirty feet ahead of him—steep, but not as steep as the near side where he'd fallen. Thin dark tree trunks staggered along the incline would be enough to pull himself up.

The bridge soared above him, dark and imposing, the frozen, windswept river snaking below. Somehow, he'd slid beneath it.

I can see, he thought dimly. How could he see so clearly?

The fall had rattled him more than he'd initially thought. He shook his head to clear his brain. Mindful of the ice, he turned slowly and took in the sight directly behind him.

Less than five feet away, The Ski-Doo jutted from the ice. It had landed rear-first. The twin headlights beamed upward, highlighting the diving snow in an eerie red glow.

Pops and groans echoed as the hole in the ice surrounding the Ski-Doo widened. Deep cracks spidered out from the snowmobile. Small avalanches of snow collapsed into the widening cracks, spilling into the black water with little *pfft, pfft* sounds.

He could hear them, even over the moaning wind and the creaking branches. He could hear every *snap* and *crack* as the frozen slab splintered.

His heartbeat quickened, his mouth going dry.

With a great groan, the snowmobile shifted and began to slide. It lifted for a moment as if bobbing in the current, then it crashed onto its side, the red headlights wavering crazily before shining directly into his eyes, blinding him.

Instinctively, he lifted a hand to shield his face.

The plane of ice shifted and crackled and popped as the river swallowed the snowmobile in a single, greedy gulp.

He froze, willing it to be over, for the river to be satiated.

It was not.

It was like him—never satisfied, always hungry, always craving more.

Adrenaline shot through his veins. Remaining motionless wouldn't help him now. He spun and scrambled on hands and knees toward the far bank, toward safety.

A great crack snaked beneath him. Then another and another. The surface opened up below him, and he slipped into the breach. Dark water closed over his head.

The shocking cold nearly stopped his heart. He flailed wildly, pushing himself upward, breaking the surface. His lungs seized, and for a moment, he couldn't pull in air.

Sputtering and coughing, he scrabbled for the nearest slab. The current dragged at his legs, threatening to pull him under the ice and away.

He held on, lifting his legs in the water and inching himself onto the ice, grappling for handholds, scraping with his gloved fingers, pulling himself out little by little.

He remained focused but not afraid. A river would not take him. The cold would not take him. He was the one who ruled fate, who broke everything beneath his iron hand.

This was a challenge, a test of his will. Like every hunter, he relished a challenge.

This, though, only infuriated him.

His rage fueled him as he pulled himself across the ice, crawling with legs and arms splayed, snow driving into his face, his eyes, his mouth.

His thoughts narrowed to a single splinter of desire—Hannah. The soldier. The dog. What he would do to them. How he would make them watch. The dog first. Then Hannah. Then the soldier. Or maybe the soldier second. Hannah and the child she carried—his child—last.

He crawled like a worm, inching forward on his belly. The ice groaned and quaked beneath him but did not give.

Finally, he reached the firm ground of the riverbank. He pulled himself to his feet.

He shivered uncontrollably, his body aching, his thoughts thick and slow and growing heavy. His soaking clothes were already turning brittle, freezing against his skin. Hypothermia would set in within minutes.

He felt for his rifle strap. It was gone. He cursed through chattering teeth. He'd lost his Winchester in the water and hadn't even noticed. He was too cold to worry about it now.

He pulled a small penlight from a zippered pocket in his coat, fingers shaking so hard he nearly fumbled and dropped it. He shoved it between his teeth so his hands were free to pull himself up the embankment, using branches and tree roots and whatever he could grab.

At the top of the embankment, the trees thinned into what he hoped was a yard. People loved homes overlooking the river. Why should this place be any different?

The penlight only allowed him to see a few feet in front of him. He staggered through the snow and the darkness. One boot in front of the other.

He would not die today. If only the good died young, then he was destined to live forever. He was unstoppable. Ruthless.

As relentless as the blizzard itself.

37

QUINN
DAY TWELVE

L oki swished his tail in Quinn's face for the umpteenth time. She pushed him aside, but he kept coming back for more. "Ugh! Loki!"

"Loki's fine," Gran said, and gave him an affectionate pat. He purred and rubbed his head against her hand. "Aren't you, boy?"

Quinn, Milo, and Gran were seated around the kitchen table working on constructing a solar oven out of aluminum foil, cardboard boxes, duct tape, a piece of Plexiglas, and a few other supplies. Gran had explained they could use it to heat food and disinfect water, even in winter as long as they had sun.

Quinn snorted. "Fat chance in Michigan."

The fire in the woodstove crackled and popped almost merrily. The delicious, yeasty scent of homemade bread filled the kitchen.

Gran's Mossberg 500 leaned against the cabinet next to her cane. Quinn's loaded .22 rifle and a box of ammo rested on top of the sideboard behind her, within easy reach.

Hel, the snotty ruler of the underworld, lorded over his

domain from his favorite spot on top of the refrigerator. How he got up there, Quinn had no idea.

Thor wound himself around Milo's legs, his tail sticking straight in the air, and meowed to be petted. Odin and Valkyrie were sleeping, curled up on the rug in front of the woodstove.

Loki, the mischievous, disobedient tabby, kept jumping on the table. Quinn would swat him away. Three minutes later he was back again, rubbing against the sides of the cardboard box, almost knocking over the lamp, or poking his tail in Quinn's nose.

"He's so irritating," Quinn said.

"I think he's cool," Milo chimed in.

"Of course you would."

"You must like cats a lot," Milo said to Gran. "That's a lot of cat litter to clean."

"Tell me about it." Quinn rolled her eyes. "Call her the cat lady of the apocalypse."

"If the shoe fits," Gran said proudly.

"So what happens to the cats if we have to bug out?"

Gran gestured at herself and her cane and gave Quinn a rueful smile. "Where? And how? Besides, my babies aren't going anywhere. You think we could herd these crazy felines all the way to Florida?"

"If anyone can, it would be you."

Gran snorted.

Quinn shrugged. "Well, anyway, if it comes to it, we can always eat the cats."

Gran whipped her cane around and smacked Quinn on her butt before she could dart out of the way. "More likely, I'll eat the sassy human first."

Milo's eyes went wide, his head pinballing back and forth as he followed the exchange.

"Don't worry," Quinn said. "Gran seldom eats the guests. You're safe. Probably."

Gran winked at Milo. "Desperate times call for desperate measures."

He smiled. "I know you're joking."

"Don't be so sure," Gran deadpanned.

Odin roused himself from his nap by the woodstove, yawned, and trotted over to the table. He leaped onto Gran's lap with a lazy yowl. He turned in a circle, kneading his paws on her thighs, and curled into a fluff ball.

Gran paused in her work to scratch him behind the ears. Within seconds, he was sleeping again. Odin was the fattest, laziest cat on the planet. All he ever did was eat, poop, and drag himself from one nap to the next.

Quinn rolled her eyes. "Cats are useless in the apocalypse. We should get a dog."

Gran patted Odin's sleeping head. "Say that again, and you can sleep in the garage."

Quinn managed a grin. It was almost real. "I bet it'll smell better."

After her talk with Bishop and with Gran, she was starting to feel a little better. It still hurt. She was still scarred and haunted by nightmares. But she didn't feel so alone.

Gran clucked her tongue. "What am I going to do with you?"

"What are you going to do without me is more like it."

Milo put the aluminum foil down on the table, bent down, and scooped Thor into his lap. "I think Quinn's pretty awesome."

Quinn felt herself smiling, despite herself. "See? He thinks I'm awesome."

Gran rolled her eyes. "Speaking of being awesome . . . I want you to check on the neighbors for me."

"So you do have a heart."

"Please. Even the Grinch has a heart. I've been checking up on them most days in the mornings, as you very well know. But my hip is bothering me, so you can do it today. That's why God gave old people grandkids."

"I don't believe in God."

"Lucky thing God believes in you, or you wouldn't exist. Now go." She gestured at several grocery bags piled by the front door. "There are a few boxes of macaroni and cheese and cans of baked beans in each bag. And I refilled two plastic two-liter bottles with filtered and disinfected water for each house. It's not much, but it's something."

Quinn stared at her with her hands on her hips. "You're still giving food away?"

Gran flashed her a sharp look. "My pastor believes I'm an angel of mercy clothed in light. I aim to maintain that reputation."

Quinn snorted. "Doesn't the devil masquerade as an angel of light?"

"Come closer so I can wash out that smart mouth with soap, girl."

Quinn danced out of her reach. "Not a chance."

Milo giggled. Gran reached over and pretended to pinch his cheek. Her smile was genuine.

Quinn's heart squeezed. They were a long way from okay, but they were starting the long, slow process of picking up the pieces.

There were still moments when Quinn caught Gran staring blankly out the window, her eyes wet. Or sometimes, she'd simply stop in the middle of whatever task she was doing, her gaze going distant. She'd stay like that for a few minutes, then shake herself out of it, mutter under her breath, and return to work.

Quinn cleared her throat and swallowed the sudden surge of emotion. "So what's the real reason we're going door-to-door? I know it's not just the kindness of your heart."

Gran's expression went serious. "We can't do everything ourselves. Pretty soon, we're going to start having to work together. For firewood, for food collection and preparation, for hunting, for security. A few people can't do everything. We need our neighbors. We need a community."

Quinn sighed. "I guess you're right."

"I'm always right. I was planning on getting a neighborhood watch together so everyone can keep an eye on this street. But it starts with trust and goodwill."

"What if they come and just try to steal your stuff now that they know you still have food and supplies?" Milo asked.

"Good question, Small Fry."

Gran nodded. "We want to take care of those less fortunate if we can, but we have to do it carefully, anonymously if possible, and we also have to make sure we have enough for our own family first. It's a fine balance. Which is why you're going to say the same little spiel at each house. This is the last of what we have. Everything was about to expire, so we decided to share it and check up on everyone and make sure they're okay." She narrowed her eyes at Milo. "You got that?"

Milo wrinkled his nose. "Isn't that lying?"

"It's being smart," Gran said. "Period. End of story."

"Okay." Milo finished petting Thor and set him down on the floor. The cat wrapped around his legs and meowed plaintively for more.

"Tell them to meet at my house tonight at seven, and I'll serve the last of my homemade bread and honey butter. That should get them here."

Quinn and Milo put on their winter gear and gathered the bags of supplies. Quinn moved aside the blanket they'd tacked over the doorway to preserve the heat. The windows were already covered with aluminum foil to reflect all the heat back into the house.

She removed the rolled-up blanket stuffed against the bottom of the back door and painstakingly removed the duct tape she and Milo had stuck around the frame.

The cats circled around their boots, sniffing and meowing eagerly, excited to get outside and hunt for birds and mice. Valkyrie darted between their legs in a sleek black streak. Unlike the other cats, she seemed to love the snow. Against the field of white snow, she looked like a miniature panther stalking her prey.

Gran's neighborhood was full of older one and two-story homes set back on a few acres of wooded lots. Quinn piled the supplies on an old sled Gran had kept since Quinn was little. Milo sat in the front, holding the sides and grinning like a little kid.

He *was* a little kid. He should get to be one. He was damn heavy, though.

She lugged the sled through deep snow toward the next house, grunting from the effort and gritting her teeth. "Next time, you're pulling me, Small Fry. You aren't so small, after all."

The sun was shining. The sky was blue for once. Gran said another snowstorm was coming. Quinn didn't know how she knew. Some ancient art of farmers being able to read the sky was all Gran would say.

Even with the sun, the air was still bitterly cold. Her hands stiffened as she gripped the rope and yanked the sled behind her. In only a few minutes, her feet felt like blocks of ice.

The first two houses were empty. Large red Xs were spray-painted across the front doors. A couple of the windows had been broken. Tire tracks and trampled snow across the wide expanse of the front lawn told the story—these houses had already been looted.

One belonged to a young couple with a baby. Gran said they

were visiting the wife's parents in Orlando. They were probably still there. At least it was warm in Florida, and people weren't freezing their asses off.

The second house belonged to a distinguished accountant in his fifties who Quinn rarely saw outside, other than when he gathered his mail from the mailbox. One of the teenagers down the street mowed his lawn in summer and shoveled the driveway in winter. Gran said he would chat with Gramps, but few others. No one knew where he was, but he clearly wasn't here.

The third house belonged to the Cleary's, a middle-aged couple with a brood of kids who were always screaming, running around, and riding their bikes across Gran's lawn in the summer.

Quinn didn't much care for them, but orders were orders.

She marched up to the front door, dropped the sled rope, grabbed one of the bags, and banged against the wood with her fist.

"Maybe they aren't home, either," Milo said from the sled.

"They're home." The sound of boys yelling and shrieking filtered through the door. She waited for a few impatient seconds and banged again.

It was too damn cold to wait around forever. She was about to turn and go when the door opened a crack.

An object eased through the crack and pointed at her face—a shotgun.

38

QUINN
DAY TWELVE

"What do you want?" Mrs. Cleary glared down the shotgun barrel at Quinn. "Go away."

Quinn's heart jumped into her throat. She threw up her hands. "Woah! Relax, lady. It's just me. Molly's granddaughter from down the road."

"We ain't got no handouts to give. So just get yourself out of here before I do somethin' we both regret."

The shotgun barrel was trembling. Mrs. Cleary's hands were trembling. Her eyes were red and bloodshot.

She was a short, heavy Caucasian woman with stringy blonde hair stuck to her chapped, reddened cheeks. She wore several pairs of sweatpants. A couple of sweatshirts bulged beneath her zipped coat.

Behind her, Quinn glimpsed a bunch of kids bundled in coats and hats piled on the couch, watching her with wide, fascinated gazes. There were at least four of them—all boys, all under the age of ten.

Quinn shook the bag. Cans clinked against each other. "You got it all wrong. We're the ones bringing food. Gran asked me to check on you."

Mrs. Cleary took a step back. Slowly, she lowered the shotgun but kept her hands on it, still wary. "Food?"

"Mac and cheese. Beans. I think there's some canned alphabet soup for the kids. Gran and I don't really like the boxed mac and cheese." Actually, Quinn loved it, but she didn't want to make the lady feel bad.

Milo popped up beside her. "It's the last of what we've got."

The woman didn't blush or apologize. She placed the shotgun against the wall inside the front door and gestured for Quinn to come in. "Never can be too careful. Not anymore. We already had two attempted break-ins. Someone broke into our shed a few nights ago and took the rest of our firewood. It's all gone now."

Quinn stomped her boots and stepped into the cold house, Milo right on her heels. "That sucks hairy balls."

A couple of the boys on the couch snickered.

Mrs. Cleary shot them a look. "Come and have a seat. I have a bit of lemonade left that I was warming with the last of our firewood. I'm sure the boys would love to see Milo."

Milo shyly edged toward the boys. One of them bounced on the couch. Another was pouring over a comic book. Two of the boys, the younger ones, looked wan and lethargic.

Their big eyes in their small faces tracked Quinn's every move. Or rather, the food in her hands.

"I'm hungry!"

"Can we eat now?"

"Please, please, please!"

"Just let me cook it first," Mrs. Cleary said.

Quinn handed the bag to Mrs. Cleary, who immediately headed for the kitchen. She pulled a can opener out of the drawer and opened three cans of alphabet soup. She poured them into a pan, then pulled out another pan and filled it with water from a jug on the counter.

She opened both boxes of macaroni, took out the cheese packets, and stuffed a handful of hard noodles into her mouth. She closed her eyes. "We've got no milk or butter. But it'll do. A bit of extra water will work. It's edible. The boys will eat it."

"Maybe you should ration the food a bit," Quinn suggested. "Make it last longer."

Mrs. Clearly acted like she didn't hear her. She moved back into the living room and set both pans over the makeshift wire grate she'd positioned over the fireplace for cooking. The flames danced and hissed.

The fire let off the only heat in the entire house. The air smelled dank and musty. The boys looked like they hadn't had a bath since the day the power went out—and smelled like it, too.

"Tell me as soon as it boils," Mrs. Cleary instructed the oldest boy, who was busy showing Milo his comic book. She removed the coffee pot and headed back to the kitchen. She shivered. "It's so damn cold in here. I can barely feel my fingers, even with gloves."

"You should move everything into the living room and block off the room with blankets to trap the heat," Quinn said.

Mrs. Cleary's shoulders slumped. "Try telling that to those rambunctious boys. Though the youngest two . . . I think they're coming down with something. Hopefully it's just a cold, right? When the firewood's gone, I guess it doesn't matter anyway."

"What about the shelter?"

Mrs. Cleary shuddered. "I suppose we'll have to. But have you seen it? It's where hope goes to die. I've been doing everything I can to keep us from that place. Even with the food pantry handouts and the new distribution center at the middle school, it's not enough. And now, with no firewood . . ."

"You can burn furniture." Quinn pointed to the heavy

wooden mirror hanging over the couch and the large secretary desk looming in the corner. "Burn everything you have."

The woman took six clean mugs out of the cupboard and poured the hot lemonade into each of them, half-full. She passed them out to the boys and handed one to Quinn, taking none for herself.

"We got that mirror in Gatlinburg on our honeymoon," she said quietly. "My husband Jim is a financial consultant for Chase Bank. They had him in California to consult on this business deal. He was supposed to be home on the twenty-third. But ice on the plane's wings got the flight canceled. He took a Christmas Eve flight instead. He was in the air when it happened."

She waved a hand in the air helplessly, angrily, as if "it" could encompass every horrible thing that had taken place in the last two weeks. "I keep telling the kids he'll be home soon, but the truth is I don't know if he ever will be."

Quinn didn't know what to say. Her chest ached for this family. For all the suffering people in Fall Creek, in Michigan, in the whole damned country.

Millions of people. Her mind couldn't grasp the enormity of it.

"That's why I don't want to go to one of those FEMA emergency shelters. How will he find us?" She shook her head wearily. "We can't leave. We have to be here. Just in case."

Quinn swallowed. "Gran wanted me to ask for your help to set up a neighborhood watch. To keep an eye on things and help each other out."

"Good idea. I'm so tired trying to keep watch myself." The woman pushed her dirty hair out of her face and sighed. "I'm just so tired."

Quinn handed the hot lemonade back to Mrs. Cleary without taking a sip. "You need this more than I do."

The woman didn't argue. She took the mug gratefully, hungrily. Even though steam still wafted from the liquid, she swallowed it down in several rapid gulps. Like she hadn't imbibed enough calories in days. Probably, she hadn't, saving it all for her boys instead.

Ten minutes later, Quinn and Milo were back outside, trudging from house to house. Several people had left home already, either staying at the high school or taking FEMA up on their offer of transportation to the regional emergency shelter.

At least a half dozen folks remained, battling the elements and their hunger to last as long as they could. This was a rural town, with rural, independent people.

They didn't want to give up their homes, their lives, and their freedom at a government-run shelter crammed with a bunch of scared, hungry, sick, and smelly people.

Quinn sure didn't.

One intrepid couple in their fifties—Mr. and Mrs. Lunslow— knew how to hunt and had bagged a deer yesterday. They rejected the food Quinn and Milo offered them, telling them to save it for those who really needed it.

Instead, the Lunslows gave them some deer jerky and agreed to the neighborhood watch meeting. Two other families, a gay couple, and a single lady in her forties also agreed.

Quinn was surprised that she didn't know everyone on the street. And that everyone—even strangers—had been kind and helpful. That's what she got for being so antisocial.

Maybe Gran's "everyone works together" spiel wasn't as lame as she'd first thought.

She could barely feel her fingers or toes by the time they reached the house right before Milo's. She tugged the sled behind her as she waded across the yard of a daffodil-yellow colonial.

The Bernsteins lived here. She remembered them from the

public funeral. The wife collapsing to her knees, that high, keening wail of grief. A sound to split your heart wide open.

"We don't need to check our house!" Milo said through chattering teeth. "We know it's empty."

"Yeah, well, this is the last house, and we're heading back. We're not freezing our butts off, not even for Gran."

She left the sled at the base of the steps and grabbed one of the last plastic bags. She trudged up the porch, snow crunching beneath her boots, and banged on the door. No answer.

No one had spray-painted an X across the door. The windows were unbroken, the curtains drawn. She'd seen them at the funeral three days ago. They should be home.

She knocked again. "Hey! Anybody here? We've got food for you!"

Still nothing.

She glanced back at Milo. He watched her, wide-eyed.

She looked back at the house. Still and silent. No smoke poured from the chimney.

An uneasy feeling wriggled in her gut.

39

QUINN
DAY TWELVE

"Should we just leave it at the door?" Milo asked. "For when they get back?"

Quinn frowned. "Someone will steal it."

A Christmas wreath hung on the navy-blue door. Christmas lights were strung along the porch railing and wound up the white pillars on either side of the porch. A four-foot evergreen tree smothered in snow sat in a pot to the right of the door.

She kicked the snow at her feet, revealing a welcome mat. She bent and checked beneath it. Nothing. She moved aside the pot and felt the porch slats. Her gloved fingers closed over a key.

"What are you doing?" Milo asked.

"The right thing," She had no idea if it was. She could open the door and get blasted by a shotgun, just like with Mrs. Cleary. She didn't think so, though.

Something about this place felt *wrong*.

It took three fumbling tries to get the key in the lock. The door slid open. Snow tumbled onto the hardwood floor of the foyer.

It was dark inside. Dark and quiet.

She turned back to Milo. "You still have that little flashlight your dad gave you?"

He pulled it out of his pocket and handed it to her.

"Stay here."

"I'm not scared. I want to come with you!"

"It's not about being scared. I need a lookout. If anything happens, you go running to Gran, got it?"

He bit his lower lip unhappily, but he nodded.

Quinn stepped inside. She scanned the house with the small Maglite. Deep shadows draped the normal house stuff—overstuffed chairs and couches and bookcases in the living room, end tables and bookcases and cabinets.

A dark Christmas tree sagged in the corner, molting pine needles.

No sounds of life.

A smell, though. She sniffed. So faint she might have imagined it. She couldn't place it, but it was freaking unpleasant.

Her heart rate quickened. She switched the Maglite to her left hand, slipped her right hand into her coat pocket, and gripped the handle of her slingshot. Too bad she didn't have a knife or a gun instead. She needed to start carrying her .22 with her wherever she went, not just at Gran's house.

Maybe it was nothing. Maybe the Bernsteins had moved on to the school shelter, and she just hadn't known about it. Maybe the police hadn't marked the house as unoccupied yet. Or they were in line at the food pantry or distribution center, waiting for hours for a few cans of beans.

So many maybes. None of them explained this feeling of trepidation. The tightness in her chest or the hairs lifting on the back of her neck.

She could turn around and leave right now. She didn't.

The house was cold. Her breath puffed in white clouds in front of her. Her slick, wet boots squelched across the foyer. Wooden stairs loomed straight ahead.

She peered above, saw nothing but darkness. Heard nothing but her beating heart and shallow breathing.

She took each step slowly, listened to the squeak of the treads, straining for any strange sound over the roar of her pulse.

She reached the top of the stairs. Dim light filtered through a window at the opposite end of the long hallway. She moved cautiously toward the doors, which she assumed led to bedrooms.

She pushed open the first door. An office—a big white modern desk from IKEA, white bookcases, canvas paintings of oceans and beaches on the walls.

Her apprehension grew. She felt trapped. Claustrophobia tightened around her like a net. She wanted to run. To escape.

But from what?

There was nothing here. Nothing but silence and shadows and the cold, creaking house.

Her hesitation made her angry. At herself, at everything. She fought her own fear. She wasn't going to become a scared little church mouse, jumping at every sound. Heck no.

She moved on. The next door was a bathroom—cream walls, burgundy striped towels, the shower curtain closed. The door on the left was a guest bedroom—double bed neatly made, end tables uncluttered and dusted.

One more bedroom across the hall. The master bedroom. The door was closed.

She stood in front of the closed bedroom door, hesitating. Her heart hammered against her ribs. Her mouth so dry she could barely swallow.

A seed of fear sprouted in her gut. She pushed it away, hard. It was stupid. The whole thing was stupid.

She should leave this whole eerie place behind. Turn around and head back downstairs to Milo and the sled and the weak sunlight pushing through the clouds. Flee to Gran's comforting, warm, *safe* house.

The church flashed in her mind unbidden. Creeping through the cold dark hallways, Milo's slick hand clenched in hers, her pulse a roar in her head, blind panic a frantic flutter in her chest.

She closed her eyes, opened them. She wasn't there anymore. She was here.

The monsters were dead.

More monsters would come. She wasn't naïve or stupid. They might already be here.

But she wouldn't fear them. Wouldn't allow that fear to control her.

Quinn steeled herself, aimed the Maglite at the floor, and reached out her hand. Turned the knob and swung the door inward.

The smell hit her like a physical force. The stench so strong, she tasted it. Metallic and tangy. Like rust. Or copper.

A denser smell beneath it—something tainted.

The master bedroom was dark. She couldn't make out any details. The heavy drapes were drawn over the windows. She waited, allowing her eyes to adjust to the darkness.

She lifted the flashlight and slowly took in the room.

A dresser on each wall. Closet doors, another door leading to a master bathroom—both open. The carpeted floor neat and clear. Two end tables with useless lamps bracketing a king-sized bed covered with a beige comforter.

Beneath the comforter, two shapes on the bed.

Quinn sucked in her breath, sharp and sudden, nearly gagging from the rancid stink.

A wave of dizziness crashed over her. She braced herself with the door handle. Forced herself to take another step into the room, then another.

She approached the bed. A part of her screamed at her to get out, to leave, to run, to close her eyes and pretend she hadn't seen what her brain was translating.

She needed to do this. For their sakes and hers, she needed to see.

Mrs. Bernstein lay curled like a comma on her side, an arm pillowed beneath her head. Her husband curved around her. Loving, protectively.

The gun in his limp right hand. The blood so dark in the shadows, it appeared oily black, coagulating beneath his head. A bottle of water and two bottles of prescription pills on Mrs. Bernstein's end table—both empty.

Her mouth filled with a coppery taste like rusty pennies. The rancid stench threatened to overwhelm her senses. The coldness of the house had retarded the bodies' decomposition but hadn't stopped it altogether.

Quinn staggered backward, covering her mouth with her hand.

Did they decide to do it together? Or did she go first, and her distraught husband chose to follow her into death?

She understood their grief. The overwhelming loss. Even the burden of survivor's guilt. She understood the fear. The hunger and desperation. The cold, brutal future that awaited them all.

But giving in? Giving up?

Quinn couldn't understand that. It didn't matter how hard things got, how overwhelming the odds. She would never give up. Not on herself. Not on the people she loved with every ferocious beat of her heart.

Never.

A sound of a door opening jerked her from her shock.

"Quinn!" Milo shouted from downstairs, alarm in his voice. "Come quick!"

40

QUINN
DAY TWELVE

"What the hell is going on?" Quinn stormed up to Gran's house, Milo bouncing in the sled at her heels.

Three ancient trucks and four old snowmobiles with attached trailers were parked in front of Gran's driveway. Quinn had been so focused on what she'd found, she hadn't heard them arrive.

A dozen men and a few women dressed in gray camo uniforms beneath their coats and armed with semi-automatic rifles crowded in a loose ring around Gran's front porch. The militia.

Gran stood in the open doorway, dressed in jeans and one of Gramps' old red and black plaid shirts, her chin jutting defiantly. Thor and Odin curled around her ankles. She gripped the Mossberg 500 in her hands, though it was pointed down.

The militia gave way as Quinn burst through the line. She didn't give them a choice in the matter. Milo scrambled after her. She turned to face them at the bottom of the steps, trembling with adrenaline, still shaken from the double suicide.

She remembered all of them. Their faces were seared into her memory. The two who'd dragged her own mother through the streets of Fall Creek. The ones who'd lined up at the courthouse steps and stood guard.

Mattias Sutter wasn't here. The leader. The one who'd pulled the trigger.

A Caucasian man in his late twenties stepped forward. He was slim but still strong and rugged, with sun-weathered features. Even though he was young, his face held a dour, brooding, world-weary look. Like he was tired of all this and just wanted to go home.

He wore gray fatigues with LUTHER emblazoned across the patch over the right side of his chest, a US MILITIA patch over his left. A pistol was holstered at his hip; a tactical knife sheathed on the opposite side. An AK-18 hung from a two-point sling.

If their fancy show of weapons and might were meant to intimidate, it didn't work. They didn't cow her. Quinn squared her shoulders and glared at him.

"My name is James Luther." The man ignored Quinn and looked directly at Gran. "We serve under Mattias Sutter, the commander of the Volunteer Militia Brigade of Southwest Michigan. Mrs. Dương, we're here on behalf of the superintendent and the township of Fall Creek."

"What do you want?" Quinn snapped.

A hint of surprise flickered across the man's face.

If they thought they were gonna be greeted with a welcoming committee, they had another think coming.

A bunch of toy soldiers rolling in like Fall Creek's saviors? No. That didn't sit right with her. They didn't belong here.

The sooner they left, the better.

"We're requesting that homeowners donate a small percentage of their food, water, and sanitation supplies to the community distribution center we've set up at the middle school for those families who don't have enough."

"Gran's already donated plenty," Quinn said.

"How much?" Gran asked.

"Ten percent."

"This is a request?"

"If everyone donates to the community, then we—"

"Is it a request? Is it voluntary?"

Luther grimaced. The men behind him shifted uncomfortably. "Ah, well—"

"The answer is no," Gran said. "I choose to donate to my community on my own terms."

"I'm sorry, but we're going to have to insist."

Gran frowned slightly. "So not a request, then."

"I'm sorry, ma'am, but no."

"At least you're a polite jerk," Quinn muttered. "Like that freaking matters."

Luther's eyes narrowed.

A Hispanic man in his early forties with a buzz cut and trimmed beard stepped in front of Luther. He was an oak tree, thick and solid, with a face like a slab of granite. "I'm Lieutenant Sebastian Desoto, second-in-command. I assure you, this is for the good of everyone."

Quinn rolled her eyes. "On whose authority? I don't see any badges."

"The superintendent and the Fall Creek law enforcement." Desoto patted his pants pocket and pulled out a folded piece of paper. "We have official authorization."

Quinn shook her head. She couldn't see Chief Briggs going along with this. He was an ornery old man who hated people butting into his business. Noah, either. "You can wipe your ass with that paper. That's all it's good for."

A few neighbors came out onto their porches in their coats or wrapped in blankets. Curtains moved behind windows. No one said anything. No one did anything, not even the people she'd just given food to. They just watched, shivering and stony-faced.

"I'm sorry, but we're going to need to see your pantry and cupboards," Luther said.

"Hell, no!" Quinn said. "You can't do this. It's an invasion of privacy. It's against the law!"

"Think of it as a tax." A shadow passed across Desoto's hard, flat face. His jaw bulged. He was losing patience. "Everyone pays taxes. *That's* the law. We're adjusting to face a new crisis no one saw coming. That's all this is. Now stop being overdramatic and let us do our damn jobs."

Quinn glared at him, fury boiling through her veins at his curt dismissal. At all of this, everything. "Everything in this house belongs to my grandmother," Quinn said. "She bought it and saved and made it all. It's hers. You can't take it."

She slid her hand inside her pocket and gripped her slingshot. Not that she could do anything worthwhile with it, not with a dozen guns against her.

"Quinn," Gran said tersely. "Pick your battles."

Desoto's lip curled. "Listen to your elders, girl. Don't make us do something you'll regret. We are authorized to use force if we must."

A few of the men adjusted their grips on their weapons. Quinn's gut lurched in dismay. She had no choice. Gran had no choice. These jerkwads had the guns.

Whoever had the biggest guns had the power. Just like before. Just like in the church.

Just because these soldier boys claimed they were doing this for everyone's benefit didn't make it true. It didn't make them the good guys. They could just steal most of their "tax" for them-selves. There was no one to hold them accountable.

"I'm gonna tell my dad on you!" Milo said. "He's a police officer!"

Desoto smiled. He had wide white teeth. A shark's smile. "Go right ahead."

Milo was right. Noah would help, but Noah wasn't here. Quinn stared daggers at them, but she took a step to the side, pulling Milo out of the way.

For Gran's sake. And for Milo's.

"Thank you," Luther said politely.

Quinn spat in the snow. "You can stick your thanks right up your ass, you sorry sack of rat turds."

41

QUINN
DAY TWELVE

The militia strode past Quinn and Gran and into the house. Two remained outside to guard the trucks and snowmobiles. The truck beds were half-loaded with goods they'd already confiscated from other law-abiding citizens.

A female soldier took Gran's shotgun. "Just until we're gone," she said almost apologetically.

Being nice about it didn't make what they were doing less wrong.

"Come on, Milo." Quinn grabbed Milo's hand, and they ascended the steps into Gran's house.

The living room and kitchen were crowded with too many people.

Loki and Thor hissed and scrambled for the safety of the bedrooms. Valkyrie circled the strangers, her tail standing straight up. The fearless hunter of the bunch, she looked like she wished she were big enough to pounce on these bozos.

Quinn felt the same way. She wanted to scream. To push and shove the toy soldiers right out the door.

This was her sanctuary. Hers and Gran's. They didn't belong here.

She hated all of them.

Desoto slammed open Gran's pantry. He whistled as he perused the full shelves. "Look at this. Women and children are starving, and here you are, hoarding everything you have."

"We're not hoarding!" Quinn said.

"Quinn." Gran tugged on her arm. "Shut up."

Quinn pressed her lips together. She watched helplessly as several men brought in crates to steal Gran's supplies. They filled the crates and took them out to the truck.

The soldiers hesitated. Desoto ordered them to fill more. A man and a woman returned with four more crates. They filled those, too.

Milo pointed at the stack of crates. "That's way more than ten percent!"

Quinn folded her arms across her chest. "He's right."

Desoto threw her a disdainful glance. He looked at them like they were scum on the bottom of his shoes. "There are exceptions for *hoarders*."

"Exceptions? What the hell does that mean?"

"It means you're stealing from the community. Keeping things to yourself in a time of great need."

"That's a load of B.S. and you know it!"

Desoto shrugged. "It doesn't really matter what you think."

"You're a thief!"

Desoto whirled on her. He was faster than she had expected. In one swift stride he was looming over her. So close, she could count every pore in his skin. "Your feisty teenager shtick only goes so far. I'm running out of patience."

Quinn didn't cower. She refused to cower.

"Don't you hurt her," Gran snapped.

"Desoto, we've got enough now, yeah?" the female soldier asked. She stood in the doorway between the kitchen and living room, a concerned look on her face.

She was a mousy woman in her twenties, with dull brown hair and brown eyes. She didn't look like much of a soldier. "We should be going."

"Not yet." Desoto didn't take his eyes off Quinn. He smiled that broad white shark smile again. "Take more."

"Gran will starve if you take all her food!"

"Calm down," Desoto growled. "We aren't taking anywhere near everything. Yet."

From the top of the fridge, Hel hissed angrily. The white fur of his back stood on end. His tail twitched back and forth, and his eyes held a wicked glint.

Desoto glanced up at the cat and took a hasty step backward. "That thing dangerous?"

Quinn glared at him. "I sure hope so."

"You know, I'm going to remember you." Desoto gave her another predatory grin before stalking outside to oversee his men. Hel hissed after him.

Quinn stood there, fuming. She hated Desoto. Loathed him.

One of the soldiers—the one called Luther—put his hand on Quinn's arm. "Miss? Are you okay?"

She turned and bared her teeth. "Get your hands off me!"

Luther took a step back and raised both palms in a placating gesture. "Sorry, sorry."

"Yeah, well that's not good enough. Why don't you do something about that 'sorry?'"

His gaze darted guiltily to the floor. He didn't say anything.

"This isn't okay, and you know it. Is this what you thought you'd be doing? Stealing from little old ladies?"

"Believe it or not, we're doing this to help," he said quietly.

Quinn snorted. "You go ahead and tell yourself that while you're drifting off to sleep in your soft warm bed in your new house with heat and electricity. How is that helping?"

"Things must be difficult for your grandmother. And for you. We can give her a ride to the high school shelter. Or if she wants, we can even get her to one of the busses escorting people to the regional FEMA shelters. We can take you as well. Don't worry. We're here to make sure she's well cared for."

"You don't get to make that choice for her or anyone else." Quinn jabbed her finger toward the emptying pantry. "You're as bad as a gang of thugs. That worthless piece of paper doesn't mean a thing! It doesn't change who you are!"

"Quintessa!" Gran angled her chin at the men with guns, her eyes flashing a warning.

Several of the toy soldiers standing in the living room had stiffened and adjusted their rifles, their attention turning toward Quinn, their expressions hardening.

Quinn bit her lip until she tasted blood. Gran was right. She knew it. She was on the verge of crossing a line she may not be able to step back from.

"I'm sorry you feel that way. I truly am." Luther averted his gaze and walked away.

Milo grabbed her hand and squeezed it. She let him. She stood beside Gran and Milo, seething, while the jerkwads took load after load from Gran's stocked pantry and cabinets.

All her hard work, all her careful planning. Gone in an instant.

Gran held Thor in her arms and stroked his fluffy back. The lazy cat seemed to sense that something was wrong. He stared at the fake soldiers with unblinking yellow eyes.

Gran said nothing as they tromped out, leaving a path of dirt and snow from their filthy boots all over the floor.

"Did you raid the superintendent's pantry, too?" Quinn yelled at their backs.

Luther hesitated on the porch steps. He flinched.

He had a bit of a conscience, then. So what? It hadn't stopped him, or any of them, from taking whatever they wanted. It wouldn't stop them the next time, either.

"Yeah," Quinn muttered. "I didn't think so."

After the rumble of the militia's truck engines had faded, Quinn stomped back into the kitchen and stared at the trashed pantry shelves, aghast. "They took half! Half! Why didn't we stop them!"

"There is a time to fight, and a time to wait," Gran said. "A time to speak out, and a time to hold your tongue. You need to learn which is which."

Quinn blinked back stinging tears. She wanted to scream. She wanted to strangle something—or someone. She was so furious Gran's words barely filtered through her mind. "That Desoto jerk took more just to spite us!"

"Yes," Gran said, an edge in her voice. "Yes, he did."

Quinn felt herself deflate. Guilt pricked her. "Because of me and my big mouth."

"Probably." Gran sighed. "But there's no use crying over spilt milk. What's done is done."

"I'll have my dad arrest him!" Milo piped up. "I bet he'll throw them all in prison for the rest of their lives!"

"I wish." Quinn glanced down at him. "Don't worry about it, Small Fry. Gran and I are brilliant, you know. We'll figure something out. You hungry?"

Milo shook his head. "My stomach kinda hurts."

He needed a distraction. So did she. "You feel like reading? I'll let you pick any science fiction book you want. Even Stephen King."

Milo's eyes got huge. "Even *The Stand?*"

"Quinn—" Gran said.

Quinn shrugged. "What? I'll skip all the scary and violent bits."

Milo made a face. "Those are the best parts!"

42
QUINN
DAY TWELVE

I t was late afternoon by the time Quinn extricated herself from Milo and at least a dozen chapters of *The Stand*. He'd fallen asleep midchapter, which wasn't like him. He'd prop his eyelids open with toothpicks if it bought him another few pages.

He was emotionally drained. They all were.

"You guys hungry?" Gran sat in the La-Z-Boy in the corner, her feet up on the ottoman, taking a rare break. Thor and Odin were both nestled in her lap. "We can whip up some peanut butter and jelly sandwiches. I know Milo would like that."

"What are we going to do?" Quinn worried at her eyebrow piercing. "We're really in trouble now, aren't we? I—I'm sorry, Gran. I messed up."

Gran shook her head. "What's done is done."

"I don't want to live in a stupid shelter. Just shoot me now."

"Gramps always said something like this might happen. So we were careful."

"Careful?"

"I have something I need to show you." Gran shooed Thor and Odin off her lap, picked up her cane, and shuffled to the basement door in the kitchen. She picked a flashlight off the counter and handed it to her. "Go down there. Tell me what you see."

"I was already down there two days ago searching for all those old pool noodles for your poop buckets."

"Don't knock my poop buckets." Gran grinned. Wrinkles spidered across her face. "Look again."

Quinn rolled her eyes but obeyed. She trudged down the stairs, shining the beam on the narrow wooden steps. Cobwebs clung to the wood and concrete. The basement smelled damp, the air dusty and stale.

The basement was nearly as big as the house, with a low ceiling and cold concrete floor. Water stains decorated the bare concrete walls. The furnace stood in one corner, on the other stacks of cardboard boxes and totes of stuff Gran and Gramps never got rid of—clothes, picture frames, and camping, hunting, and fishing stuff.

She spun in a slow circle and sighed. "I don't see a damn thing, Gran!"

"Behind the crochet supplies!" Gran called down, a chuckle in her voice. She was enjoying this way too much. "And watch your language!"

Behind the chest-high stack of totes, there was just a dark shadow. Quinn walked over to it. She stretched out her hand. A black felt cloth was strung across the wall. In the dim lighting, it looked like nothing, just a shadow.

"Squat. It's by your feet," Gran said.

She squatted, felt around the base of the wall behind the felt curtain. Her fingers touched something cool and metallic. A latch. She opened it.

It was a false wall. Behind the wall stretched another ten feet of low-ceilinged root cellar. Quinn gaped.

She played her flashlight beam across rows and rows of

shelves. Every shelf was stuffed to the gills with survival supplies. To her right was food storage; to the left, supplies like batteries, flashlights, candles, lamps, headlamps, bottled water, and bleach.

"Gran! What the heck is all this?"

"Hmmph." Gran's boots and cane clomped down the stairs. "What's it look like, girl?"

For maybe the first time in her life, Quinn was speechless.

"We've been setting aside a few things here and there."

"For how long? Several decades?"

"Pretty much." Gran unhooked a battery-operated lantern from the wall and switched it on. She pointed to one of the shelves. "Whole wheat, salt, honey, and powdered non-fat milk. The fantastic four. Nutritious, store well, and last forever. Well, close enough. The powdered milk, I have to rotate every couple of years, but the other three last much longer."

The food supplies Gran had gathered were stored in opaque, moisture-and-air-proof white restaurant-quality food storage buckets. She'd stored the powdered milk in white-painted glass jars with moisture and oxygen absorbers.

Gran also had cooking oils, sugar, legumes, black and kidney beans, vinegar, and spices. First aid supplies. Water purification tablets. Bandages and gauze, antiseptic, and pain relievers, cold medicine, bottles of antibiotics, and antibiotic creams. All meticulously labeled in Gramps' precise handwriting.

A clipboard and pen hung on the wall next to the closest shelf. Quinn placed the flashlight between her teeth and rifled through the meticulous lists of supplies, the amount of each item, the last time they were rotated.

She glanced back at Gran in surprise. "Why didn't I know about this?"

Gran leaned heavily on her cane. "Because Octavia couldn't

know about this. She would've done something. Told someone. Stole it and tried to sell it for drug money. We couldn't risk it."

"You could've told me," Quinn said, feeling hurt.

"You didn't need to know."

She jutted her lower lip in a pout. She knew she was being childish, but she couldn't help it. Gran and Gramps had kept a giant secret from her. "And now?"

Gran shrugged. "Now you need to know."

"I wouldn't have told Octavia. You could have trusted me."

Gran's face softened. "It wasn't about not trusting you, Quinn. When you were little, you might have accidentally let it slip. And once you got older . . . I think we were just so used to keeping it a secret, we just kept on in the same way. And it wasn't like we were carting in truckfuls beneath your nose. We didn't have the money for that. It was always a few things here and there, a couple extra cans each grocery trip. After thirty years, it adds up."

Quinn shook her head in amazement. "You can say that again."

This was a good thing. A very good thing. It was an immense relief that she didn't have to worry about starving to death, didn't have to worry about Gran, either. All this food. It would feed them for years if need be.

In her mind, she apologized to Gramps for all the times she'd rolled her eyes for his lectures on preparedness. All Gran's seemingly pointless old-fashioned skills were now saving their lives.

"I can't believe I almost forgot about this one." Gran pointed to a galvanized steel trash can in the corner. The lid was sealed with conductive tape. "Gramps made it. It's a homemade Faraday cage. The lid is super tight. He lined it with cardboard and extra aluminum foil on the inside for extra protection."

The Faraday cage would have protected the electronics inside from the EMP. It took a few minutes for Quinn to get it open. She set the lid aside and pulled out a hand-crank radio, a pair of walkie talkies, a couple of LED flashlights, and a Kindle e-reader.

"That e-reader is full of reference and survival books. Medicinal herbs, edible plants, wilderness first aid, how to survive nuclear fallout, how to build a spring house and a latrine. And the Bible, of course. The usual beach read fare."

Quinn snorted to keep from crying. She imagined Gramps carefully and lovingly packaging each item, hoping it would never be needed but preparing all the same.

"Just in case I wasn't around to teach you." Gran shrugged. "No one lives forever, you know. Not even me."

"I'm pretty sure you're too ornery to die." Quinn set everything on a nearby shelf and pulled out the last few items—an old iPod and a solar charger.

"It took him a long time to save up for that solar charger." Gran cleared her throat, her voice suddenly rough. "We got a cord that will work with the e-reader, too. The iPod . . . it's loaded with all his favorite songs. He wanted . . . he wanted you to still have music while you painted."

Quinn swallowed and wiped hastily at her eyes. "Gran, I—"

"Oh, hush, child." Gran waved her hand in the air. "Don't get all soft on me now."

"Well, then . . . thank you."

"We'd have put a lot more in there if we'd had the money."

She pocketed the iPod and the charger. She couldn't wait to share it with Milo. How big his eyes would get, how his whole face would light up. She couldn't wait to crank it up and hear the songs Gramps had picked just for her. "This is—it's perfect."

"Quinn?" Milo's voice echoed down from the kitchen. "Where are you?"

"We're in the basement." She straightened quickly. It was best if Milo didn't see what was down here. "On my way!"

"I'll pick out a few things to bring up," Gran said.

"Don't try to bring up any boxes yourself," Quinn said. "I'll come down later and carry up whatever you set aside."

She hurried through the hidden room into the basement and up to the kitchen. She nearly tripped over Loki on the stairs. He meowed and darted ahead of her. He dashed through the kitchen, into the living room, and hopped onto the couch at Milo's feet.

Milo lay curled on his side, his thin arms cradling his stomach. His black curls stuck damply to his cheeks and forehead. His skin was pale and waxy. Too pale.

"Look what I found! Hidden treasure!" She was about to pull out the iPod but hesitated. Instead, she bent over him and pressed the back of her hand to his forehead the way Gran had done with her a hundred times.

Her chest tightened. He was burning up.

"Milo? You okay?"

"I don't feel so good." Milo turned his head and vomited all over the floor.

43

PIKE
DAY TWELVE

There it was. A tan two-story house looming out of the darkness. A big deck. Two pairs of French double doors. The glow of candles in the windows.

Pike couldn't see the smoke spiraling from the chimney, but he smelled it.

His face was half frozen, but he still managed to smile, chapped lips splitting—but he didn't care. A house with people inside. A family, maybe. If he was lucky.

He stumbled up the deck steps, shuffling through the knee-high snow, stumbling over his own numb feet. He knocked on the glass, so softly at first no one heard it inside. He gritted his teeth and banged louder with his fist.

A man came to the French doors, dressed in heavy winter gear, a hunter's camouflaged cap pulled low over his forehead, a Remington hunting rifle gripped in both hands.

He pointed the rifle at Pike's chest through the glass. He did not open the door.

They stared at each other for a moment, the man's mouth moving—a threat, no doubt, *Get the hell out of here or I'll shoot,*

245

don't think I won't—but Pike couldn't hear a word outside in the blizzard.

A little boy of five or six wandered into the kitchen behind his father, rubbing his eyes sleepily, his hair mussed. He wore plaid Christmas pajamas beneath a red winter coat, scarf, and boots.

Pike lifted both hands in a gesture of surrender, a symbol of peace. He opened his stiff fingers and held the object he'd barely managed to pull out of his pocket a moment earlier. His Michigan Corrections Officer badge.

The man's expression transformed from suspicion to relief, and then concern. Pike's smile widened, his mask slipping into place.

The badge was his secret weapon. He could've broken in. He didn't need a gun to end these people. A couple of kitchen knives. His own bare hands—even frozen and numb. He had no doubt he could do it, even against an armed opponent.

Men used to hunting defenseless prey animals had no idea how to kill a man. It was psychological more than anything—that instinct to avoid killing their own kind. They hesitated, all of them. Well, most of them.

That moment of indecision—that's when Pike would strike. Or even before, when the man was still running through his litany of threats, still trying to remain human, only turning to violence as a last resort.

That was usually their fatal mistake. Violence was most effective as a first resort, not last. Never last.

But not in this case.

Pike was in a weakened state. He wasn't so arrogant that he didn't know his body's limitations. He needed aid. These people could provide that aid.

The man unlocked the French door. Pike had to kick away a

layer of snow before they could open the door enough for him to slip inside.

The man's wife materialized and helped him to a kitchen chair, murmuring over him, calling for a daughter to bring blankets, hurry now, ordering her husband to start some soup on the stove and for heaven's sake, get this man's frozen clothes off.

Pike's smile widened.

He would let these people do their good deed. Let them care for this poor police officer who'd fallen into the river in the line of duty, chasing a pair of killers out of this town, risking his life to keep them all safe.

Maybe he would kill them. Stack them like firewood before their Christmas tree with its tinsel and ornaments—still standing beside the roaring fireplace.

Or maybe he wouldn't. He could be magnanimous. As generous as a god on Mount Olympus looking down upon the scurrying ants. Crush this one. Let that one go.

Maybe he would save his bloodlust for the girl and her soldier.

He smiled and thanked the little boy, who knelt at Pike's feet and unlaced his waterlogged boots. The wife—middle-aged and pretty in a bland, harmless way—helped him remove his coat and wrapped a blanket across his shoulders.

Once he was thawed, dry, and warm, dressed in fresh clothes and full of delicious hot vegetable soup, he pulled out his cigarettes and Zippo lighter. They were both waterlogged. But he had a second pack—unopened, still in its cellophane seal. He ripped it open, put a cigarette to his lips, and flicked the lighter. *Click, click, click.*

The family gathered around him, watching him curiously, a little warily. He did not ask if he could smoke. He didn't care about their wishes. He cared nothing about them.

He lit the cigarette and dragged in deeply, blew out a

mouthful of clove-scented smoke. Slowly, his nerves settled. His mind sharpened, his thoughts crystalizing and clarifying. *Click, click, click.*

Yes, he would save himself for them. He'd let himself recover, rebuild his strength. If he was stuck in this blizzard, so were they. They were here, too, trapped in the same town.

They must think him dead. Let them think it.

When he finally came for them, when he exacted his particularly savage and satisfying brand of vengeance, how surprised they would be. How shocked.

He imagined their faces, visualized each moment as the horror finally registered—the widening eyes, their mouths gaping, the leap of the pulse in their vulnerable throats.

The girl first. Hannah and the child she carried. His child.

Maybe he would kill the squalling creature, like the last one. Or maybe he would be magnanimous and allow it to live. Maybe he would take it home and offer it to his mother as a gift, as the grandchild she'd always wanted. If it was a boy, he might even mold it in his own image.

He had no desire to raise the thing, but there was a certain delicious irony in the idea of Hannah's child in Fall Creek, where no one would ever know who it really was or how it came to be— or what became of its mother.

So many tantalizing options.

He would enjoy every damned second of it.

44

NOAH
DAY TWELVE

"We did it," Noah said. "We ended this. We caught the men who did this to your family."

Bishop stared blearily into his mug of steaming hot apple cider. His hands were wrapped around the mug for warmth. "I know. I was there."

Noah shifted on his bar stool. Bishop didn't seem happy, didn't seem satisfied. "We gave you justice."

"What is justice, Noah? Stringing those guys behind the snowmobile and torturing them? Is that what justice looks like?"

Noah glanced around the bar. They were at the Fireside Tavern across the street from Crossway church, where Bishop was still running the food pantry several hours a day.

It was only nine a.m., and both Bishop and Noah were taking a much-needed break.

Donovan Miller, the tavern's owner, didn't have a generator but was running a few portable camping heaters until he ran out of propane. The cold sunlight streaming through the windows provided enough light during the day.

There wasn't much liquor left, but Bishop didn't drink

anyway. Noah nursed a glass of rum. He would limit it to a single drink since he was technically on the job. Not that he would collect a paycheck anytime soon.

Normally, he never drank during work hours. But this wasn't normal. His head was pounding, and his stomach felt sick. He wanted to feel triumphant. Victorious.

One look at Bishop's face had stolen his thunder.

He lowered his voice. "They tortured your family."

"I know. I know that more than anyone. But there is a way to seek justice that brings peace to a community. That was not it."

Noah sipped his drink and glanced at the room behind him. A few couples huddled at the tables along the bar's far wall.

Dave Farris waved. He was sitting with Mike Duncan, Mike's nephew, Jamal, and Darryl Wiggins, the manager of the bank—which was still closed. All three were council members. They were leaning forward, conversing in hushed tones.

Everyone seemed subdued after the execution two days ago. If they weren't at peace, at least they weren't rioting anymore.

Noah turned back around. "What should we have done then? Let them live? Lock them up and waste manpower we need elsewhere on guarding them indefinitely? Feed them precious resources while our own children go hungry?"

Bishop winced.

Noah regretted his words immediately. "I'm sorry."

Bishop's eyes were red-rimmed and glassy from days of grieving. His broad, brown face was the same face Noah had known for years, and it also wasn't.

There was a hollowness—an absence, like grief had carved out a permanent place in everything that made Bishop *Bishop,* irrevocably altering him forever.

Noah knew that kind of grief. Knew it intimately. Absently, he touched his wedding ring, twisted it on his finger. Even his own loss and sorrow was no match for the wife and children ripped from Bishop's arms in an act of barbaric, savage violence.

Bishop unwound his hand from the steaming mug and touched Noah's forearm. "I know, friend. I know you risked your own life to catch those men. I thank you for it. Please don't take my reticence as ingratitude. I—I'm still processing. Still working through things in my own head and heart. Wrestling with God like Jacob did, if you will."

"Take your time. Take all the time you need."

Bishop was silent for a few minutes. "I'm human, too, Noah. I can't pretend I don't have anger in my heart. That I didn't want those men dead, that I didn't imagine ripping their limbs from their bodies with my own bare hands, over and over." His deep baritone voice went ragged with pain. "That I don't see my little girls' faces, every single second of every single day. The fear and terror I couldn't comfort. The pain I couldn't stop. That I don't see Daphne's beautiful eyes judging me for eternity for failing to save them."

He picked up the mug, glared at it in futile despair, and slammed it back down on the counter so hard the cider splashed over the sides.

A couple of people glanced at them, realized who it was, and looked quickly away. Their expressions full of pity mixed with guilt and relief.

Noah's chest tightened. He'd experienced years of the same looks. He'd hated them then, too.

"I am not against self-defense or violence when necessary to protect those who need protecting," Bishop said quietly. "I have served my country. But this . . . the way it was done . . . it was vengeance, not justice. The world is cold and growing colder. It is full of fear and anger and hate. If we aren't careful, we will become the same as the enemy we claim we are fighting against."

Noah flinched. A vision of Billy's broken, bloodied face flashed through his mind. Julian aiming the pistol, Noah standing there, doing nothing. "We won't."

"How do you know? How will we hold onto our humanity? Our souls?"

Noah didn't know about souls. That was the terrain of the spiritual, the role of the church.

The role of the lawman was to keep law and order and protect people. When the bad guys were willing to do anything to win, the good guys had to play just as dirty to beat them.

He told himself that over and over. Maybe eventually he'd believe it.

"To survive, maybe we need to set our humanity aside for a while."

Bishop stiffened. "That is not how I will choose to live."

Noah shook his head, suddenly angry, though he wasn't sure why. "Then maybe you're a fool."

"Maybe," Bishop agreed readily. He wasn't a man easily insulted or provoked. "I don't pretend to have all the answers."

Noah deflated. "No one does."

After a few moments, Bishop sighed. "I've come to terms with myself, my faith, my God. I won't break. For a while, I thought I might. But I know now that I won't. I won't let them turn me into a man of bitterness and hatred. I am who I am. I choose love over hatred. Joy over bitterness."

Noah waved his hand. "How can you still talk about joy and love after all of this?"

"Because of hope," Bishop said. "And faith. I believe I will see my wife and daughters again. But it's not my time yet. While I am still here, I will do good. That is my choice. No one can take that from me."

He was still a man ravaged by grief, but there was something else in his eyes. A sense of resolution, maybe even of peace.

Noah wanted that sense of peace radiating from Bishop. He longed for it, yearned for it, but he'd never experienced it himself. Not even a fraction of it.

Bishop had lost everything and still believed.

"You're a good man, Bishop. I wish I was half as good as you are."

Bishop took a long swallow of his cider. He wiped his mouth with the sleeve of his leather jacket. "You are who you decide to be, Noah. That's all life is. A series of choices. And it looks like you have some big ones set before you."

Noah lowered his voice. "You mean with the militia."

"I mean with a lot of things."

Noah felt himself torn between loyalties. To Rosamond and Julian and the town. To Bishop, Quinn, and Molly, who didn't understand the compromises they'd been forced to make to protect Fall Creek.

"I have to think of the whole town, Bishop. I have a lot of responsibility."

Bishop put on his gloves and shrugged a big orange parka over his leather jacket and matching orange Hawaiian shirt. "You don't have to explain it to me. Just remember who your responsibility is to."

Noah bristled. "I know that."

Something had happened he didn't quite understand. Like a line had been drawn in the sand. And he still wasn't sure what side of that line he was on.

Bishop pushed back his stool, pulled an unopened box of Frozen Band-Aids from his coat pocket and set it on the counter. He motioned for Donovan, who accepted the exchange with a nod. Noah had paid for his drink with two rolls of toilet paper.

Bishop smiled ruefully. The smile didn't reach his eyes. "Who would have guessed how fast green pieces of paper become worthless. How quickly Band-Aids and bullets become the currency."

"And medicine," Noah said. That was one thing the militia was good for. Noah had a two to three-year supply of lifesaving hydrocortisone for Milo, thanks to Sutter.

"No doubt." Bishop ran a hand over his afro. A shadow crossed his face. "I'm praying for you, Noah."

Guilt pricked him. Before Noah could say anything, his radio crackled. "Sheridan, you there? Where are you?"

"Come in, Julian. I'm at the bar with Bishop."

"We have a problem at the shelter. A bunch of people are sick. Like, really sick. Shen Lee is already here, but there's not much he can do. Can you grab Chief Briggs and get over here as quickly as you can?"

Noah's mouth went dry. He stood up quickly, went to fish some cash out of his wallet, and realized he had nothing left. It was an old habit. "How many people, Julian?"

"Over a hundred. And more experiencing symptoms by the minute." The strain was clear in Julian's voice even through the radio. "We have several critical cases, including a five-year-old girl."

Noah zipped his coat and adjusted his scarf. "I'm on my way."

Bishop said, "I'm coming with you."

45

NOAH

DAY TWELVE

Noah surveyed the high school gym with growing horror. "What's wrong with them?"

Things were far worse than it was when he'd last visited the shelter two days ago. The entire building reeked of vomit, blood, and human excrement. No amount of bleach could cover that stink.

There was very little movement. People lay curled on their sides in the fetal position. Groans and crying filled the large gymnasium and echoed off the tall ceiling.

Their faces were ashen or sallow, hair damp from feverish sweating, bodies shivering and trembling, eyes sunken and glassy. They clutched their stomachs from the agony washing over them in waves.

Noah, Julian, and Bishop stood just inside the double doors. Rosamond had just arrived. Annette King, the high school principal who'd volunteered to run the shelter, and Shen Lee, their pediatric nurse, greeted them. Annette and Lee wore N95 masks, latex gloves, and disposable scrubs over their clothes.

"What are we dealing with here?" Rosamond asked briskly.

"Untreated drinking water." Lee snapped off a glove, ran a hand through his mussed black hair, and sighed tiredly. "We have dozens of cases of cryptosporidiosis and giardiasis."

A slightly overweight Chinese American man in his mid-thirties, Lee was a friendly, gregarious guy who liked to look on the bright side. The last two weeks had taken a significant toll on his glass-half-full philosophy.

Noah stared at him, aghast. "But we passed out fliers and went door-to-door! We told everyone exactly what to do to purify their water."

Lee shrugged. "Not enough people took it seriously. No one is used to getting sick from water. Until now. Victims are suffering from cramps, nausea, vomiting, muscle aches, fever, and fatigue, including severe dehydration. Some people had wells, but no hand pumps or way to get to the water.

"When people ran out of bottled water and the water they could find in their own homes from filled tubs and hot water heaters, they used snow, but a lot of people didn't have the patience or enough firewood to keep melting it, so some of them turned to the river."

"They may have attempted to disinfect the water but failed to use the correct amount of iodine or bleach or didn't properly boil the water," Annette said. "Unpotable water can contain viruses, parasites, and bacteria. It only takes one drop."

He already longed for the days when he didn't have to worry about deadly waterborne illnesses. Back when the water treatment plants were online. Back when water and trash were simply bills to be paid.

The toilet flushed, the faucets turned on, someone whisked away the trash and recycling twice a week, and that was that.

Two weeks ago. It felt like an eternity. A lifetime.

Now, they had to worry about everything. So many things that could hurt you. Not just thugs and gangs with guns and deadly blizzards, but microscopic bacteria and parasites you couldn't even see but would kill you and everyone you loved anyway.

Noah covered his mouth and nose with his scarf. Rosamond, Julian, and Bishop did the same. Annette already had her mask. It didn't do much good.

A sour sensation lurched through his gut as the stench clawed down his throat. He feared he might vomit all over his boots right then and there.

"What about the truck of supplies the militia brought in yesterday?" Noah asked. "Where are all the bottles of water?"

"They're in pallets in the cafeteria kitchen," Annette said. "We've been passing everything out. But the fresh water supply came too late. Everyone was already sick."

"Most of the medical supplies were too basic—Band-Aids, ibuprofen, acetaminophen, cough medicine," Lee said. "Not what we really need."

They followed Lee as he picked his way across the gym floor, bypassing the cots, sleeping bags, and piles of blankets. Buckets and containers lay beside each person.

Volunteers in disposable gowns, booties and gloves, and paper masks moved among the sick. They changed buckets, exchanged soiled linens, and mopped the floor.

They tended to the sick with damp washcloths and compressed snow inside wrapped cloth as makeshift icepacks to bring the high fevers down, along with electrolyte drinks and potable water. They mopped up accidents and changed children out of their filthy clothes, piling dirty blankets in one corner.

It looked like a scene from a third-world country, not something that could happen in America. Not something that was happening right now to their town, to people they all knew.

"God have mercy," Bishop said quietly.

"We have at least ten sick people crammed into each bathroom," Annette said. "Not that it's enough. People can't make it to the latrines we've dug outside. Some can't make it to the buckets, either."

She gestured toward a hallway with a propped open door. Noah glimpsed a row of five-gallon buckets lined with black trash bags and two short two-by-fours on either side as the "seat."

They were all being used. A dozen people waited in line, most slumped against the wall or simply lying down on the cold tile floor.

"Dysentery from improper sanitation killed more than seventy thousand soldiers in the Civil War," Annette said tightly. "The same disease killed more soldiers than bullets during the Spanish American War. Well over two billion people live without access to proper toilets or drains."

Julian and Noah glanced at her.

She grimaced. "I was a high school history teacher before I was a principal."

"Someone told me once that the average person pees two pints a day and craps a pound a day," Julian said. "That's a lot of human waste no longer flushing away to a place no one has to think about. I guess now we're thinking about it."

"Pathogens in human feces can easily contaminate above and below ground water sources," Lee said. "People crap too close to the water line, or like idiots, they actually go in the water."

"I assumed everyone knew better," Noah said wearily. "Yet another item to add to the list."

"Looks like you're using a lot of toilet paper," Julian said.

"We are." Annette rolled her eyes. "Sutter's men have been bringing us what we need so far. Hopefully, we don't reach the point where we're scrounging for paper, newspapers, scraps of cloth."

"We can always return to corncobs like the pioneers," Bishop said.

"Let's hope not." Noah tore his gaze from all the sick people. "Any chance they'll get better on their own? That this will ride itself out in a few days?"

"For some, yes," Lee said. "But the children and elderly are particularly vulnerable. Many also have the flu and suffered hypothermia before they got here. They're under extreme physical and psychological stressors. The brutal cold has already worn down their body's natural defenses."

Rosamond folded her hands in front of her. Her normally perfect, manicured nails were chipped. "This is a crisis."

"It is." Gray creases lined Annette's eyes, her skin sallow. She looked worried, exhausted, and near sickness herself. She and Lee both had been working themselves to the bone. For no pay, for no reward other than to help others.

Just like every other volunteer here, at the food pantry, and everyone pitching in to help with communication, sanitation and trash, and security.

These were good people. The town was doing the best that it could. It felt like they were getting hit with one disaster after another. They couldn't catch a breath before the next catastrophe hit them.

Noah didn't need to see any more. He squared his shoulders. "What do we need to do?"

Lee gazed down at his clipboard. "We need fluids. IVs. Antibiotics."

Noah wheeled to Rosamond. "Any working nearby hospitals? Urgent care centers?"

"All the smaller medical clinics and hospitals have been shut down, their personnel and supplies moved to larger facilities to consolidate resources and power," Rosamond said. "Officially, the governor is directing all who need medical attention to the Red Cross emergency tent hospitals set up at the FEMA regional centers."

"And unofficially?"

"Dave Farris's contacts on his ham radio have been much more forthcoming." She grimaced. "The Red Cross emergency hospitals are so overwhelmed that people are dying like flies just while waiting to be triaged. The flu and pneumonia are spreading through the camps like wildfire, and they can't seem to stop it. We could bring our people to the operating hospitals in St. Joe or South Bend, but they're likely to die in the parking lot before even seeing a doctor."

"There has to be something we can do," Bishop said.

Noah scratched at the stubble along his jawline. "We search the clinics and urgent care centers. In their rush to leave, some things might have been overlooked or left behind."

"Last I heard, Lakeland Hospital in Niles was still operating," Lee said. "Albeit on a reduced basis. Their generators might have run out by now, though."

"It's something," Noah said.

Niles was a town with a population of about twelve thousand people located fifteen miles to the southeast of Fall Creek along Old 31. The much larger city of South Bend lay ten miles further south, just across the border into Indiana.

"Old 31 is dangerous," Rosamond said. "Every day, we hear new reports of increasing gang activity out of Benton Harbor. Scavengers and refugees fleeing the cities are starting to get desperate. Many of them are armed."

"Where are all the super soldiers?" Bishop asked tightly. "Aren't they here to roar in and save the day?"

Julian shot him a sharp look. "They've already got another search team out looking for supplies. I just tried to get Sutter on the radio. They're out of range. They may not be back until late tonight.

"The rest of them are busy guarding the pharmacy, Friendly's, the middle school distribution center. At least a dozen are patrolling Winter Haven after some punks tried to set one of the cabins on fire last night. They're setting up the blockades on all the roads leading into and out of town. We need them there."

"And the chief?" Noah asked. "Where's Briggs?"

"He's MIA," Julian said.

"What does that mean?"

Julian gave a careless shrug. "We haven't been able to reach him since yesterday. No one knows where he is. He hasn't been to town hall and he's not at his house."

A hint of unease pricked him. "That seems odd."

"He's probably trying to stage a coup against the superintendent," Julian said darkly. "Canvasing neighborhoods, spreading rumors to get people on his side."

Rosamond flashed him a disapproving look. "Julian, that's not our concern right now. I'm sure Chief Briggs can take care of himself. He'll turn up. Right now, saving these sick people is our top priority."

Julian made a face, but he shut up.

"I'll head out now," Noah said.

"You're not going alone, brother," Julian said without hesitation. "Count me in."

Bishop ran a hand through his afro. "I'm coming, too."

Julian scowled. "What's a pastor going to bring to a gunfight? Gonna deflect bullets with a Bible?"

"I know my way around a gun," Bishop said mildly. "I can hold my own."

Wisely, he didn't rise to Julian's bait. Still, Noah didn't relish the thought of the two of them trapped in a vehicle together—with Noah stuck as the peacekeeper. "Bishop—"

"All of you go," Rosamond said crisply. "You may need the manpower. Take the AK-47s with you."

"I'll make you a list of antibiotics," Lee said.

Annette put her hand on Noah's forearm. "Thank you."

Noah strode for the gym doors, Bishop on one side, Julian the other. If only Julian and Bishop could learn to tolerate each other. He loved Bishop and trusted him with his life, just as much as Julian.

They wove around the pallets and cots of dozens of sick, moaning men, women, and children. Noah's gut twisted with anxiety. They needed to hurry.

The radio at his belt crackled. "Hello?" a young female voice said.

Noah unclipped the radio and brought it to his mouth. "That you, Quinn?"

He'd finally found a working radio and given one to Milo to keep in his fanny pack along with his pills and emergency dose syringe. He wouldn't allow a lack of communication to put his son in danger again.

The radio spat static. "It's Milo," Quinn said. "He's sick."

46

NOAH
DAY TWELVE

Noah and Bishop headed straight for Molly's while Julian gassed up the truck and collected their tactical gear, rifles and shotguns, extra ammo, and body armor.

Quinn was beside herself with guilt. "It was the lemonade," she said, her expression stricken. "It's my fault."

"Just tell me what happened," Noah said.

"We've been so careful with the water. We went to visit the Cleary's. She was heating water for the lemonade, but she took the pot from the fire before it was completely boiled. I didn't even think . . . I didn't know they were getting their water from the river. I didn't know. I should have. It's my fault."

"And you didn't drink it?" Noah asked.

She shook her head, pulled nervously at her lip ring. "I gave it back to Mrs. Cleary. She needed the sugar and the calories more than I did. She's been giving all her food to the kids . . ." She shoved her blue hair behind her ears and looked at Noah like she was drowning. "Those kids. They'll all be sick, too."

"We'll get them," Bishop said. "I'll go there right now and load

the family into my truck. We'll drop them off at the shelter so at
least Lee and Annette can watch over them."

"Should we take Milo there, too?" Quinn asked.

"I'll take care of him here," Molly offered. "There's nothing
that nurse can give him that I can't right here. At least until you
come back with IV fluids." She hesitated. "I have antibiotics I'm
willing to share with him. Not enough for everyone at the shelter,
but for Milo."

"Thank you," Noah said, immensely grateful. The thought of
Milo at that disgusting shelter terrified him. "Truly, I can't thank
you enough."

Gran brushed him off with a wave of her hand. "I haven't had
someone to baby in way too long. Quinn was always too prickly."

Quinn rolled her eyes. "Whatever, Gran. Everyone knows
you're the prickly one."

Noah knelt in front of Milo, who lay on the couch beneath a
fuzzy blue blanket. No fewer than four cats were curled up on
various parts of Milo's body—two at his feet, the orange fluffy one
nestled beneath Milo's chin, and a sleek black feline perched on
Milo's shoulder. The black cat watched Noah's every move with
suspicious yellow eyes, her tail twitching.

Noah checked his pulse. Steady. Felt his cheeks and forehead.
He was burning up.

Milo was so small. His tiny body couldn't take the strain. And
with his Addison's disease, a physical stressor like a serious illness
could send him into shock, even with his medication.

Noah couldn't abide that thought.

"Any stabbing pains in your belly?" he asked. "Light-
headedness?"

Milo smiled weakly. His damp curls were plastered to his
flushed skin, his eyes sunken. "No, Dad. Just hurts like I wanna
throw up. You don't have to worry all the time."

"I do. It's my job."

Noah caught Quinn giving Milo a wink. "Just look at him. Your dad's a humungous worrywart."

He appreciated her attempts at levity. Milo needed it. He needed it, too, but he was too anxious to relax. "He needs to drink something."

"I have a homemade oral rehydration solution that works excellent for dehydration and diarrhea," Molly said. "I'll make it for him and write it down so you can give the recipe to the shelter.

"A half level teaspoon of salt with six level teaspoons of sugar, mixed carefully in one liter of clean drinking water. Measure accurately and mix. A half cup of orange juice added will help with the taste and add potassium. Or add some Jell-O mix in powder form. That will help until you get back."

Noah stood, swallowed hard. He could hardly bear the thought of leaving his son. It was the last thing he wanted to do. But he didn't trust anyone else to find the lifesaving supplies they needed. "Make sure he gets a triple dose of hydrocortisone."

"Got it," Quinn said.

"Take his temperature on the hour," Noah said. "If it goes above 104 degrees, give him the emergency injection of glucocorticoid. It's only supposed to be a stop-gap until he gets to a hospital, but it's all we have, and it's the only one—"

"I said we've got it!" Quinn gazed up at him, her eyes steady, her expression unflinching.

"We'll give him acetaminophen every four hours and alternate with ibuprofen," Molly said calmly. "If that doesn't bring it down, we'll use compressed snow wrapped in washcloths and put them under his armpits, behind his knees, and the groin area. We'll do whatever we can to keep from using that emergency syringe."

"You go be a superhero, or whatever it is you do all day," Quinn said. "We'll take care of Milo."

Bishop took hold of Noah's arm. "She's right. There's nothing more you can do here."

Noah left Milo reluctantly, but he knew his son was in good hands, with people he trusted.

Bishop agreed to drive while Noah sat stiffly in the passenger seat with the AK-47 in his lap. He wore his department-issued ballistic vest, with his service pistol holstered at his hip along with a battle belt containing four preloaded magazines. A Remington 870 12-gauge shotgun rested on the floor between his feet.

Julian took the rear seat on the driver's side. He wore the same body armor and carried a second AK-47. They constantly scanned the road ahead of them, the shoulders on either side, the trees and buildings for potential ambushes.

"Keep alert," Noah said. "We need to be ready for anything."

Bishop tightened his grip on the steering wheel. They rode in the black 1978 Ford F250 4x4 with "Fall Creek Police" spray painted on the sides in white paint. "Got it."

Many of the stalled vehicles had been pushed to the shoulder. Deep snowdrifts lined the road in some spots. Old 31 had been cleared several days ago by the National Guard, but fresh snow had fallen since then. It was slow-going even with snow tires.

The windows were rolled down so they could aim and fire easily if necessary. Noah shivered. The wind froze his face. At least they weren't hungry.

By the time they'd set out, it was well after noon. Annette had sent them off with peanut butter and jelly sandwiches in baggies and bottled waters for lunch, which they'd inhaled in seconds.

Just past the bridge over Fall Creek, they'd encountered the militia blockade. Six soldiers guarded the road. They'd blocked most of the road with a short maze of cars, leaving enough room for a single vehicle to weave through slowly.

To keep anyone from simply driving around the blockade, they'd used a tow truck to stack vehicles about thirty feet on either side of the road, and even dragged over several felled trees as a further deterrent.

A dozen planks of wood spiked with large nails were placed in the road on the opposite side of the roadblock. Two militia darted ahead and removed them as they waved the truck through.

"Be back before dark," James Luther said.

Noah noticed a lumpy tarp just off the road to the left. Several pairs of feet stuck out from one end. Bodies. "What's that?"

Luther frowned. "About ten gangsters rolled through last night, pretending they were refugees seeking shelter. Guns hidden under their coats. When we didn't allow them through, they thought they could get the upper hand. They couldn't."

Noah nodded, relieved. The militia was doing their job. They were doing exactly what they were supposed to do. Protecting Fall Creek.

"Stay safe," Luther called after them.

The day was cold and heavily overcast. Thick, iron-gray clouds hung above the tree line. It would snow again soon.

The emergency channel on the radio had issued a snowstorm watch. It was supposed to hit sometime tonight or tomorrow. A blizzard, possibly the worst one in years.

They needed to be back in Fall Creek before it hit. They couldn't afford to get trapped in whiteout conditions with the life-saving supplies the town needed—Milo needed—stuck under a tarp in the bed of the truck.

He just wanted to find what they needed and get back as quickly as he could. His teeth chattered as the frigid wind whipped inside the cab through the open windows.

The truck rumbled past more houses. The occasional farm.

Snow-covered fields. They passed a cemetery on the left, the headstones barely poking above the snow. A farmer's market with American flags on the roof rippling in the breeze.

"Watch these dense trees and houses near the road for potential threats," Bishop warned.

Noah tensed, kept his eyes peeled for any signs of danger. He forced himself to remain present, but his concern for Milo kept intruding.

"We'll find what we need in time," Bishop said as if reading his mind. "Have faith."

"I wish I could believe that."

"God is with us, whether we live or die. We're all in His hands."

"No offense," Noah said, "but I'd much rather have Milo in God's hands *alive*."

"That's what I'm praying for."

From the backseat, Julian snorted. "Fairytales don't save people. Guns do."

"Faith isn't a fairytale," Bishop said evenly, but Noah sensed the strain in his voice. "And we have no disagreement on the necessity of guns. Just on how—and when—to use them."

Noah sensed Julian bristling. "Yeah, well, you always think you know better than everyone else, don't you? Things don't change, Bishop. You're still that—"

"There's a delivery truck ahead on the right," Noah said quickly as a distraction. He pointed ahead. "More than one."

Bishop tapped the brakes as they approached a row of three long-haul trucks along the side of the road.

Noah twisted in his seat. "We should stop, see if they have any supplies."

"They're already looted," Julian said. "They were probably cleaned out the first week, if not the first day."

He was right. The rear doors were hanging wide open. Empty boxes, plastic wrap, and trash were scattered across the snowy road, embedded into dirty snowbanks.

Even with working generators, hospitals would quickly run out of supplies without long-haul trucks to deliver them. The best medical care in the world used to be a simple drive or 911 call away. Even then, people died all the time. What would happen now?

The cab went tense and quiet. The truck jolted through the heavy snow.

"What's that?" Julian asked. "In that field on the left?"

Bishop slowed the truck to less than ten miles an hour.

A large, oddly shaped object protruded from the middle of a snowy cornfield. The thing was covered in snow, but it didn't take long to realize what it was. A wing jutting into the sky. The long cylinder of the fuselage. The wide white nose plowed into the ground. A small private plane.

"Dave said a bunch of people reported plane crashes on the ham radio, remember?" Julian said. "This EMP thing took out planes, too."

"Most of them were probably able to glide into an emergency landing," Bishop said. "The pilot must have been flying over, lost all his electronics, and attempted a landing in the closest field he could find."

"Still," Julian said. "Can you imagine if a big jumbo jet came down right on top of you?"

Noah shuddered.

They kept driving. As they drew closer to the city limits, warehouses and businesses dotted the landscape. A church. A liquor store. All dark, all empty—at least, they appeared empty.

They rounded a bend, a YMCA on the left, the St. Joe River on the right.

Noah tensed. "Bishop."

Bishop immediately slowed. "I see it."

Julian leaned forward between the seats. "We've got trouble."

47

HANNAH
DAY TWELVE

Time passed in a hazy blur. Hannah lay on the mattress, covered in blankets and propped up with several pillows. She'd changed into a long, frilly white nightgown several sizes too large. It probably belonged to the grandma she'd imagined earlier.

She couldn't give birth in pants, so a nightgown it was.

Ghost lay beside her. Stretched out, he took up nearly the length of the mattress and half the width, a mountain of heat and fur.

She didn't mind. His warm, soft presence centered her, kept her anchored and present to this reality, and not the reality of her nightmares, the memories that haunted the corners of her mind.

The contractions were coming four minutes apart now. The pain came and went in waves. But it wasn't just the pain or the preeclampsia she feared and dreaded. It was something else.

She clung to Liam's watch, studied each ticking second and minute like it could give her the answers she so desperately craved.

Counting kept her in this place, kept her present. Fifteen contractions in the last hour. Only nine the hour before. While her labor pains intensified, Liam busied himself securing the house.

He'd nailed slabs of plywood he'd found in the garage over the sliding glass doors—both the broken and unbroken sides. He added a layer of industrial-sized black trash bags and thick duct tape for good measure. It kept the wind, cold, and snow out.

He'd wedged doorstops beneath the front and rear door leading to the garage and secured the windows. Wood shims in the windows ensured that even if the glass was broken, they couldn't be opened.

He removed the blackout curtains from the kids' rooms and duct-taped them over the living room windows to block the firelight.

In the blizzard, it was doubtful anyone would see them, but Liam was cautious. Always considering the what-ifs, the worst-case scenarios, even before she did.

Another moan escaped her lips. Ghost raised his head and whined softly. He pressed his snout against her cheek, reassuring her.

After circling the house and checking the windows again, Liam warmed pans of water by the fire. A pile of clean towels stacked on the lintel, ready and waiting. He set down the pan and came and knelt at her side.

His expression was grim, his eyes filled with shadows she couldn't read. "What can I do?"

She shook her head. "Nothing. Just . . . will you stay?"

His mouth pressed into a thin line. He looked nervous and uncomfortable. He glanced back at the kitchen, then down at his hands. When he met her gaze, his eyes were steady. "I'm not going anywhere."

The truth was, she was terrified. She was glad he was here. She needed him here.

He raked his hands through his chestnut hair. Tufts stuck up here and there on his head. "Are you scared?"

It was a surprising question, coming from him.

"Yes." She looked down at her belly. "Are you?"

He didn't say anything for a long moment. She thought he wasn't going to answer. Finally, he sighed. "Scared out of my mind."

She glanced away from him, toward the fire. Watched the leaping, flickering flames until her vision swam. "I don't want it."

"Don't suppose you would."

"Does that make me a bad person?"

He didn't hesitate. "No."

The fire blurred into tongues and fingers of flame. The warm crackling filled the room. *You're safe. You're safe here.* She closed her eyes. Wetness clung to her eyelashes. "I wanted another baby after Milo. It didn't happen like I thought it would."

He didn't say anything, just waited patiently. Waiting for her to be ready to tell. Or not tell. It was up to her.

She felt the darkness rising, the fear and panic and horror. The pain and anguish and dread rushing back like a nightmare, like the worst dream you've ever had, only this one was real.

"This isn't my first pregnancy . . . with him. There was another . . . another baby." She'd never said the words before. Never had anyone to say them to. The truth had corroded inside her with no way to get out, a toxic poison spreading into every corner of her being.

"I'm here, if . . . if you want," Liam said slowly, haltingly. He cleared his throat. "If you want."

There was no judgement in his voice. His usual gruffness was gone. He was nervous, awkward, as lost as she was.

She did want to. She needed to say it, to tell someone. She

trusted Liam. Not just with her life, but with this, too. With everything.

He was reticent, reserved, fierce. But he was not unkind. Nothing about him was unkind.

She endured the tide of pain, teeth gritted, willing herself through it as the pain gradually diminished, seeping out of her body until the next time it washed through her, as brutal and relentless as waves crashing over and over, eroding the shoreline. Eroding her resistance, her will.

"I begged him to let the baby go," she said softly, brokenly. "He could've dropped him off at a fire station or a hospital, in any town or city, even a hundred miles away. No one would ever have known the truth. The baby could have lived. Could have grown up with parents and a dog and a swing set in the backyard, every-thing . . . everything he should have had. A childhood. Someone to hold him, love him.

"But Pike, he . . . he won't let anything go. Not ever. I belonged to him. Like property. Everything I am, everything I had. The baby wasn't real to him, wasn't a person. Was just a thing, something to taunt me with, to torture me. And then, when he was born . . ."

Her voice trailed off. The images came bright and sharp behind her eyelids, whether she wanted them or not, as sharp and ferocious as the pain.

She was back in the basement. Four concrete walls, concrete floor, the mattress, the bathroom, the barred window with dim fingers of daylight slipping through. The window the only evidence that the world outside was still spinning, continuing without her in it.

The mattress reeking of sweat and blood, agony wracking her body, dismantling her, cell by cell, piece by piece, until there was nothing left but the pain.

She was alone. No hospital, no nurse or midwife, no mother or husband to hold her hand. No one to tell her what to do. No one to tell her whether what was happening was normal, that she would get through it like billions of mothers before her, that this incredibly violent and painful thing was as natural as breathing, all part of the circle of life.

She'd given birth before, in a sterile white hospital with brisk doctors and nurses in scrubs, with reassuring smiles. With monitors and blinking machines and IVs dripping meds that obliterated the pain, dulled the fear.

Milo had been breach, a scheduled C-section. She'd never even gone through labor. It had all been planned, scheduled, scripted. The blue sheet went up, separating her from what was being done to her body. She was present, but not an active participant.

She'd lain there, nauseous and nervous, numb from the chest down, feeling the weird painless tug and pull as the doctors poked and prodded her internal organs.

When they lifted the blue-tinged, goopy infant above the blue paper sheet, she'd experienced a frisson of wonder and delight and love—oh, such love, so strong and fierce it had taken her breath away.

She'd loved Milo the instant she'd laid eyes on him.

The second birth was nothing like the first. Instead of anticipation—dread. Instead of wonder—fear. Instead of joy—terror.

Instead of order and cleanliness and sterile precision, there was panic and fear and misery.

What did she know about centimeter dilation or timing contractions? No one to tell her, "when the contractions are five minutes apart, do this" or "when your water breaks, do that."

Squat. Breathe. Push. Scream.

It was a miracle the baby was born alive.

For three days, she'd held him to her breast, nursed him, burped him, wiped his pee and poop with torn sections of a sheet she had washed in the sink.

She did not name the child. She couldn't bring herself to do it. She could not love him. He was Pike's. Not hers.

And then Pike came. She would never forget his expression when he saw the tiny infant in her arms, that red slash of a smile, his eyes flat and cold.

She said, "Pike killed my baby."

48

HANNAH
DAY TWELVE

The familiar pain came again, in her mid-back pushing down and outward through her pelvis. The pain was stretching and widening her, relentless and persistent, demanding that everything else—her very self—fall back and make space.

Make space for new life.

In her mind, she met the hurt with her fists clenched. It felt like she was fighting her own body. Fighting herself. She wasn't ready. Didn't want it.

The contraction dwindled and she sucked in a sharp breath, opened her eyes. She stared at the fire, afraid to look at Liam. Afraid to see the disappointment in his eyes.

"None of that was your fault," Liam said gruffly. "Nothing you could've done."

But he didn't know how cold her heart was. He didn't know that even as she begged for the baby's life, she'd felt nothing for him, nothing but a hollow emptiness pulling her under into darkness, so much darkness.

"I—I didn't love him. I couldn't."

Liam leaned forward and took her hand. Her bad hand. The

ugly, misshapen one. He didn't flinch away. He held it between both of his rough and calloused ones.

Tears welled in her eyes and leaked down her cheeks.

She'd never cried for him. She hadn't been able to cry for him.

She had allowed her baby to die. She hadn't fought hard enough, hadn't risen from her bloodstained mattress and thrown herself at the monster, sacrificed herself even knowing they both would die.

Shame spread deep into her bones, settled there like an ache. She should've *tried*. Who was she for not even trying? For lying there numb and horrified, forever trapped in that moment like a fly encased in amber. What kind of mother?

A low sob escaped her lips.

"You couldn't have stopped it," Liam said, as if reading her thoughts. "You survived."

"What if I can't love this one? What if—?"

"Tackle one problem at a time." Liam squeezed her bad hand gently. "We'll deal with that when the baby comes."

He said *we*. He was here. This time was different. She wasn't alone.

The headache struck her anew with explosive force. It felt like an ax was cleaving her skull apart.

And then the pain rolled through her—immense, consuming— and her thoughts fled, ripping away from her on red tides.

The contraction started somewhere in her back and moved layer by layer toward the deepest part of her pelvis. It radiated outward, spreading, spreading, pushing through her belly, her chest, her thighs, her spine, like it wanted to press right out of her skin.

The quality of the pain changed. More intense. More intimate.

It felt like her deepest insides being pried apart—her bones, her flesh—wrested open to release something new.

She growled and groaned through it, frantic for the pain to drop off but it didn't. Pain in her belly, her pelvis, her head throbbing with it. Darkness hovered in the corners of her vision.

The preeclampsia, she thought dimly. Her blood pressure was too high, skyrocketing, and she had no idea what to do to stop it.

The pain reached a peak but instead of ebbing it pulsed deeper, harder, so strong she couldn't breathe, forgot to breathe. It was so insistent, so tenacious, she couldn't shake it off. Couldn't keep going. It was taking over her, obliterating her.

She cried out, desperate, panicked.

"Hannah!" Liam called. "Hannah!"

His voice distant, receding.

She couldn't see him anymore, couldn't feel him.

And then blackness was spilling into her vision and she was spinning, spinning, spinning into emptiness, into open space, into deep gray water with no bottom and no surface. She swam and swam and couldn't reach shore, couldn't break the surface, was trapped in a space where light and color no longer existed.

The pain vanished. There was only this, only blankness.

Some small fragment of her mind understood, then. She was balanced on the brink of something. Unlike the times her mind disappeared and went somewhere else, then came back, this was eternal. This was forever.

It could all be over—the pain, the cold, the anxiety, despair, shame, and grief. The fear.

It was a gift. An offering.

She only had to let go.

49

NOAH
DAY TWELVE

Noah stared out the windshield. His pulse thudded loud in his ears. Adrenaline surged through his veins. He tightened his grip on the AK-47 but kept it low below the windows.

Just past the YMCA, they approached a train bridge above them. The river blocked them to the right, a tall concrete embankment to the left.

Directly ahead, several vehicles blocked the road. A snowplow was situated on the right, a school bus on the left. A narrow space wide enough for a single car to drive through was left open in the middle with a gray truck parked sideways in the center of the road about fifteen yards back from the blockade.

A dozen figures cloaked in heavy winter gear crouched behind the bus, snowplow, and the truck. Their heads, shoulders, and long guns were visible, their rifle barrels pointed at the F250.

"Bishop," Julian warned.

"I know!" Bishop swung sharply to the left, attempting to hang a U-turn and get them the hell out of there. He didn't have enough room with so many stalled cars and the sharp drop-off to the river on their right.

He bumped over the curb and tried to slam the brakes. The grille nosed into the fender of a burgundy Toyota parked along the shoulder. Metal squealed and made a horrible scraping sound. The truck came to a sudden, jarring stop.

They were sideways in the middle of the road about twenty yards from the makeshift barricade.

"Drive!" Julian shouted.

Bishop revved the engine, tried to reverse. Snow and dirt spit from the tires. The wheels spun and went nowhere. "I can't! We're stuck!"

"Don't move!" a male voice shouted into a megaphone. "Throw your weapons out of the windows!"

"We're cops!" Noah shouted out the open window. "Put down your guns!"

"We will shoot you!" the man continued as if he hadn't heard him. "Toss out your weapons and get out of the vehicle. Lay down with your hands on your heads!"

They didn't even wait for them to comply. Three *booms* shattered the air, one after another. A round pinged off the front fender.

Noah's heart bucked in his chest. He and Bishop ducked down in their seats. Julian slid as far down as he could, spitting curses and checking his spare mags.

The passenger's side faced the blockade. Noah had the least protection. Unlike in the movies, the flimsy metal of a vehicle's door offered little to no cover against a high-powered round.

"That was too close for comfort," Bishop muttered.

"You think?" Julian said. "We need to get out of this sardine can and give ourselves some room to maneuver. Maybe we could've hung a U-turn but genius over here got us stuck. Now we're screwed."

Two more shots rang out. They didn't hit the truck. Warning shots, for now.

Bishop twisted around, struggling to unsnap his seatbelt in the cramped space. He placed one hand on the driver door handle. "Ready?"

Noah and Julian nodded tightly.

Bishop flung open the door and lunged out. Noah scrambled after him, his rifle knocking awkwardly against the dashboard, nearly getting tangled in the seatbelt. He yanked hard and the weapon came tumbling out with him.

Julian cursed as he leapt out through the rear door and landed awkwardly.

Noah hit the snow on his hands and knees and crawled forward to the cover of the engine block. Bishop and Julian crept up beside him. Noah and Julian gripped AK-47s; Bishop had grabbed the shotgun.

The cold air numbed his cheeks, ears, and nose. The snow leaked through his jeans and chilled his legs. His rapid breaths curled in front of him like white mist.

"You're the lawmen," Bishop said. "What's the plan?"

"We're not giving up our weapons," Noah said. "No way."

Julian scooted onto his knees and slid his rifle over the hood. Another gunshot splintered the air, and he ducked behind the cover of the engine block. "They're shooting at us. We shoot back. And we shoot to kill."

Bishop risked a peek over the hood. "They don't look like gangsters or thugs. They're just regular people. Look at their faces. They're terrified."

"I'm too busy watching their guns and trying not to get killed," Julian snapped.

"They're just scared," Bishop said. "We can talk this out."

"Scared people are dangerous. I don't care who they are."

Julian glared at Bishop. "That imaginary line between good guys and bad guys? It doesn't exist."

"Yes, it does."

Adrenaline spiked through Noah. His guts turned to water. "We shouldn't enter a firefight if we don't need to."

Julian shot him a scornful look. "Newsflash! We're already in one."

"They're shooting over our heads," Bishop said.

"They're terrible shots. So what?"

Noah's head hurt. The stress and the adrenaline were making it hard to think, to weigh the facts. It was true that none of the rounds had hit the truck after the first one.

He had no desire to instigate another bloodbath. He also had no desire to get killed today, either. He couldn't afford to lose anyone else. Not Julian. Not Bishop.

"They sealed their death warrant by firing the first shot!" Julian's jaw clenched, a muscle in his cheek jumping.

"They're just trying to scare us off," Bishop hissed. "We hurt or kill one of them, that changes."

Anger mixed with disdain contorted Julian's features. Without waiting for a response, he popped up, aimed, and fired at the bus. He punched two holes through the windshield. The glass spiderwebbed into gummy shards.

Boom! Boom! Two shotgun blasts in response.

"Next shot is a kill shot," Julian said.

Noah ducked low. Julian was wrong about this. He felt it, deep in his gut. Julian was out of control. There was a darkness in him, a rage Noah didn't understand. He might get them all killed.

Noah had to stop him from doing something they couldn't take back. Every second they wasted here was another second Milo inched closer to death. It had to be fast.

He balanced his rifle against the wheel well, fumbled in his pocket for his badge, and yanked it out. He glanced at Bishop, his heart in his throat. "Cover me."

Bishop nodded. "Stop shooting!" he shouted in his deep baritone. The sound carried in the stillness, echoing off the snow. "A police officer is coming out and he's unarmed!"

"What the hell?" Julian growled. "Noah, don't—"

Noah stood and moved around the nose of the truck. He raised his hands in the air, holding the badge high, and stepped out into the road.

50

NOAH
DAY TWELVE

Noah strode forward, arms in the air, waving his badge. His boots almost slipped in the wet, sloshy snow. His lungs burned as he gulped in frigid, shallow breaths. "Police! We're not a threat. Don't shoot!"

Dread mingled with the anxiety twisting in his gut. This was either the smartest or the stupidest thing he'd ever done. At least he knew that Bishop and Julian—no matter how disgruntled—had his back.

If he got shot, these people would pay dearly for it.

Noah stopped halfway between the two groups. "The two men with me are excellent marksmen. You shoot me, you'll lose several of your own people."

"You could have shot to kill," Bishop boomed. "You didn't. We could've shot to kill. The guy in the Detroit Lions cap over there had his head and shoulders exposed the entire time. We could've easily taken him out."

The guy in question flushed and yanked off his hat, as if that would make a difference.

"No one's gotten hurt yet," Noah said. "We can still walk this back."

"Tell your friends behind you to drop their guns!" a woman shouted.

"That's not going to happen," Noah said. "You drop yours."

A man heavily garbed in winter gear stepped out from behind the bus. Noah glimpsed a weathered oval of pale face and wisps of graying hair. He gripped a revolver in both hands and aimed it at Noah.

A middle-aged black woman followed close behind him, her shotgun up, stock pressed against her shoulder, ready to fire. "Don't even move."

Noah remained still. He held the badge high. "I am a police officer from Fall Creek."

"You can say you're anybody," the woman said. "You may have killed the cop and stolen his badge."

"My police ID card is in the wallet. It has my name, rank, agency, and my photo."

"Throw it to us," the man said.

Two men moved out from behind the snowplow, both armed with hunting rifles. One was black, the other Hispanic. In their forties and a little heavy, they were wearing jeans and wool coats, hats, and scarves. They looked like teachers or accountants, not thugs.

That didn't mean they weren't dangerous. Anyone was capable of anything if they were pushed far enough, if they were desperate enough. He knew that.

An image of Billy Carter's bludgeoned face flashed before his eyes. His body still lying in that filthy, trash-littered trailer where they'd left him. Where Noah had left him. He blinked the bad memory away.

Noah tossed the badge at the woman's feet. She kept her eyes and gun on Bishop and didn't move. A brunette with glasses and a yellow knit cap came up behind her, grabbed the badge, and examined it. She carried a pistol and a hunting rifle slung over her shoulder.

The two women conferred with the older man in low voices. The old man nodded as they came to some sort of agreement.

The old man turned to Noah. "Who are you?"

"My name is Officer Noah Sheridan. Officer Sinclair is with me, as well as Atticus Bishop, the pastor of Crossway Church in Fall Creek."

Noah sensed movement behind him. Footsteps crunched through snow as Bishop circled the truck and came to stand beside Noah. "We just want to talk."

The older man gestured at his people. "Stand down. Lower your weapons."

The men and women obeyed. Three more people came out from behind the blockade, forming a group of around ten. Their expressions were bleak and haggard. They still looked wary, but they dropped their weapons to their sides.

Noah lowered his hands. Bishop lowered his shotgun.

"Julian," Noah said. "You can come out now. Please don't shoot anyone."

Julian broke cover and stalked up to the group. He'd shouldered his rifle, but his service pistol was drawn in the low ready position.

"There's no need for that." Noah reached out and pushed Julian's gun down. "These folks mean us no harm. They were simply protecting their town."

"What's left of it," said the woman in the yellow knit cap.

Julian muttered a curse and shot a dark look at Bishop, like he blamed him for this predicament. Reluctantly, he lowered his pistol to his side.

The older man hitched up his coat and holstered his revolver. "My name is Mick Sellers. Newly appointed head of security operations for the town of Niles. Served twenty years with the Marines, so I suppose I got the job by default. Too bad it doesn't pay worth a hill of beans. At this point, I would take the beans."

Noah stuck out his hand. "I wish I could say it was a pleasure to meet you."

The man shook his hand with a pained grimace. "I apologize for the misunderstanding. I wish we could offer a warmer welcome."

"You have a lot of looting issues?" Bishop asked.

"Of course. That's how it is everywhere, I imagine. But it's not just that," Mick said gravely. "Three days ago, we were attacked."

Noah stiffened. "Attacked by who?"

"Good question. We aren't sure. There were almost thirty of them. Well organized and well-armed. They came in guns blazing. Our stores and pharmacies were already bare. They seemed to know that and left them alone. They stripped the two emergency shelters, stole the rest of the gas from three stations, and hit about thirty homes as well. Killed seven people who tried to defend our supplies."

"Sounds like a gang out of Benton Harbor." Julian hung back, scowling, refusing to holster his service pistol. Probably still stewing over the fact that he couldn't arrest everyone for drawing on him.

Noah ignored him. He loved Julian, but he could be a jerk.

These people weren't the enemy. They had enough enemies already. There was no reason to create more.

Mick stomped his feet and shivered. "Don't know about that. They seemed too professional to be a gang or a ragtag group of scavengers."

"You think militia?" Noah asked.

"Maybe. Could be a rogue military or National Guard unit as well, I suppose."

"It wasn't just us," said the woman in the yellow hat. "Saginaw got hit four nights ago. We just got reports that Bridgman was attacked last night. Same M.O. They swept in just before midnight. Struck with precision and lethality. Some of the Bridgman folks tried to fight back. Thirteen of them are dead."

A chill ran down Noah's spine. Could Fall Creek protect itself from organized, professional killers? Would Sutter's men be enough if such a group turned their attention to their small town?

"We asked for National Guard protection, but we got nothing," Mick said. "The governor's too busy trying to contain the violence in Detroit, Grand Rapids, Kalamazoo. Everywhere but us. But we got desperate people here, too. We're sitting ducks." He patted the revolver at his side. "So we took it upon ourselves to protect our town. They come again, we'll be ready."

"Smart thinking. We're doing the same."

"How's Fall Creek holding up?" the woman asked.

Bishop's face contorted. For a moment, he looked like he might lose it. He took a step back and rubbed the back of his arm over his eyes.

"We've experienced our share of violence," Noah said quickly, giving Bishop time to regain his composure. "It's been . . . difficult."

The wind picked up, kicking up swirls of snow and biting Noah's exposed face. Julian's teeth were chattering. Only Bishop seemed unaffected by the cold. He wasn't even wearing the hood of his bright orange parka.

"The whole world's flipped and gone crazy on us." Mick blew into his cupped hands. "Well, you didn't come all this way to stand out here and freeze your balls off. How can we help you?"

51

NOAH
DAY TWELVE

M ick Sellers wished them the best of luck and provided an armed escort through Niles.

Niles was a bust. Mick and the others had explained that the hospital was barely functional. FEMA planned to shut it down within the next couple of days and move all medical resources to the functional hospitals in Kalamazoo, about sixty miles northeast.

The doctors, nurses, and medical staff were completely over-whelmed. The last medical delivery had been the day before Black Christmas. The FEMA distribution trucks had delivered some supplies to local hospitals, but they were used up within a day or two.

The local walk-in clinics, doctor's offices, and urgent care centers had already been emptied and consolidated. But they couldn't return home empty-handed. They had to keep searching, hoping a few critical supplies had been overlooked.

They continued east to Buchanan then doubled back and headed west on Highway 12 to Edwardsburg, north on Highway 62 to Cassopolis, then northeast to Dowagiac.

The story was the same everywhere.

Noah had only been outside of Fall Creek a single time since Christmas Eve, and that was at night. In only two weeks, Southwest Michigan already looked like a third-world country.

Most of the shops, businesses, and restaurants were ransacked and looted. Windows broken. Front doors torn off their hinges or shattered. Angry graffiti scrawled across the store fronts.

The neighborhoods were no better. Trash piles lined the curb. As people ran out of trash bags, they used plastic grocery bags. When they ran out of those, they'd dumped their waste in heaps at the edge of their yard.

Debris blew across the roads, through people's yards, snagging on fences and trees. Torn plastic grocery bags fluttered and rippled in the wind like flags.

Noah pointed to their left. "Possible threat at our nine o'clock."

"I see them." Julian said.

Three teenage boys lurked in the shadows between a bank and a looted McDonalds. Likely lying in wait for a working vehicle to rob or steal. They were armed with baseball bats and tire irons. No guns that Noah could see.

Still, they needed to err on the side of caution.

Noah casually slung the rifle through the opened window.

The punks saw it. Their eyes got huge and they gestured wildly to each other. Within seconds, they'd vanished behind the bank. They would wait for easier prey to come along.

The truck was a sweet prize, but not at the expense of a gunfight they would lose. They weren't that desperate yet.

How long until they were? He kept thinking about the townspeople of Niles, their haggard faces, and what Mick Sellers had said about the vicious attacks on local towns.

Fall Creek had to be ready when these pros came for them.

Noah pushed that thought out of his head. That was a

problem for another day. Besides, they had the militia. This was the reason they'd made such drastic compromises. Threats lay in wait everywhere.

The horrible stench of urine and feces wafted from many of the houses. In these larger towns, people relied on city water and sewage, not septic systems.

Noah coughed and covered his nose and mouth with the crook of his elbow. His eyes watered. "How can people live like this?"

"They must've continued using their toilets until the sewage backed up into their houses," Bishop said. "No one told them how to build latrines or makeshift toilets."

They passed a large, stately craftsman-style home on the corner. A man and his two teenage sons were working in the driveway, hacking at a tall wooden bookcase with saws and axes and creating a pile of firewood. A wooden dresser waited behind them.

A few people had broken off the wooden spindles along their wrap-around front porches. Other homes boasted fresh stumps in their yards, the pretty maple and magnolia trees chopped down— though the unseasoned wood would be difficult to burn.

"They should be combing the woods collecting deadfall," Noah said. "That oak tree over there is still standing, but it's dead. They should've gone after that one first."

"At least they're burning whatever they can," Bishop said quietly.

They searched urgent care clinics, home healthcare offices, and long-term care-facilities. The nursing homes had run out of fuel for their generators and transferred their residents to larger facilities under the guidance of the Red Cross and emergency officials.

Every building was already cleaned out of everything, even trash bags and medical exam gloves. Julian guarded the truck while Bishop and Noah searched. Again and again, they came up with nothing.

Once, Julian was shot at by a couple of punks looking to steal their truck, but Julian shot back. The punks disappeared.

No one else dared to accost them. Though several times they caught glimpses of shadows moving behind shattered windows, slipping from building to building. No doubt, they were being watched.

If they were stuck out here after night fell, they'd be in trouble. The punks and thugs and criminals wouldn't hesitate then.

They had to find something, and soon.

With each raided and empty clinic, Noah's anxiety grew. His chest felt like a giant hand was squeezing his heart tighter and tighter. His thoughts spiraling with concern for Milo, for all the sick and suffering at the shelter.

What if they failed? How many people would die? What would happen to Milo?

Hours passed. The day was so overcast, they could only tell the time by Noah's mechanical watch. Early afternoon moved into early evening. The clouds grew thick and dark.

Julian grew more agitated. Even Bishop was on edge. Noah felt the tension crackling like static between them like electricity, like its own sort of brewing storm.

They were running out of time.

52

NOAH
DAY TWELVE

The truck eased along Main Street in Dowagiac, a town of about five thousand people about fifteen miles east of Fall Creek. They passed a car wash, a Burger King, a Subway, a vacant gas station, a tire shop, and a corner convenience store.

The convenience store was a ransacked mess. So was the veterinarian's office next to it, the "Companion Care Animal Clinic" sign still wrapped in Christmas lights and holly.

Bishop slammed on the brakes. The tires locked. The truck fishtailed for a moment before jerking to a stop in the middle of an intersection.

Noah nearly slid off the seat and crashed into the dashboard. His heart stuttered in his chest. He brought the rifle up awkwardly and pointed it out the window. He craned his neck, searching the empty streets for danger.

The traffic lights were dark. An SUV and a compact car were stalled in the oncoming lane two dozen yards ahead, so covered in snow that the makes and models were impossible to discern.

A Rite-Aid stood on the corner to their right, windows broken, no movement in the shadows. The same with the office building on their left. It was two stories and impossible to see into the second-story windows. The hairs on the back of his neck lifted.

"What is it?" he asked. "What's wrong?"

Bishop banged his fist on the steering wheel. "That's it!"

"This better be good," Julian snapped. "Because your driving sucks."

"Daphne." Bishop sucked in a breath, mopped at his face with one arm. "She's a vet tech." His jaw stiffened as he caught himself. "She was a vet tech. She used to complain when the girls got sick and we had to pay so much for antibiotics. She said animal antibiotics are nearly the same. They have amoxicillin for cats and dogs. Fish antibiotics."

Relief surged through Noah. "Seriously?"

"Yes. And it's not just the antibiotics that are the same. So are the intravenous saline fluids."

"Fantastic," Julian said, his voice dripping with sarcasm. "You sure took your sweet time telling us."

"I'm sorry. I truly am. I've had a lot on my mind."

"Give him a break, Julian," Noah said. He was just thrilled they had another option. "Let's do this."

Bishop switched off the engine, and they scanned their surroundings again before climbing out. Julian remained behind to watch their backs and guard the truck.

The front door to the clinic was locked, but the front plate glass windows had been bashed in. Shards of glass glittered everywhere. Bishop and Noah cautiously climbed through.

The place was dark and freezing cold. Noah flicked on his weapon mounted light. He pulled his Maglite from his belt and tossed it to Bishop. With their weapons in the high ready position, they cleared the reception area, examination rooms, and office.

Some of the shelves were already cleaned out, but nowhere

close to everything. They found boxes of kitty litter, flea collars and heartworm meds, and various bags of cat, dog, and bird foods.

"People should come here to get supplies for their pets," Bishop mused. "They need to eat as much as we do."

They moved cautiously down the darkened rear hallway, leading with their weapons. They cleared a staff room and janitor's closet. In the last room, they found the medical supplies.

Bishop leaned the shotgun against the wall near the door and shone the Maglite across rows and rows of bottles and boxes of medications, gauze and bandages, and various knick-knacks. Cute images of puppies and kittens decorated the labels.

"Praise God." Bishop dumped out a box of heartworm meds and went directly for the animal antibiotics. He swiped his arm across the shelf and spilled dozens of pill bottles into the box. "Amoxicillin. Gentamicin. Clindamycin. Doxycycline."

"Hot damn. We just hit the motherlode."

They had brought crates, heavy-duty large trash bags, and a dolly in the back of the truck, but there were plenty of cardboard boxes here, several of them already empty. Noah dropped the rifle on its sling, grabbed a box, and started collecting supplies.

"Do you feel guilty for just taking stuff? I'm an officer of the law. I'm supposed to stop people from stealing and looting."

Bishop ran his hand through his wiry hair. His afro sprang back into place. "I don't pretend to have all the answers. Or to always know what's right. But I believe that preserving innocent life supersedes lesser sins. When the country goes back online, we can come back and pay the business owner for the things we took to keep our loved ones alive. If he or she were here now, we would pay them, or we'd move on and look for another abandoned store. There's a difference between taking things left behind and stealing from a person who needs those supplies to survive as much as we do."

Noah managed a tight grin. "Thanks for easing my conscience, pastor. I knew we were friends for a reason."

Bishop snorted. "Is that why we've remained friends all these years? You think befriending a preacher will save you by proxy?"

"That is what I thought, yeah."

"Unfortunately, it doesn't work that way."

"Well, then I've got no use for you."

In the harsh play of shadow and light from the flashlight beams, he caught the slight twitch of Bishop's lips.

Maybe Bishop really would be okay. Not today. Not tomorrow. But someday soon. Maybe they would all be okay.

Noah found the bottles of saline fluids labeled NaCI 0.9% and carefully stacked them in an oversized cardboard container along with IV start kits plus syringes and needles. The needles were different, but Bishop assured him they'd work for people.

"What about these butterfly needles?" Noah asked.

"Absolutely. Those will work great for children, the elderly, anyone dehydrated. I also found a big box of reusable icepacks. We can fill them with snow instead of using the wet washcloths. They're useful for all kinds of bumps and bruises."

Once they had the first stack of boxes ready to go, Noah grabbed the Maglite and headed back through the building to the entrance to retrieve the dolly from the back of the F250.

Outside, the temperature was dropping rapidly. It would be dusk in less than an hour.

Julian leaned against the truck, his rifle in the low ready position. He stomped his feet, shivering. "Well?"

"We found what we needed." He unloaded the dolly and lugged it awkwardly over the snowy curb. "Any trouble?"

"Nah. All the smart people are hunkered down inside, taking shelter from this storm headed our way."

Before he could head back inside, Julian seized his arm. "You need to be careful."

"Careful about what?"

He narrowed his eyes and lowered his voice. "He's making you soft, Noah. He's becoming a liability."

Noah shook his head. "They were townspeople. Our neighbors. We were right not to shoot. We're all on the same side."

Julian didn't say anything. His disgusted expression spoke for him.

Noah jerked his arm away. He didn't have time to deal with Julian's foul mood. He thought of Milo, felt the seconds ticking away, his anxiety growing. "I have to get back inside. We've got a few more loads."

He went back inside and loaded more boxes on the dolly. He couldn't get Julian's words out of his head. They buzzed relentlessly in the back of his mind.

He knew where Bishop drew the line. He knew Julian didn't believe there were lines, not when survival was at stake. That was its own kind of line in the sand.

The question was, where was his own?

53

NOAH
DAY TWELVE

Noah dumped bottles into the box and reached for more. His fingers were stiff from the cold, almost numb.

He glanced at Bishop. "We almost opened fire on people just trying to protect their town."

"But we didn't," Bishop said.

"Because you kept a calm head. Julian, he was going to—"

"You stepped up and prevented a bloodbath."

"Did you ever kill someone in combat?" He felt embarrassed that he'd never asked. "I'm sorry. You don't have to answer that."

"Yeah. In Syria. More than once."

Noah swallowed the thickening lump in his throat. His chest tightened. "I never killed anyone before the raid on the Carter compound. Never even shot with the intention of hitting another human being."

Bishop glanced at him. "It's not an easy thing to carry that weight."

Noah seized several bottles of fish antibiotics, squeezing so hard his fingers ached in protest. Bishop had no idea. "It isn't."

"I believe in self-defense. I'm not afraid to take up a gun. I only wish—" Bishop turned away for a moment, struggling to compose himself. When he spoke again, his voice was rough. "The Israelites defended themselves with swords and arrows. In fact, they were the aggressors dozens of times. The tip of God's righteous spear. Sometimes, killing is necessary."

Bishop gazed down at his hands, his expression grim. "The thing with killing is it becomes easier the next time. And easier still the time after that. It becomes harder and harder to hold back. To stop. You start to fear yourself."

Noah didn't say anything.

"Violence begets violence. Blood begets blood. There is killing that is righteous and killing motivated by rage and vengeance. Fair and scrupulous justice brings peace. Vengeance births more bloodshed. It takes wisdom to discern the difference."

Julian hadn't just killed someone. He'd murdered him.

And you stood by and watched it happen.

Guilt snarled in his gut, clogged his throat.

He was a cop. An officer of the law. In the real world, before this disaster, Julian would be on leave right now, pending the IA investigation that would find him guilty, guilty as hell.

And what was Noah?

He thought of the Crossway Massacre. The images burned into his mind. The blood sprayed and spattered across the walls, the pews, the carpet, the bodies.

He saw Billy Carter's swollen, bloodied face. Saw Julian squeezing the trigger, shooting a round through his skull at point-blank range. An assassination of an unarmed suspect.

They'd taken the law into their own hands. Acting from rage and hatred, not justice.

That was the difference Bishop meant.

Shame warmed his cheeks. He touched his wedding ring beneath his glove. What would Hannah think of him now?

"Anything you want to share, old friend?" Bishop said it lightly, but Noah knew he was serious. He was offering Noah an out. A chance to confess. To unburden his conscience.

But Noah didn't want to take it. Wasn't ready to take it.

"I'm here, you know," Bishop said. "I'm always here."

They didn't say anything after that. They both worked in silence, buried in their own heavy thoughts. After another load, Noah quickly counted the supplies. He was anxious to get back, to make sure Milo was okay.

"We have enough for the sickest ones. But what if others get worse? What about the next crisis?"

"We'll figure it out." Bishop tossed him a small white pill bottle. "Catch!"

Noah squinted to read the label. Prednisone tablets, 5 milligrams, 100 tablets. His heartbeat quickened. Milo was supposed to take hydrocortisone for his Addison's disease.

Prednisone wasn't recommended for pediatric patients due to its side effects, but keeping his son alive was the priority. Prednisone would do the job.

"Dogs get Addison's disease, too. And other inflammatory, auto immune, and allergic conditions. I'm so sorry, Noah. I should have thought about it earlier."

Noah shook his head, almost too overwhelmed with joy to speak. "How much is here?"

Bishop flashed the Maglite across the middle shelf. "Hard to say. A lot. Maybe a year for a kid like Milo?"

Noah exhaled slowly. He wasn't a praying man, but he whispered a quick prayer of gratitude to whoever—God, the universe, fate.

They carted two more loads and stacked them in the back of the truck. Finally, they cleared the last shelf.

"I think we've got it all," Bishop said.

"We did it." Noah's throat tightened. "We're going to save them."

"We are. We will."

Bishop put his arms around Noah and pulled him into a bear hug. Noah returned the hug. He felt the subtle quake of his friend's broad shoulders as he fought to hold himself together.

Tears wet both their eyes. For everything. For their triumphs and successes, for their pain, suffering, and loss. Neither of them needed to say the words aloud. What it meant to have a friend standing beside you, no matter what.

Bishop pulled away and wiped his eyes. He hefted the shotgun and headed for the door. "Let's get this home to our people."

54

NOAH
DAY TWELVE

The snow fell from the sky in thick wet sheets, heavier and heavier. By the time they returned to Fall Creek, it was nearly nightfall and their headlights were a wash of whirling white flakes.

But it didn't matter. The storm didn't matter. They had what they needed.

Over two dozen volunteers under the direction of Shen Lee helped set up the IVs and disperse the antibiotics at the shelter. The anti-diarrhea recipe that Molly had created helped immensely.

Mrs. Cleary, the mother of the four rambunctious boys, had died. Coupled with her lupus, the strain had been too much for her body to take.

Her death was tragic. Every death was tragic. Noah had witnessed enough death in the last two weeks to last him several lifetimes. He felt himself becoming numb to it. Inured.

If he didn't put up some kind of barrier, didn't harden his heart, it would wreck him. There were too many people depending on him. They needed him to be effective, not a sobbing desolate heap on the floor.

He shut out the tragedy and allowed himself to be grateful. No one else had died that day. Things could have been so much worse. And the community was coming together. Everyone pitching in, everyone helping.

Noah didn't wait around at the shelter any longer than he had to. He left Julian at the high school with most of the supplies and drove straight to Molly's home. Bishop came with him to help with the IV, since he had medic training.

Noah glanced at the gas gauge. The needle bounced near empty. The gas station would've been out of gas if not for the resupply the militia had brought in yesterday. Now, all he had to do was stop in and top off the tank in the morning.

He cared deeply for this town and the people in it, even loved several of them like family. But his priority was and always would be one person only.

They were snuggled in the warm, toasty kitchen when Noah and Bishop arrived with the IV start kit and antibiotics in hand. Molly and Quinn had dragged the sofa into the kitchen for Milo so they could stay warm together. Music played softly from Quinn's iPod—the Monkees' "I'm a Believer."

Quinn sat on one end of the couch, reading a chapter of *The Stand* aloud. Milo's head rested in her lap. He lay draped in blankets on the sofa, a fat orange cat sprawled across his chest, the tabby and the black one curled into furry balls at his feet.

At the sight of his son, immense relief radiated through Noah's entire body. The feeling was so overwhelming, his legs nearly buckled.

Molly looked up from the kitchen table, a bunch of dried herbs and spices spread over old newspapers in front of her. Milo's fanny pack rested at her elbow, the vial and syringe unused.

Molly frowned at Noah. "Took you long enough." She shifted to Bishop. A wide smile split her wrinkled face. "Pastor, lovely to see you again."

"It's wonderful to see you, too, Molly."

Molly beamed at him.

Quinn gave Bishop a lazy wave, but her smile was genuine. "Hey, Hawaii Five-o."

Bishop glanced down at his orange Hawaiian shirt beneath his unzipped parka. His eyes were shadowed, but his smile matched hers. "A fitting nickname. I approve."

"I thought you would."

Noah barely heard them. His focus was on one thing. He crossed the kitchen in a few steps and knelt beside Milo. "How do you feel, son?"

"Better after Miss Molly's medicine," Milo said with a weak smile. His normally olive complexion was still too pale. His big dark eyes were glassy with fever. "It tastes like Cherry Jell-O. I missed you, Dad."

"I missed you, too." His chest tightened. "You'll feel a whole lot better soon, I promise. Have you had your pills yet?"

Quinn snorted. "Of course."

"And his fever?"

"It hit 103.5," Quinn said, more serious. "It's coming down. We've been watching it like a hawk."

Noah choked up. "Thank you."

Ten minutes later, Bishop had the IV hooked up to Milo's arm, the lifesaving fluids shooting straight into his bloodstream.

After chatting with Quinn for a few minutes, Bishop took the truck back to the high school shelter to help, promising to return in a few hours for Milo and Noah.

It didn't take long for Milo to start perking up. Soon Milo felt well enough to read them a few of his favorite lines from *The Stand*, which Quinn had so graciously lent him.

Noah raised his eyebrows. "For an eight-year-old? Really, Smurf?"

Quinn lifted her chin. "Don't diss our literary tastes."

"Yeah, Dad," Milo chimed in. "I'm literary!"

He looked so happy, Noah didn't have the heart to stop him.

Noah helped Quinn reheat some of Molly's homemade tomato soup and grill some garlic bread on the woodstove. Molly criticized their cooking skills. Quinn rolled her eyes. They danced around to Aerosmith's "Dream On" and Journey's "Don't Stop Believin'."

It almost felt like home. A real home.

The cats meowed and purred and generally made themselves pests by winding around his ankles and attempting to trip him. The fluffy white cat, Hel Destroyer of Worlds or something, perched on top of the refrigerator and followed Noah's every move with a diabolical glare.

"Your cats are trying to kill me."

"Probably," Quinn said with a wicked grin. "Watch out for that one up there. He's not called Ruler of the Underworld for nothing."

Milo giggled.

It was the best sound he'd ever heard. Abruptly, he thought of Hannah. His hand strayed to his wedding ring. She would have liked these people. She would've loved them.

"You two should come live with us," Noah said, an ache in his chest. "In Winter Haven. It's a big house. We have room."

Molly raised her gnarled eyebrows.

"The other families are doing it, too. It only makes sense. They're four- or five-bedroom houses with basements, three or four bathrooms. People living together can share the work and the security, as well."

Milo grinned. "You can be my sister, Quinn!"

Quinn scowled. "You wouldn't like me much if I was your sister. I'd have to give you noogies and wedgies and put a 'no boys allowed' sign on my door."

"Then I'll put dirt in your shoes and frogs under your pillow."

"Except I like frogs and dirt, so you'll have to do better than that."

He chewed on his lower lip, thinking. "I'll be stealthy. You'll never see me coming. Like a super ninja."

Quinn ruffled his hair. "Touché, Small Fry."

Molly's tough features softened. "Your kindness is noted, Noah. But this is my home. My husband and I shared forty years of memories here. We may not have electricity, but we know how to make do. We'll be fine."

Quinn wrinkled her nose like she wasn't quite as excited to make do without electricity, but she didn't argue. Her lip and eyebrow piercings glinted in the firelight.

Milo's face fell. Quinn leaned over and whispered something in Milo's ear. It was just loud enough for Noah to overhear. "We can still be besties, but only if you pinkie swear not to tell a soul."

Milo grinned and happily hooked his pinkie with hers.

Outside, the snow blew. Wind whistled around the corners of the house. Ice crystals ticked against the dark glass.

Inside, it was warm and safe. Milo was okay. People had food, water, and firewood for another day. The town was protected.

"Things are looking up," he said. "I think we might actually make it."

Quinn shot him an incredulous look. "You really believe that?"

"I do."

Quinn scrolled through the iPod touch and chose a song. R.E.M's "The End of the World as We Know It" blasted from the speakers.

"So you disagree, then," Noah deadpanned.

Quinn's grin faded. "Those militia bozos took half of Gran's pantry. Did you know that?"

"The council agreed on ten percent."

"It wasn't ten percent. They took more because they wanted to. Because they could."

Noah pursed his lips. Unease slithered through his gut. He pushed it down. "I'll talk to Sutter. I'll get it back for you."

The look Quinn gave him was skeptical at best.

"I will. Don't worry. Things will be better now. I promise."

She shook her head and gazed out the window. "I think you're wrong. The real storm is just beginning."

55

LIAM
DAY TWELVE

Liam couldn't help himself. His defenses were down, his nerves worn raw.

The terrible memories rose up in him unbidden. Grief and sorrow threatened to overwhelm him. He'd done this before.

Every time he looked at Hannah, he saw Jessa. Felt the blood on his skin, the knife in his hands, the desperation and despair wringing his heart.

He'd saved the baby—his nephew—but not the mother. Not Jessa.

He'd lost his sister-in-law. Lost the only woman he'd ever loved. All the skill and talent in the world, and he couldn't save her.

He stared down at his hands.

He was built to do damage, to wound, to kill. His hands were made for hurting, for destroying the enemy, for making sure the bad guys never reached home.

He did the dirty work so others didn't need to. He stood on the wall so others wouldn't have to.

Killing was the only thing he was good at. He knew the best

way to break a man's neck, how to slit a throat, every pressure point and artery in the human body and how long it took to bleed out. He could assassinate a man at nine hundred yards.

Now that expertise was utterly useless. He had field medic knowledge like all Special Forces, but he feared it wouldn't be enough. Not for this. Not for what was at stake.

Hannah and the baby inside her. They'd been through too much. Struggled and fought and bled together.

He wasn't going to fail at this again.

He would not let her die.

Hannah's face was twisted in absolute focus and concentration, in immense pain. Her long brown hair damp and curling against her forehead, her cheeks. Her body went rigid, the tendons standing out in her neck.

Hannah cried out. A high, panicked animal cry of terror and suffering.

Liam's heart kicked with adrenaline—and fear. "Hannah!"

He squeezed her hand. It was her "bad" hand, her deformed fingers stiff and unyielding beneath his own. There was nothing ugly about her. Nothing.

Her hand was a war wound. A battle scar. He had plenty of his own.

She didn't react to his touch. Her closed eyes moved rapidly beneath their lids. Her skin bone-white, every freckle standing out like blood.

Dread twisted in his gut. "Hannah. Can you hear me?"

She mumbled something unintelligible. She was delirious.

He bent over her, grasped her shoulders, shaking her gently and calling her name. "Hannah, Hannah! Come back. Wake up. Open your eyes."

She didn't wake up. She didn't open her eyes. Her body went limp in his hands.

His brain cycled through options and assessments. His training took over, the muscle memory of emergency medical care in the field, of men staunching amputated limbs and bleeding out in the sand.

He placed the pads of his fingers against her pulse. Dim, thready, so faint he wasn't sure he'd felt anything at all. He placed his hands on her chest. He leaned close, felt no warm breath against his cheek, no slight rise of her ribs.

Hannah wasn't breathing.

Fear scythed through him. He tilted her head back slightly and lifted her chin, making sure her airway was clear. He performed thirty chest compressions, hands clasped, one on top of the other. He did it again and again.

Her lips were warm but lifeless. Her sternum felt fragile as glass beneath his hands. "Breathe, damn it, breathe!"

Ghost leapt to his feet. He circled the mattress, alternating whining and growling, pausing to sniff Hannah's slack face, her limp shoulders. He gave a low, bewildered whimper that sounded entirely human.

"I'm trying," Liam said, his voice raw as he started another set of compressions. "I promise I'm trying."

Tears gathered in his eyes and leaked down his rugged cheeks into the stubble of his beard. He barely noticed. Didn't care.

He only wanted her to live, for her to open her eyes and look up at him with that brilliant, beautiful smile so he could tell her he was sorry, sorry for everything.

For Hannah. For Jessa and Lincoln. For his little nephew. For this damned world that stole everyone who mattered, everyone who was kind and good and worth anything.

Eternal seconds passed. Time slowed. The fire crackled and popped. Ghost whimpered. His own pulse thudded loud in his ears. *Come on, come on!*

And then he was praying, begging, bargaining with whatever God lived up there beyond the stars, a God he'd turned his back on long ago. *Just let her live. Her and the baby. Take me instead.*

He'd give up a thousand lifetimes to save hers. Gladly exchange himself for her. Would make any Faustian bargain.

He was the one who didn't deserve to be here. Who'd wasted years of his life in bitter isolation, at war with the world.

She wasn't Jessa. Could never be Jessa. No amount of bargaining or begging or devil's dealing would ever bring Jessa back.

Liam had lost her, had lost his twin brother.

Lincoln, with his bright laughter, his gregarious nature, boisterous and outgoing and nothing like Liam. Lincoln who had always been there for him, even in their childhood, the years lost to a drunken, raging father.

Even separated by hundreds of miles and years of estrangement, his twin had always been there for him.

And Jessa, his heart, the first and only woman he'd ever loved.

He wept. Wept for the things broken inside him he could never fix. All the ways he'd failed the people he was supposed to protect the most. The selfish mistakes and omissions and self-denials that allowed him to retreat from the world, to isolate himself from the bitter disappointments—but also the joys, the victories, the small moments that meant everything.

The tears ran free, without shame as he bent over Hannah's inert form, pumping her chest, willing breath into her lungs.

Hannah wasn't gone yet. Hannah was here in his arms, *right here.*

A girl both fragile and incredibly strong, much stronger than he'd given her credit for. She was brave and determined, a spine of steel beneath that meekness, that fear.

After all she'd been through, after everything that sadist Pike had done to her, she still clung to hope, still had goodness in her.

He didn't understand it. He was bitter and cynical. Because of the things done to him, the things he'd done. He didn't understand it, but he respected it—respected her. Cared about her in a way he'd thought he never could.

She deserved to live. Deserved to find her own way in this doomed world, deserved a chance to make herself new again.

He poured his breath into her, poured his want and need, his grief and sorrow, the last flickering ember of hope.

Come back. Come back to me.

And then it happened. Hannah's body bucked beneath him. She coughed, her chest seizing. Her eyes flashed open. She inhaled a gasping, fluttering breath.

Liam reared back on his heels. He sagged with relief.

She blinked slowly, her eyes focusing on his. The dimness clearing. The soul returning to its body, retethering itself to Earth.

Ghost let out a joyous bark. He nosed her face as if checking to make sure she was really there. She lifted one hand and touched the scruff of his neck. He stood at the head of the mattress keeping watch.

Liam swallowed the lump in his throat. Scrubbed at his face with the back of his arm. "Welcome back."

"Was I—" she asked weakly.

"For a minute there, Ghost and I thought that you were . . ." He paused, unable to continue. Too many emotions ripped through him—relief, gratitude, and something else, something deep and powerful and too alarming to name. "I thought I'd lost you."

She reached a trembling hand to his face, brushed his cheek for a fraction of a second, her fingers hot on his skin.

"You brought me back."

His pulse jumped in his throat. "You brought yourself back."

She considered that for a moment, breathing hard, then nodded. She was alive again, but it wasn't anything he had done. Whatever brought her back had come from her, from within Hannah herself.

Her face contorted, agony twisting her features. The next contraction was upon her. Life pushing, forcing its way into the world, not to be denied.

"Are you ready?" he asked, moving to position himself between her legs.

Her eyes locked on his. "I'm ready."

56

HANNAH
DAY TWELVE

It was here. It was time.

Her face was bathed in tears and sweat. The pain was filling her up, overflowing, an urgent desire to push, push out this thing bearing down on her. Hannah pushing fiercely, with everything she had, to bring this baby into the world, come what may.

It was coming and she was doing it, doing this. Making it happen.

There was no riding it out. The tremendous pressure a tidal wave. Hannah clutched the sheets with clawed fingers, her deformed hand bent and mashed against the mattress, but she didn't even feel it, felt only the agony, the *need*.

She bucked and groaned and cried and pushed, straining with all her might, all her strength, bringing every ounce of her will to bear on this one quivering point: get it out.

It felt like she was being split open, but this time she knew she wasn't. This was part of the process, this opening up to let life out, to let it through.

She accepted it instead of fighting it.

Chose it, just like she'd chosen to keep swimming against that warm, colorless sea, all that gray nothing. Chose to fight her way back to this place, to accept the pain and the grief and the fear, to keep going.

She wasn't a warrior, wasn't strong or brave or mighty. She was stubborn and maybe that was what it took, in the end. Her stubborn refusal to give up, ever, at anything. Even this.

She felt it then. The baby coming, not sliding out of her easily but fighting for every inch, and she thought, *Fight, child, fight.*

The pain clenched down, burning, ripping, tearing at her, and she pushed and pushed and fought with it, alongside it.

Abruptly, the pain released her. The baby came out.

Her eyelids fluttered. The red haze before her eyes slowly cleared. She fell back against the mattress, utterly spent.

Dimly, she felt Liam between her legs, knew he'd caught the infant.

It was over. She'd done it.

There was no sound. No sound at all but the crackling fire and the clatter of Ghost's toenails across the wooden floor as he circled, circled, alert and watchful.

Nothing from Liam. Nothing from the baby.

Babies are supposed to cry.

Her heart constricted. Ice cold streamed through her aching, trembling body. She struggled into a seated position, everything weak and floppy like her limbs were liquid.

"Liam." Then louder. "My baby."

57

LIAM
DAY TWELVE

The baby came out with the cord wrapped around its tiny neck.

The crown of the head slipped out, the shoulders smeared in blood. The small chest, the belly and two legs, and then she was out, the umbilical cord trailing after her as he gathered this miraculous creature into his hands.

Hannah's daughter was blood-drenched and gray.

He thought of the nephew he'd saved, but had left behind.

The loss had left a hole clean through his center. His whole body ached—his bones, his chest, the space beneath the vault of his ribs.

This was a different baby. But also, it wasn't.

It might break Hannah to lose this child. He knew it would break him.

There was no NICU here, no incubators or ventilators or trained nurses and doctors to whisk the child away and perform emergency surgery.

Everything depended on him.

You know what to do, Jessa's voice whispered in his mind, appearing when he needed it most. *Remember what I told you.*

He did remember. He remembered every second of that horrific, bloodied hour.

He stopped thinking, only acted. His fingers were already moving, seeking the edges of the swollen bluish rope blocking the infant's airways.

Swiftly, he balanced the fragile child on his thighs, the feet aimed toward his torso, the head at his knees, and praying it wasn't too late, praying the noose had tightened only in the last few moments of birth.

Hannah was calling his name, her voice thin and reedy and frantic, but he couldn't answer her, couldn't risk even a breath to respond.

The totality of his immense focus was on saving her child.

He pulled at the cord, gentle but insistent, his hands steady but his heart trembling from the tension. He needed to be absolutely precise. No mistakes. Zero margin for error.

Each ticking second brought this child closer to death.

He unwound the squishy, pulsing cord, unraveling it, finally freeing the infant's tiny neck. He gently rubbed her sternum with two fingers.

She looked like an alien creature, bluish and filmed in blood and white goop. So much like his nephew that it physically hurt. An ice pick plunged into his heart.

Breathe, breathe, breathe. He repeated the words in his mind. A chant, a plea, a prayer.

She moved. Her tiny hands balled into fists. She scrunched up her eyes. Her little rosebud mouth opened.

The child gathered her breath and howled. A thin, insistent, fierce cry.

Relief flooded his veins. The tension in his shoulders eased. He let out his own held breath.

She was stubborn, then. Just like her mother.

He clamped the umbilical cord a few inches from the baby with precut strips of a sheet, then made a second tie a few inches from the first, between the baby and Hannah.

Jessa hadn't needed the second tie. It had been too late for her. Grief flared through him. He remembered what she'd said about the mother bleeding out from the afterbirth. He made sure the ties were tight and effective.

He carefully sawed the umbilical cord with a sterilized kitchen knife, cleaned the infant gently with warm water and towels, then placed her in Hannah's arms.

He sat back and watched them in the flickering firelight, a fierce tenderness pounding in his chest. Ghost sat beside him, plumed tail thumping softly. His furry chest puffed out like a proud uncle.

Liam had joined the military at eighteen to escape a home haunted by rage and violence. But that wasn't the only reason. He'd believed in the cause. Defend and protect. Keep the innocent from harm. Stop the bad guys.

That beating core of him hadn't died with Jessa and Lincoln.

He'd thought it had. But he was wrong.

It was still there.

He felt it again, growing and strengthening with every beat of this child's tiny heart. She was the definition of innocence, of vulnerability.

He would protect her and her mother with his very life.

His hand moved to his pocket unbidden. It wasn't even a conscious thought, but something deeper, instinctive. He tugged out the small knit cap with green and gray stripes. A little lumpy, a little crooked, but soft and handcrafted with the best intentions.

He knelt carefully on the mattress beside Hannah. She looked at him, sweaty and exhausted, triumph shining in her tired eyes.

He pulled the knit cap gently over the baby's head. It fit perfectly.

Before, it had represented his mistakes, his grief, his shattered heart.

It meant something else, now. Something that felt a lot like hope.

58

NOAH

DAY THIRTEEN

"We have much to be proud of tonight," Rosamond Sinclair said to the council. "Much to celebrate."

She sat at her usual place behind the giant island in the open-concept great room of her home. Lanterns and candles flickered, lighting the space with a warm radiance. Rosamond had reserved her precious electricity for heat to augment the roaring fireplace.

The council members sat in a loose circle on stools, tufted chairs, the coffee table, and the two sofas, drinks in hand. Rosamond had passed out beer, tequila, and whiskey.

"This is the last of it, so drink up!" she said.

Outside, it had been snowing hard all day. Another foot at least, with plenty more coming.

Rosamond had almost canceled the meeting, but it was as hard to notify everyone of the cancelation as just having the meeting as planned. And since everyone already lived in Winter Haven, it was a short, if brutal, trip.

Noah took a swallow of smoky whiskey and relished the burn. He clinked his glass with Samantha Perez and Jose Reynoso, who sat on either side of him on the sofa across from the kitchen island.

Even Mattias Sutter, ever the gung-ho soldier greedy for more violence, seemed content to relax and enjoy the warmth, company, and libations.

The mood had lightened considerably from only a few days ago. The journey ahead of them was still dark and cold, but they'd glimpsed a few glimmers of hope.

The virus or bacteria had passed. Everyone other than Mrs. Cleary was making a full recovery, including Milo. Mrs. Cleary's four boys had recovered, but they were grieving and devastated.

Annette King, always kind and a bit of a bleeding heart, had offered to take in the four boys until a permanent home for them could be established. CPS wasn't a simple phone call away anymore.

They would take care of their own.

Sutter's men had brought back another delivery of food and supplies this morning, including a load of bleach to disinfect enough river water to last Fall Creek another month.

Molly had told Noah that they could also use pool shock to disinfect the water, which would be much easier to find in bulk. Noah had passed it on, and Sutter added it to their growing list.

The town had food, gas, and diesel for a few more days.

Rosamond clapped her hands to regain everyone's attention. "Of course, we still have many difficulties facing us."

"It's nothing my people can't handle," Sutter said.

Rosamond smiled smoothly. "Agreed. However, a town hall to get everyone up to speed and allow the people to share their thoughts is valuable. It's better to gauge things early on than to find ourselves surprised later."

Sutter shrugged. He didn't seem to care what the people thought. "Most of 'em accepted the tax. A few were . . . unhelpful. And we've gotten significant pushback from townspeople against

Winter Haven. Several attempted break-ins. We now have a dozen men patrolling the perimeter twenty-four-seven."

"I suppose that's to be expected, unfortunately. We'll give them a forum to vent and reinforce the need for Winter Haven to remain a resource for our town leadership." She cleared her throat and steepled her fingers. "I also propose we send out a few search teams to look for local residents that never made it home after the EMP. Not the ones in other states and countries, but we have at least twelve residents who work in South Bend and other nearby cities who are still MIA."

Everyone knew she really meant her son, Gavin Pike, Julian's older half-brother.

Reynoso and Hayes raised their hands. Julian did not.

"Thank you." Rosamond pursed her lips and narrowed her eyes at Julian. An instant later, her expression cleared. "Lastly, we have a bit more unsavory business. Chief Briggs has chosen to abandon Fall Creek."

A flurry of murmurs. Noah glanced around the room. Chief Briggs was nowhere to be seen. He hadn't been around yesterday, either. Or the day before.

"He moved on to St. Joe," Julian said from his stool at the island next to his mother. "He took one of the snowmobiles. The purple Yamaha."

Now that Julian mentioned it, Noah recalled the conversation. The last several days had been brutal. Everything was a blur. Certain things were better left forgotten in a dusty, ignored corner of his brain.

"What do you mean, 'abandon?'" Sam asked, dubious.

"His daughter and son-in-law live in St. Joe," Rosamond said. "You know he was adamantly against certain suggestions and improvements here. I hope he finds St. Joe more to his liking."

Wiggins gave a satisfied smirk.

Murmurs and confused, uneasy whispers circulated around the room.

Rosamond clasped her hands together and gazed around the room, making eye contact with each individual. "That is his choice. We will not resent or disparage him for choosing the well-being of his family. But that does leave us in want of a police chief."

Next to her, Julian began to stand.

Noah found himself already grinning. Julian was ambitious. He'd always wanted to be the police chief, or to move to a larger city and work his way up to commissioner. This was his moment.

Noah set his drink on the coffee table so he could clap the hardest for his friend. He and Julian exchanged a glance. Julian beamed at him, eager and triumphant.

"I hope you don't mind if I chose the new chief myself. Expediency and efficiency are key during trying times. As is a shared vision of unity. A community leader willing to serve as much as to lead."

Everyone listened intently, their full attention on Rosamond. She was smiling, eating it up, relishing her command of the room. She'd always had that special talent.

"After much thought and consideration, the new police chief of Fall Creek is . . . Noah Sheridan!"

The room went dead quiet.

Noah stiffened. His gaze flashed to Julian. His friend. His best friend. He didn't feel glad, validated, or affirmed. His heart sank to his stomach.

A shadow crossed Julian's face—resentment and anger. His jaw bulged, his mouth thinning.

Maybe no one else saw it. Their eyes were on Noah. But Noah saw it. His gut clenched.

Reynoso slapped Noah on the back. "Stand up, man!"

Hesitantly, Noah stood.

The room broke into applause. Whether they really meant it, he didn't know. After all, he'd once been the social pariah, suspected of killing his own wife.

That was the past. That was done and gone. This was now.

Rosamond stood and smoothed her skirt, flicked invisible lint off her shoulder. "Noah Sheridan proved himself in the Crossway massacre. He proved himself again at the raid of the Carter compound. He brought back the critical IVs and antibiotics that saved over eighty of our own neighbors, family, and friends. We could not do better than Noah, I promise you that."

Sam raised her glass with a hearty cheer. "Hear, hear!"

Dave and Mike were smiling. So was Annette. Even Reynoso, a better friend to Julian, seemed happy for him, pleased with the decision.

"I—I don't know what to say," Noah stammered.

"Say yes!" Rosamond beamed at him.

He hesitated. Everyone's eyes were on him—Julian's, Rosamond's, and Mattias Sutter.

His mind roiled, trying to take it all in, to untangle the strings attached and the possible repercussions. And not just with his friendship with Julian.

He understood instinctively that he would be making certain concessions the second he agreed to the promotion. He understood who was really in charge without a word said aloud.

In Fall Creek, the police chief was the window dressing.

But even as window dressing, he could still have influence. He could still watch over the people he cared about. At least, that's what he told himself.

He saw Billy's face in his mind's eye.

A low desperation thrummed through him. He'd lost Hannah. He couldn't lose Milo.

To keep Milo safe, he was willing to do anything.

He was going to have to do things he didn't like, didn't agree with. He understood that, now.

Next time, he would have to pull the trigger himself.

He swallowed.

"Well, Sheridan? Don't keep us hanging!" Dave bellowed.

"I accept." His throat was tight, his mouth dry. He didn't look at Julian again. He couldn't. "Thank you so much. I promise I will do everything in my power to protect and safeguard Fall Creek."

"From now on, everything that goes wrong is his fault," Rosamond quipped, to more laughter and applause.

"Seriously, though. I've said this before, and I'll say it again." She waited for everyone to quiet down as her gaze settled on each council member. "You are all family to me. We are family to each other. We do what we have to do. And we will survive!"

More clapping. More cheers. It sounded genuine now. Maybe it was.

As his friends, coworkers, and fellow council members slapped him on the back and offered their congratulations, Noah glanced around for Julian. He needed to make sure this wouldn't come between them.

They were friends. They were closer than brothers.

Julian would sulk and pout for a few days, but he'd get over it, just like he had when Noah was chosen as first string wide receiver over him.

Rosamond probably believed the council would assume nepotism if she'd appointed Julian as police chief. It wasn't personal. It wasn't a slight to Julian. Noah would explain that to him.

Only he couldn't, because Julian wasn't in the room.

He'd already left.

59

QUINN

DAY FOURTEEN

"You're stealing our food!" a woman shouted.

"That's our livelihood!" a second man in the crowd yelled. "You have no right!"

Quinn shifted uncomfortably in the hard metal chair. A screw dug into her back through her coat. Even with all the bodies packed in the building, it was still chilly.

She sat stiffly next to Gran. "This is stupid," she said too loudly.

A few people glanced back at her, frowning. She frowned right back at them.

She worried at her lip ring and leaned closer to Gran. "Why are we even here?"

"Just to see the lay of the land," Gran said quietly. "We need to figure out who we need to be concerned about."

Superintendent Sinclair had called a town hall meeting in the historic courthouse building. A few hundred metal folding chairs were lined up in an enormous two-story room featuring gilded arches, white pillars, and shiny wood flooring.

The town had once held ballroom dances here in the roaring twenties. Or so Gran had told her.

Even though the winter storm hadn't let up in two days, the place was still packed. Every seat was taken, and several dozen people stood in the back or leaned against the walls along the sides.

At the start of the meeting, the superintendent had announced Noah's new role as the chief of police. It couldn't come soon enough as far as Quinn was concerned. Maybe something good would actually happen now.

Everyone clapped for him, but they were tense and restless and in no mood to be easily placated. Neither was Quinn.

In the front row, Milo had clapped and cheered excitedly for his dad. He was back to his spunky self, thankfully. After his near scare, Noah was keeping him close.

Rosamond Sinclair went on to discuss possible places for an indoor community garden and the drop-off points for the growing trash problem. They'd marked off areas for people to dump their garbage instead of letting it accumulate in their front yard and stink the whole town up.

"We already explained the food tax to everyone," the superintendent said into the megaphone. Her voice was calm and steady, but her shoulders were stiff, her mouth tight. "When everyone participates, we come together as a community, as a family. We're not here to take from you but to give what you need. Any food or supplies you need, including firewood, can be obtained at the middle school disbursement location or Friendly's for refrigerated and frozen items."

"We didn't need handouts when we still had what was ours," Quinn muttered under her breath.

Gran shushed her with a swat to her leg.

"What about Winter Haven?" Mr. Blair stood up in the center

row. He still wore his expensive wool peacoat, was still tall and scowling, but his face was lined with worry and thinner, an unkempt beard bristling along his jawline. "Why does the council all get heated houses with power but the rest of us don't?"

Murmurs of agreement rippled through the crowd.

"That's not fair!"

"We've got a family of six kids, but Julian Sinclair has a huge house all to himself!"

"I haven't had a shower in a week!"

"The shelter is crowded and overwhelmed! Why aren't we staying in Winter Haven?"

"We deserve the same privileges you have!"

"Why the hell are a bunch of strange military men taking over OUR houses! Winter Haven belongs to us!"

Principal King stood up from the front row. She raised her hand and the superintendent offered her the megaphone. "As a council member, I want to assure you that we are trying our best to be wise with the resources at Winter Haven. I have personally asked three other families to move in with me at my house—"

"That's not even your house!" someone shouted from the back. "It belongs to the Dalsons, not you!"

Principal King flinched a little. "And I will give it back when they return. As I was saying, Dave Farris and Mike Duncan have also opened their Winter Haven homes to several families. I'm sure other council members will as well."

Darryl Wiggins, who was sitting in a chair behind the superintendent, grimaced. He probably had no intention of sharing anything.

"I'm also opening my home up to an orderly shower rotation," Principal King said. "There's not much hot water, but at least you can get clean. Please, come to me if you'd like to get on the schedule."

"How generous of you," Patty Snyder groused, every word dripping sarcasm. "And all this time, I thought we were actual friends, Annette."

Someone shouted a foul insult.

The principal's face drained of color. She opened her mouth but didn't say anything, just stood there, looking hurt and shocked.

Quinn felt a little sorry for the woman. Principal King wasn't a bad person. But she could see why people were upset. She was upset herself, but for a different reason.

The crowd erupted into a dull roar of anger and frustration. Everyone looked exhausted, weary, afraid, and anxious. Their clothes were wrinkled and grubby, their hair disheveled. Their faces were pinched with worry.

Even with the militia handing out food to everyone, it wasn't nearly as much as they were used to. It still didn't do a thing to replace all the things—and people—they'd already lost.

"That's enough!" Noah shouted. He raised his hands, trying to placate the people. "I understand you're upset. But there's no reason to be disrespectful. We're neighbors and friends. We can discuss things together and come to an agreement—together."

It didn't work. They shook their heads angrily. Several people hissed and booed.

"Easy for you to say," Mr. Blair said. "You're not starving or freezing to death, are you? You've got one of those sweet digs yourself."

Patsy shook her head. "Looks like the superintendent did a great job buying people off."

"Listen to your new police chief," Rosamond yelled into the megaphone, actually raising her voice. People weren't in any mood to listen.

Mattias Sutter stepped forward and held out his hand for the megaphone. The superintendent handed it to him without hesita-

---

tion. His second in command, Sebastian Desoto, stepped up beside him.

Quinn's gut clenched. She hated Desoto. Hated the dismissive, demeaning way he'd treated her and Gran. How he'd viewed Fall Creek with derision.

She hated Mattias Sutter more. Maybe it was irrational, but she didn't care. Her feelings were her feelings.

She'd watched him point a gun at her mother and shoot her point-blank in the head. He was the one who'd pulled the trigger. For that, she hated him with an intense, primal loathing.

It didn't matter if Octavia deserved it. Didn't matter if execution was the right thing to do or that she was glad those monsters were all dead.

The terrible memories flashed behind her eyes. Screams echoed in her ears, gunshots, shattering glass. Bodies falling and jittering. Juniper crying, shrieking her name over and over, the same terrified cry that still haunted her nightmares. Maybe it always would.

She blinked, curled her hands into fists, forced the memories down deep.

"You will be quiet now, or this meeting will be canceled effective immediately," Sutter said in a steely voice.

A dozen militia stepped forward from either side of the room, their hands on their weapons. A half dozen more stood at attention behind Sutter and Desoto.

They'd been silent and innocuous until now, until they were needed. Their guns were still holstered, still resting on their slings, but the warning was clear.

The crowd remained disgruntled, shifting and murmuring unhappily, but they obeyed. They had no choice.

Anger flared through her. She reached into her pocket and felt for the handle of her slingshot. She needed to feel it, needed the reassurance.

She imagined pulling it out, loading the three-eighths-inch steel ammo and yanking the bands taut against her right cheek beneath her dominant right eye, her anchor point. Imagined lining up her shot between the angled fork and releasing, sending the ammo right into that cockroach's beady eyeball.

She was sitting less than ten yards from him. It'd be a direct, straight shot. No tough angles. No wind inside. She could shut out the distraction of the crowd.

She could hit that target. Easy-peasy. The steel ball would punch right through the soft meat of the eye socket and into his brain—

Gran seized her forearm and gave her a sharp look, like she knew exactly what Quinn was thinking—and just might do.

Quinn sighed and settled back in her seat. Gran was right. Don't be stupid. Think things through. Sometimes sitting around thinking about things wasn't enough.

"This is not a democracy," Sutter was saying. "That died with the electricity. We do not have to explain nor justify anything to you. Winter Haven is ours, not yours. You don't like it, we'll escort you personally to the next FEMA bus."

Another wave of discontent roiled through the crowd.

Beside Sutter, Noah remained still and quiet. His face was tense, his lips pressed into a thin line like maybe he disliked Sutter as much as Quinn did.

But he didn't say a word. He didn't stop Sutter.

"We're the ones ensuring you have food and shelter. Don't forget that. You want to eat? This is the way things are." Sutter glared around the room. "Get with the program or get the hell out."

Sutter handed the megaphone to the superintendent, spun on

his heels, and stalked toward the back door. Two militia were waiting and opened the door.

Superintendent Sinclair quickly retreated after him. Julian backed away, watching the crowd, then followed. Noah gestured for Milo, who jumped up and ran to him. Noah gripped his hand, turned, and strode after the others.

No one shouted after them. The crowd had gone quiet and subdued. Cowed by the men with guns and the not-so-veiled threats. The message had come through loud and clear.

If they wanted their children to keep getting fed, they needed to shut up and fall in line.

That, and Sutter was the asshole in charge. Rosamond wasn't standing up to him. And neither was Noah.

That bothered her the most. What was Noah thinking? He couldn't be okay with this. She knew him. He was her friend. He was the chief of police now, which meant he should be doing *something*.

"Go home," Desoto ordered the crowd. "Eat your dinner and be grateful."

"Sanctimonious jerkwad." Quinn rolled her eyes as she helped Gran to her feet and gave her the cane.

Gran's expression was grave, her eyes flashing. She was as upset as Quinn.

Gran valued her freedom as much as Gramps had. Nobody in Quinn's family had ever appreciated being told what to do—and certainly not by small-town tyrants.

She tapped her lip ring, frowning. "Noah just stood there. He didn't do anything."

Gran sighed. "I know. I saw."

Apprehension tangled in Quinn's gut. Noah would help. She didn't have faith in much, but she had faith in him. "Things are going to get worse."

"Yes, I believe they are."

"They're only giving stuff away to hold it over people. And that's only going to go so far. They're going to start hurting people, worse than they already have."

Gran grunted. "Too smart for your britches, aren't you? You sound just like your grandfather."

"Damn straight." Quinn swelled with pride. She straightened her shoulders and jutted her chin. "Before, you said there was a time to wait and a time to fight back. Is it time yet?"

"Maybe it is."

"So what are we going to do?"

Gran said, "That's what we have to figure out."

60

JULIAN SINCLAIR
DAY FIFTEEN

Sometime during the third day, the snowstorm worsened into a full blizzard. It raged across southern Michigan with no signs of abating. Whipping wind and driving snow created near white-out conditions.

Everyone else was inside, seeking shelter and warmth. Julian Sinclair should've stayed inside like everyone else. But he couldn't keep the thing burning like a lump of red-hot coal in his pocket a moment more.

The hoarse wind howled and moaned as it tore at Julian's parka and fur-lined hood. His eyes watered and his nose ran. He ducked his head against the driving snow, swiping at his snow goggles with his gloved hand, but it was no use. He could hardly see.

But he didn't need to see. He knew exactly where he was going.

The parked snowmobile idled on the bridge over Fall Creek. Julian stood at the guardrail, bracing himself against the wind and looking over the frozen expanse of the river.

Directly beneath him the water surged deep, the current strong. The black ice was thin.

He slid his backpack off his shoulder, fumbled to unzip it, and pulled out the brick. He hefted it in his hands. It was heavy and solid. Perfect for his purposes.

Rage boiled through his veins. Bitterness and indignation. After everything Julian had done for his mother. For this town.

His entire life, all he'd done was work to please her.

He hated being a cop. He loathed living in his older half-brother's shadow. Gavin Pike had always been the favorite. The one willing to do anything Rosamond Sinclair wished, and then some.

But Pike had disappeared into the ether. Maybe he'd never come back.

Julian tried to conjure up something like concern or worry or sadness, but he couldn't. As far as Julian was concerned, his brother could disappear forever.

Pike was a psychotic asshole. He always had been.

It didn't matter how he smoothed his cruel edges for public consumption. Julian knew who he was. What he was capable of. How he enjoyed hurting those he felt were beneath him.

Smaller, weaker, younger brothers, for example.

But Julian hadn't stayed weak and small. He was strong now. Powerful. Pike had left him alone for years. But Julian hadn't forgotten.

Pain was a hard thing to forget. Sprained wrists. A broken finger or two.

But it hadn't mattered what his brother did, then or now. He'd always been firmly ensconced as their mother's favorite.

Hadn't Julian done his best since this whole crisis started? Whatever the superintendent wanted. When she demanded he jump, he'd simply asked how high. He'd slid perfectly into place as his brother's replacement.

He'd done what he knew she needed even before she'd had to ask. He'd taken care of any threat. Hadn't the aggravating problem of Chief Briggs disappeared, too?

His hatred for Pike had always seethed just below the surface. His revulsion for Atticus Bishop. Now, a new loathing sprang into existence.

When it was finally the moment to step into the glory he deserved, Noah Sheridan had slipped in like a rat and stole it right from under him.

Julian shivered against the harsh cold. His chest burning as the frozen air was dragged deep inside his lungs. Ice collected in his nostrils, froze his eyelashes. Still, he didn't move.

Julian was the one who'd brought Noah into the family. A timid, acne-riddled kid with stunning athletic prowess, the best receiver in all of Berrien County. But lost and lonely, attention-starved and eager to follow Julian like a puppy.

With a crappy home life, Noah had practically lived at Julian's house in high school. Julian hadn't resented it. He'd been happy to share his nice house, his full pantry and stocked fridge, even his mother's affections.

In exchange, Noah did whatever Julian wanted. Even followed him into law enforcement. Julian's own little entourage of one.

Noah had grown up. Befriended Bishop against Julian's advice. Fallen in love with Hannah and married her in a whirlwind romance. Had a kid. Had marriage problems. Then the wife vanished.

Julian was the one he'd leaned on. Julian was the one who stood by his side through everything—the investigation, the suspicion and rumors, the devastation afterward.

Two-faced Noah had repaid Julian's generosity with betrayal.

Disgust roiled in Julian's gut. Noah had always been weak. Tedious in his inane allegiance to the likes of Atticus Bishop, a self-righteous ass who hid his immense arrogance and greed beneath a pious mask, fooling everyone.

Julian wasn't fooled. He saw the ugly truth staring him in the face.

Bishop wasn't the only blight on Fall Creek.

He wiped off the snow accumulating on his goggles. The brutal cold tunneled straight through his gear. All the warmth had been sucked out of the world.

The frozen darkness seemed like it was absorbing him into itself. The cold filling him, embedding itself like icy marrow into his very bones.

There was only this—Mother Nature's savage fury and his own cold and brittle heart.

He would have to be better. Work harder. Earn his mother's respect. Prove to her how wrong she was—what a mistake she'd made by choosing Noah over Julian.

As for Noah . . .

Noah was the enemy now.

And Julian planned to make him pay.

He unspooled the cord he'd brought with him, his fingers already stiff and slow. He cursed as he nearly dropped it. He had only a few minutes before hypothermia set in. He needed to hurry.

His gloves were too thick. He pulled them off and stuffed them into his pocket. His bare hands instantly felt scalded.

He managed to knot one end securely around the brick. He pulled an object out of his coat pocket and carefully tied the other end of the cord in a tight loop. He pulled it, testing to make sure it would hold. It did.

Bitter acid stung his throat. He shouldn't even have taken it. It was an error. A mistake in a string of mistakes. He couldn't fix everything, but he could fix this one little problem.

A surge of guilt mingled with the bitter anger. He hadn't known, he told himself. He hadn't known what they would do. The same mantra he'd told himself a thousand times over the last week.

What happened wasn't his fault.

He'd only done what he had to do. The fallout wasn't on him.

The vicious wind howled. The snow poured down. He could barely see ten feet in front of him. That was fine. The storm shielded him, protected him. Hid him.

No one saw the snowmobile parked in the center of the bridge. No one saw the yellow headlight beams piercing the darkness or the lone man, his tiny figure nearly obscured by the white squall of snow and wind.

And no one saw him drop the brick over the side of the bridge.

The brick tumbled end over end before smashing into the ice twenty feet below. For a terrible gut-wrenching instant, he feared the ice wouldn't give. But it did.

The thin ice cracked and opened like a maw, revealing the rushing black water below.

The brick slid into the water and dropped into the blackness.

Taking the antique iron key with it.

61

HANNAH
DAY SIXTEEN

The blizzard raged outside. Snow came down hard and fast. The wind howled and moaned. It battered the roof, the walls, the plywood crisscrossed over the sliding glass door in the kitchen. But the door held. The house held.

The snowdrifts mounded beneath the windowsills. Condensation crept across the frosted panes. It felt like they were slowly being sealed off from the rest of the world. The house gradually swallowed by snow.

They'd remained inside the house for four days. Liam had shoveled a narrow trail out the back door for Ghost to do his business.

They wouldn't be going anywhere tomorrow. Maybe not the next day, either. But that was okay.

They were safe, all four of them safe.

The rest of the world—the cold, uncertain future—it waited out there, outside. Noah and Milo and home. Cities without power. Millions of frightened, desperate, hungry people.

But all that could wait. It would wait.

Inside were the warm fire and the candles flickering low on

340

the mantle and on top of the bookcase and the coffee table pushed to the wall.

They'd pushed the bloody mattress to the opposite corner in front of the door to deal with later. Liam gave her his mattress and took the couch. He lay there now, a blanket covering him, the AR-15 propped beside him, always at the ready.

Ghost stirred on the rug in front of the fire, stretching languorously, a thoroughly pleased expression on his face. Like he'd done the hard work of bringing this tiny new creature into the world himself. Now his watch was over, his herd complete.

Hannah lay curled on her side on the mattress with the purple princess sheets, facing the fire, the swaddled infant curved into her body like a comma, one arm curled protectively above the baby's soft downy head.

Hannah was nearly naked beneath the quilt—the white nightgown Liam must have pulled or cut off so she could easily nurse. She didn't remember, and it didn't matter.

Everything that came after—clamping the umbilical cord, the messy afterbirth, the grotesque purplish placenta, like an alien life form—Liam had taken care of it.

He'd scrounged around the bathroom cabinets and found pads for her to use. They didn't have diapers for the baby, but Liam had already cut strips from sheets and found safety pins.

He'd taken care of them. Her and the baby.

Her feelings for Liam Coleman ran deep. She was grateful for his presence, his friendship, for everything. She was too tired to think about anything else.

She was exhausted and hurting and weary to the bone, but also flushed and exuberant and *alive*. She had doubted herself, experienced fear and terror, pain and sorrow.

Yet, she'd made it through. Through the labyrinth, the gauntlet, the valley of death.

She'd chosen her own way, a good way. The right way.

She wasn't ready, might never be ready for this challenge, but she accepted it anyway.

Hannah looked down at the infant at her breast, the little girl's tiny clasping hands and miniature fingers, her warm smooth skin, the downy chocolate brown hair beneath the handmade knit cap Liam had given her. Her first gift.

She was perfection. Charlotte Rose was absolutely perfect.

Hannah's heart filled to bursting with an emotion she'd feared was dead inside her, but wasn't—far from it.

Pulsing strong and steady, this mother's love.

The End

I hope you enjoyed *Edge of Madness*! Don't miss book #4, *Edge of Anarchy!*

What lines are you willing to cross to keep your loved ones alive?

Preorder the explosive fourth book in the *Edge of Collapse* series on Amazon HERE.

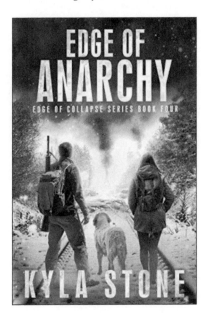

Join my exclusive VIP mailing list (I hate spam and only email 1-2 times a month), and I'll send you a copy as a thank you.

As a VIP member, you'll have first access to exclusive sales, audiobook and ebook freebies, and all my new releases. You'll also receive two of my books for free!
Join my VIP list HERE to get *Chaos Rising* now.

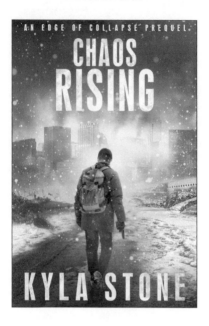

Keep reading after the "About the Author" section for a preview of *The Last Sanctuary* series. The five-book pandemic apocalypse series is 60% off and available in ebook or FREE in Kindle Unlimited.

Get it HERE.

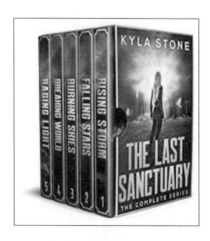

AUTHOR'S NOTE

I hope you loved reading *Edge of Darkness* as much as I loved writing it! I enjoyed blending Hannah and Liam's stories with Noah and Quinn in this book.

Hannah's birth scene was intense but an amazing experience to write. Thank you to all the men who hung in there for that!

You can expect to hear from all the major characters in the rest of the books (unless they die—I can't make any promises).

I can't wait to start exploring the major conflicts each of these characters will face moving forward. Until next time, please take care of yourself and your family.

Stay healthy and safe.

ACKNOWLEDGMENTS

Thank you so much to my awesome, amazing, and fantastic BETA readers: Fred Oelrich, Melva Metivier, Wmh Cheryl, Jessica Burland, Sally Shupe, Vanessa McCutcheon, Bonnie Smith, and Cheree Castellanos. Your thoughtful critiques and enthusiasm are invaluable.

To Beverly Laudé for patiently answering all my questions in regards to Ghost's gunshot wound. Any mistakes are my own.

To Michelle Browne for her line editing skills and Nadene Seiters for proofreading.

And a special thank you to Jenny Avery for catching those last pesky errors.

To my husband, who takes care of the house, the kids, and the cooking when I'm under the gun with a writing deadline. To my kids, who show me the true meaning of love every day and continually inspire me.

Thanks to God for His many blessings. He is with us even in the darkest times.

And to my loyal readers, whose support and encouragement mean everything to me. Thank you.

ALSO BY KYLA STONE

Raging Light

Last Sanctuary: The Complete Series Box Set

No Safe Haven (A post-apocalyptic stand-alone novel):

No Safe Haven

Historical Fantasy:

Labyrinth of Shadows

Contemporary YA:

Beneath the Skin

Before You Break

Audiobooks:

Point of Impact

Fear the Fallout

From the Ashes

Into the Fire

Darkest Night

Chaos Rising

ABOUT THE AUTHOR

I spend my days writing apocalyptic and dystopian fiction novels, exploring all the different ways the world might end.

I love writing stories exploring how ordinary people cope with extraordinary circumstances, especially situations where the normal comforts, conveniences, and rules are stripped away.

My favorite stories to read and write deal with characters struggling with inner demons who learn to face and overcome their fears, launching their transformation into the strong, brave warrior they were meant to become.

Some of my favorite books include *The Road*, *The Passage*, *Hunger Games*, and *Ready Player One*. My favorite movies are *The Lord of the Rings* and *Gladiator*.

Give me a good story in any form and I'm happy.

Oh, and add in a cool fall evening in front of a crackling fire, nestled on the couch with a fuzzy blanket, a book in one hand and a hot mocha latte in the other (or dark chocolate!): that's my heaven.

I love to hear from my readers! Find my books and chat with me via any of the channels below:

www.Facebook.com/KylaStoneAuthor

www.Amazon.com/author/KylaStone

Email me at KylaStone@yahoo.com